# MY LIFE WITH CORPSES

# MY LIFE WITH CORPSES

## WYLENE DUNBAR

Harcourt, Inc.

ORLANDO   AUSTIN   NEW YORK
SAN DIEGO   TORONTO   LONDON

www.HarcourtBooks.com

The story "My Life with Corpses" was originally published
in the *South Dakota Review*.

Library of Congress Cataloging-in-Publication Data
Dunbar, Wylene.
My life with corpses/Wylene Dunbar.—1st ed.
p.    cm.
ISBN 0-15-101015-3
1. Girls—Fiction. 2. Kansas—Fiction. 3. Death—Psychological
aspects—Fiction. 4. Self-actualization (Psychology)—Fiction. I.
Title.
PS3554.U46339M9 2004
813'.54—dc22    2003019626

Text set in Goudy
Designed by Cathy Riggs

Printed in the United States of America

First edition
A C E G I K J H F D B

*To my mother, who*
*let me read books*

Whoever is interested in life
is particularly interested in death.

—Thomas Mann

# THE CEMETERY

WINFIELD EVAN STARK is missing from his grave and in his place is my book. At least that is what an entire community of plainspoken, common sensible Kansas farmers has come to believe, that a man's coffin and the body in it have vanished, interred in their stead a "brand-spanking-new" copy of a book (an *account*, really) I wrote some years ago. Of course, I came here at once— to Laurel Cemetery, I mean—and that is where I am writing this. It is quite clear, you see, that Mr. Stark wishes that much of me, and when a man has rescued you from both corpses and corpsedom, a great deal is owed.

I have some company. My old dog, Annie, lies beside

me, and across the cemetery, the diggers are here to work, but I mean the company of those persons watching from outside the field wire fence. They have gathered from a clutch of six or seven since my arrival yesterday to nearly a dozen early this morning, and the number is growing. They watch me at Mr. Stark's empty grave and when I tour the other headstones—all the while as solemn as if they were here on the usual business. Once, I approached them to exchange greetings, but they spooked and backed away. My power to frighten these good people remains undiminished. There was a little stir earlier, too, when they saw I was holding the book, the very copy found in lieu of the old man's body and given to me last evening by Evan Crews. It was Evan, as well, who called me a week ago to say that his late grandfather had disappeared and to ask, very delicately I must admit, whether I knew where he might have gone.

"I don't know," I lied, and then corrected myself to say, "It is difficult to tell," the more usual case with what is so. While I did not know Mr. Stark's particular whereabouts, you see, neither was it true to say that I knew nothing of them at all. Half-truth is a special skill of mine, my life having required more of it than is usual.

But that was last week. What I write you now is not a fiction or even half-true but, instead, the whole of what I know, if long concealed. I have done with lying and, despite the perils that telling may present, even God's holding a finger to the divine lips would be insufficient to dissuade me from it. Just as before, you may not believe me, but that is no matter. I have appreciated for some time that what is right and true is rarely even given a pat as it trots by while the flimsiest lie is welcomed indoors, where it can take a community by the throat and never let go.

Still, knowing is not without its shortcomings and you might rather remain ignorant. If so, I will understand. Think of it as a war—it is almost that—where others will fight the battles for you. For my part, I will tell the truth and fervently hope that it is the wise, not wrong, act. The Holy Bible tells us, after all, that "wisdom is better than weapons of war, but one sinner destroys much good."

Now, as you may recall, this is what I wrote you then:

●◆●◆●◆●

# MY LIFE WITH CORPSES

## S. Oscar

You have heard the story of the boy who was raised by wolves. There were consequences: he did not learn to walk upright in the usual way; his vocal abilities were stunted. Or different, at least—the vocal chords being

used to bay and howl at a time other little boys were
mimicking consonants. He was not, did not, become
a wolf of course. But who can doubt the alternate
perspective this child, then man, forever possessed—
was possessed by—as a result of his upbringing?

My story is much the same. I was not raised by
wolves, but I *was* born into a family of corpses: parents
and a sister who, at different times, had left the world of
the living. I think my father was the last to die and, in
fact, it is only because he was still twitching in the aftermath of death when I came along that I suspected
human beings might be capable of living at all. Otherwise, my early brushes with vitality were only through
the creatures populating our small farm—the dogs, the
cattle, pigs and horses, and the wild animals—that
continuously drew my father. He brought home raccoon
babies, box turtles, a pair of owlets, jackrabbits, cottontails by the score. We would, he and I, thrill to touch
them (here, I am speaking metaphorically; the dead,
technically, do not thrill); and we would care for them
as we confined them and prevented their escape.

Even so, I had some notion early on that all was not
as it should be in my family. I specifically do not say,
please note, that I felt the wrongness. That is just the
point. There was no feeling, or very little. It is well
known that dead people do not feel, either tactilely or
in their hearts—by which I mean "emotions." I was not
dead so I suppose I could have felt something, but I was

like the wolf boy. Who could expect him to stride manfully on his two legs when all he saw around him were four-legged beasts? He would eventually come to something like that, perhaps, but why should it ever occur to him to do it in the beginning?

But I am straying from my purpose, which is to sit here and to write down, in an orderly fashion, "what it is like" to be raised by corpses. I choose to do this now for selfish reasons. I am often besieged with questions about my upbringing by the curious or even by professional persons interested in making me an object of their research. Leaving my office today and putting my dog Maggie in the car, I was again approached by a total stranger intent on eliciting some previously untold information from me. My hope is that if I set it all down here for everybody to see and digest at leisure, these constant and disturbing probes will mostly cease. If so, my most pressing concern and burden will be made lighter. I need to concentrate now and to concentrate I must be left alone much of the time. If I do not concentrate—and I am convinced absolutely that this is so—I will die.

# I. The death of my mother

My mother died in childbirth. She had been married to my father for less than two years when the baby, my older sister, came. Medicine was more uncertain and crude than it is now and she simply could not survive what were fairly ordinary complications. The doctor advised my father that my mother was not going to make it and to say his good-byes. (They neither of them at first realized that things would go on, instead, looking much the same as they did before my mother died.) He went into her room and sat beside the bed and said, "What do you want me to do with the little jigger?" I have never been told what she responded, but whatever plans they may have made together were set aside when my mother came home from the hospital after all and "life" continued as before, only now with my sister.

Once they have died, women are generally unable to give birth to any more children. Indeed, the doctor told my mother unequivocally that she should not—*would not*—have another baby. And that was true for almost ten years. During that time my sister also died and when I was finally born, as I said, my father had just died or was dying. I don't know how I was conceived and born despite all this. Mules give birth on rare occasion and that supposedly is impossible, too. Whatever the explanation, there can be no doubt that here I am.

But to return to my mother. Nothing about her outwardly revealed her deadness. She was a harmless-looking person, almost fragile, with extraordinarily soft skin that was covered with fine lines, even in the years of my early childhood. She was not what one calls "striking,"

having few features that one would remember at all.
One of these was her nose—the "Bienvenu nose."
Extremely narrow, it bowed slightly in the center with
the tip curving sharply downward, well below the nostrils. A sizable wart was positioned to one side, though
it was the precise color of her skin and, so, was not
conspicuous. Her hands were artist's hands, delicate
with tapered fingers, and her teeth—a mouthful of
them—were flashing and white when she laughed. The
teeth were false I later learned. She had lost all of her
own before I was born.

When I came to think of it at all, I assumed that
she knew she was dead because her acts were in perfect
accord with being what she was. One would suppose
that, otherwise, she would at least occasionally attempt
something that was impossible for dead people. That
would lead to a visible "accident," exposing her igno-
rance of the facts—the same way a man might fall
to the ground if he stood up on a broken leg he didn't
know he had. But this never happened.

By the time I was nine, I often thought on this at
night before I fell asleep. The paradox in a dead person's
knowing anything, let alone her deadness, however,
served mostly to tax my brain to its limits and, thereby,
induce sleep. The question, I mean, was faulty. Knowing
requires a self-consciousness that is, by definition, missing altogether in the dead. Descartes already had
unknowingly articulated the problem when he observed,

"cogito, ergo sum"—"I think, therefore, I am." I was a
child, however, who was being raised by corpses and
knew nothing of Descartes then. The truth was that my
mother could not "know" she was dead and, therefore,
did not learn that fact at any particular instant. Because
my mother was not inanimate but seemingly purposive,
however, I could be forgiven for being confused on this
matter. Being dead defined her in the way being a wolf
defines that creature. Neither needs to know she is dead
or is a wolf. They simply are.

Perhaps I ought to recount instead, then, when I
myself first knew that my mother was not alive. It was
a threshold that I can define more clearly now than
I could then. For a child born into a particular environment, all the presumptions are in favor of what exists
there. The wolf boy has no automatic reason—indeed,
no capacity—to stand to one side and reflect upon the
meaning of his circumstances and the nature of those
who are caring for him.

No. Knowledge when it comes in that situation must
hit you in the head like the clod of dirt in the old joke
about the lunatic. The story goes like this: A wealthy
society woman was being chauffeured to the mental
hospital to do charity work. As she and her chauffeur
entered the institutional grounds, she was amazed to
observe the exceptional beauty of the flower gardens
surrounding the hospital. She spied a solitary man
kneeling over a patch of nasturtiums and summoned

her driver to stop. The lady approached the lone worker, who looked at her expectantly. "Are you responsible for these gardens?" she asked. He said he was. "They are magnificent. You must come to work for me. I will pay you twice what your employer, the warden, pays you here." The man demurred and when the woman continued to press him, he explained, sadly, that he was not an employee of the hospital, but one of the patients confined there. "That can't be true! No one with your great artistry and talent should be thus imprisoned!" The man said that it was true, that he had, unfortunately, been the victim of a successful plot by family members to gain control of his fortune; that once he had been quite bitter about it but had learned to accept his fate. And, of course, he had his flowers to comfort him. The society matron was not satisfied. Would he allow her to use her influence with the warden? He would be most grateful. Would he come to work for her if she got him released? Of course. Oh, it was too much to hope that this long-standing wrong would finally be undone! The lady turned and began to walk back to her limousine, resolute in the mission before her. She was halfway to the car when a clod of dirt hit her square in the back of the head. Stunned, she turned. "You won't forget?" the man said.

That was how it was with me—moments of "dirt clod" enlightenment, when I would become aware that what had seemed normal was somehow out of kilter. These moments began early and, as you might expect, came most often when what I was doing was inconsistent with being dead and, so, disruptive to the standards of my family. Steps would have to be taken, and in those times, I see now that I knew my mother was not a living person.

The first memory I have of such moments, independent of being told by someone, is of the enemas. I do not mean to be indelicate and would not even mention such were it not for their part in explaining the nature of my experiences. But the simple fact is that my mother used these purges frequently. If I said my stomach hurt, or my head, or said I felt "funny," I was taken immediately to the toilet. There, my mother would position herself squarely on the commode and, gripping me around the middle, my bare bottom up, she would thrust the plastic nose of the squeeze bottle into my rectum. The certain pain that accompanied that intrusion was soon forgotten in the horrible knowledge that my insides were going to burst before she would cease the injection of warm water into me. They never did, it is true, but she could not have known that they would not. The only indication of my limit came from my frantic screams to stop, and to those she was completely heedless.

Some will attach a sexual note to my mother's behavior but they are mistaken. The dead have no need for sexual stimulation, perverted or otherwise, and would not seek it. No, my mother sought only to free me from the existence and occasional bad humor of a physical body that, not dead like hers, was in continual motion. I do not blame her for this. My aliveness was upsetting in a family of the dead, and its effects had to be kept to a minimum. Already, at an earlier age—I had to be told this—she had allowed the doctor to snip some skin on my private parts to stop my infantile exploring.

Two habits had cropped up that needed nipping in the bud. One was my apparent dislike for wearing clothes. I peeled off shoes and underwear as quickly as my mother could dress me. This was a problem not solved, even in part, until my school years, when a diagnosis of "weak arches" was pronounced upon me, requiring the wearing of shoes and arch supports, unless, I was constantly reminded, I wanted to be a cripple.

The other habit—touching myself "there," as my mother referred to the matter—was more easily ended. It was not healthy, she told the doctor; I would get an infection or worse. He considered the problem and using tiny, sharp scissors simply snipped a small portion of skin where it was likely to hurt the most. Did I mention I was a peculiarly bright child? I never again masturbated and long before I was past the usual age for childhood diseases I stopped feeling sick altogether. I don't think she was trying to kill me. If that had been her intention, it would have been a done deed. A child is easy prey. My mother was simply teaching me to live the only way she knew—as a corpse. A mother raccoon teaches her babies how to climb, forage for food, and cross a river.

My mother taught me how to live without feeling. More than stoicism or the courageous bearing of pain, I was taught not to feel at all—to separate myself totally from those bothersome continual indicators of life, whether they were pleasant, awful, or somewhere in between. Amazingly, at an early age, I could accomplish this as easily as breathing. Years later the fine points of this singular skill still have not deserted me.

This needs explaining. It was not, you see, that I learned simply to "hide my feelings" or "suppress" them or some other common explanation. That would assume that I had the feelings and then was taught to treat them in a particular way, and that would miss the point altogether. Feeling, in the sense I am speaking of, is a public skill. One must learn to do it in relation to others and through instruction by persons who already have mastered the trick of it. In this way, I suppose, it is very much like language. We talk to ourselves very often, of course, but not before we have learned "on the outside" to speak the language to articulate those thoughts. Similarly, mere undefined stirrings within us come to nothing much without cultivation by something "other" to instruct us in the language of our feelings.

In a normal situation, parents and siblings are the primary instructors of a child in this regard. Mine, as I have explained, was not the normal situation. As a consequence, as it was bound to do, that omission rendered my language of feelings somewhat different and in some respects completely missing. What I was able to piece together mostly came later, much later, than for the ordinary child. After a time, I was exposed to living persons much more often and could learn some from that. Although by a certain, generally young age, living persons are already becoming adept at "hiding" feelings—what I spoke of earlier—and that made my task more difficult. Later still, as a young adult, I spent one entire summer watching three different television soap operas, where I was able to observe not only a range of emotions experienced but also hear a whole grammar for naming and communicating them to others. Was it a coincidence that I experienced betrayal only after I had first copied a soap opera script in saying out loud, "I feel so betrayed by what you've done"?

Early on I had none of these tutors. Instead, what supplied any experience with feelings came from one of two sources, both related to my father. The first was my father himself and the second was the animals to which he was invariably attached. These alone, by means I will explain shortly, kept alive in me the possibility of feeling at the same time they necessarily narrowed and defined it.

I don't think I fully appreciated the nature of the difference between my family and me until I was almost twelve years old. Even then I required help from someone who already understood such things much better than I could. At the time, there were so many alternative explanations for the events of my everyday life. My theories, like classical physics, seemed to explain things well enough for a while. In false theories, however, anomalies will develop and their weight eventually brings the entire structure to the ground. So it was with me and my earlier notions. When the truth finally came, it came crashing down with terrible certainty and effect.

My mother seemed to recall many of the events of her life before her death and had the usual assortment of anecdotes that collectively outlined the course of her previous existence. I say "usual" in reference to the fact that it is ordinary for people to have such a collection. My mother's particular collection was not usual in any other sense. She recounted her stories precisely and the same way each time, unlike my father, who could be expected to change up the cast of characters with each retelling of a favorite tale. She always spoke of her experiences in a quiet and almost loving tone, as if she were speaking of a favorite doll or teddy bear that one imagined had helped her through countless private terrors. My mother-as-child was the central figure in each account and was most clearly an entity wholly apart from my mother, the corpse. I never did succeed in merging my mother the towheaded little girl with the brown-haired dead woman who raised me.

There were three stories of her young life that my mother told most often. The first concerned her violin.

The violin, with "Stradivari—anno 1730" burned into
the interior of its body, had rested on a shelf in my parents' closet from my earliest memory. I had heard her
play it on occasion. More often, I saw it when I took it
down to examine it and the odd accessories that were
contained in its case.

It was a gift to my mother-as-child from an elderly
man who lived down the road from her and whom she
had befriended. When he gave the violin to my mother,
she was only eight years old. The old man was eighty. He
had found the violin when he himself was but a child
and traveling west with his family. As he told it, he had
been walking beside a covered wagon on the prairies of
Kansas when he saw the neck of the instrument poking
out of a sand dune. He had rescued it and carefully preserved it during the rest of that journey and the more
than seventy years since. Capitalizing on his fortuitous
discovery, he had taught himself how to play. He
ultimately played so well that he was often asked to play
at weddings and funerals, with his mournful version of
"The Old Rugged Cross" being a particular favorite at
the latter. He taught my mother to play, and when she
had learned enough to play two songs completely
through, he gave her the violin for her own.

There aren't many sand dunes in Kansas, although
there are, in places, little bumps of grass and sand that,
relative to their immediate setting, might be called
that. Still, I believe the major points of the old man's

account as retold by my mother are all true. And even
as a child, I always understood the essential truth the
story was meant to convey: that my mother was a
special child who had been deemed worthy of a special
and unique gift; that she had taken that gift and honored
and cared for it and, in doing so, had proved that the old
man's assessment of her had been the correct one.

The other stories my mother told took a different
bent. Her father—my grandfather—was a rogue.
Uneducated and good-looking, he was a dangerous man.
He left Missouri at sixteen and worked his way west
hiring out as a farm laborer. By age nineteen, he had
made his way to the Bienvenu family farm, a large and
prosperous enterprise located in central Kansas. He
married Bienvenu's eldest daughter, my grandmother,
six months later. He caroused the local bars with his
children—my mother and her brother—in tow and
then, perversely, came home to beat my grandmother
for "fooling around." Surely, my mother must have
hated him, although when I knew her, my mother no
longer hated—or loved—anyone. He was the center
of two stories she repeated often.

The first took place around 1925 when my mother
was five. Grandpa stole cars. He worked with three
other men who would bring the cars to Grandpa's barn,
where the engines were swapped out and any identify-
ing numbers or features removed and destroyed. They

then drove the reworked autos off to sell in some out-of-county town.

This was steady work. It provided for his family and gave Grandpa some background for his later stints as a car salesman and deputy sheriff. Still, there were perils and one day the local law, on a tip, headed out to Grandpa's farm to have a look-see. Grandpa was gone. My mother, Grandma, and the baby were left at home with a brand-new engine in the middle of "processing." It sat under an elm tree some twenty yards from the back porch, in full view and statement of Grandpa's crime. But Grandma, on a tip of her own, was ready. Before the sheriff arrived, she overturned a barrel trough to cover the engine and sat squarely atop the trough as the police vainly searched for the incriminating evidence. Throughout the search, my mother stood at the screen door, crying ceaselessly. From fear, I supposed, fear of the strangers disrupting her home, or instinctive fear that her mother would be taken away. She never was able to explain. This happened during her life and life's events are only snapshots to the dead. What is there for them is how one appears in the picture, how the elements are arranged. So, my mother cried—she says it and I see it, but the rest is left to speculation.

The story does not end there. It has an epilogue. Some time later Grandpa took the entire family on a train trip back to Missouri to visit his brother. When they returned ten days later, the family car was not in the yard. Grandpa's gang, unable to resist the easy mark, had stolen it and taken off for eastern Oklahoma. The car was found and returned. The gang, sans Grandpa, was sent to the state prison. There, my mother said, one of the men who had been especially fond of her made her a little dresser set and sent it to her. She claimed to have kept it, although I do not recall ever seeing any piece of it.

Mother's other story can be told in a few words. It was the only one occurring close to her mature years and, in fact, took place only a few years before she died. It is simply this: My mother painted. She dreamed of being a great artist. To that end, she made plans to attend the state college and study art. Grandpa, however, was a practical man. She could attend college the one year necessary to obtain a teacher's certificate, no more, and that is what she did.

There was a finality to this that is difficult to convey. Things can be done to a person and this was a thing done to my mother. If she had lived, she might have become a great artist. But she died young and, being dead, could no longer create. Oh, she continued to paint. She even found some local acclaim painting baptisteries, the mural-sized oils hung behind baptismal tanks in fundamentalist churches. What painting she did, however, was confined to strictly representational art. The dead cannot do otherwise. As I have explained, life appears in snapshots to those not living. Thus, the only notion of the living world they are able to entertain is in the same form. To paint other than what is seen in that still life requires an ability to experience it alternatively, and that requires experiencing it firsthand. But if anything is true, it is that being dead is fundamentally a secondhand existence and, as such, certain alternatives were no longer possible to my mother.

# II. The death of my sister

There is a mistaken notion that children are, of all of us, the most full of life and that as we grow older we lose that vitality bit by bit until, eventually, we die. This is not so, as one can easily deduce by simply considering the logic of the matter. A small child, you see, is just as close to being nonexistent as, say, an eighty-five-year-old senior citizen. The difference is that the child is just emerging from that state, whereas the other is soon to go into it. The trappings of the void, however, hang on both alike.

This is precisely what I was saying earlier. Living must be learned, and it can only be learned in contact with those who are living. True, a child has an innocence that is appealing. There may even be a certain curiosity and frank interest that can be refreshing. But these things are not equal to being fully alive. It is

not by accident, you know, that "childishness" is a
pejorative term.

My sister died from brain fever when she was only
seven. Thus, she was not yet fully alive when she died.
The consequence was that she continued, in death,
much as she already was. Forever a child, just this side
of death, her perspective was distinct even from that
of my dead mother and, later, my father.

Her view of events was a simple one. More complicated matters escaped or confused her. When the latter
occurred, she laughed, as children do. My recollection
of my childhood with my sister is mostly, in fact, one of
her constant laughter. What I did or said would oftentimes produce waves of her giggles and cackling for
reasons I could not then understand.

My mother and father were not so much different.
Humor is a pretty big part of the dead life. This is a
characteristic of death that the living have accurately
portrayed, although, generally, only metaphorically.
The skeleton in a "haunted house" almost always
laughs, doesn't it?

I noticed this feature early on and long before I was
capable of understanding its meaning. Photographs from
my childhood show my family invariably smiling, pleasant. I am the exception, a frown on my face in each
picture. One shows my sister and me, in Indian costumes,
standing in front of a spirea hedge in our backyard. She
is about twelve and I am two. She stands tall, with dark

waving hair around a smiling, guileless face. I am to her waist, my headdress's single feather brushing her bare midriff. The look on my face could, I suppose, be said to be hostile, even challenging. But on close inspection, I think it was the face of someone who simply didn't understand why everyone else was laughing.

There were, in fact, many sources of humor for my family. This is so because what the dead find especially funny is anything that comes from living itself—not just feelings and emotions, the more obvious indicators we have already discussed. Any one of life's indicators was sufficiently comic to my family. (Although certainly feelings were always laughed at, and not just genuine ones, but parodies as well. I learned to escape being laughed at myself by developing a facility for burlesque, imitating outrageous displays of emotion at the very same time I was learning not to feel the real thing at all.) Fear, pleasure, compassion, some mark of creativity, the simple act of changing one's mind, the difference in one's appearance as the years pass and age shows— all are the object of humor for the dead. You need only think of a child poking a stick at a sleeping cat or throwing sticks across the fence at a big dog. When the animal reacts, there are squeals and—laughter. What is so funny? The dead could tell you.

As I said, parody was as much appreciated as reality. Television was in its so-called golden age when I was a child and my family especially loved the comedy shows with their broad slapstick humor. *Texaco Star Theater with Milton Berle, Liberace,* and *I Love Lucy* were particular favorites.

We watched these on a set placed in the living-room end of a combination living room/dining room. The dining room did not function as such. When we ate, we ate in the kitchen. In fact, we ate a good bit of food and this puzzled me when I later thought on it. Nourishment should be of no interest to dead people. But, I have come to realize, they had other reasons to eat. You probably have heard the approbative expression that "so-and-so has his feet on the ground." What you may not know is that this expression not only distinguishes a person from dreamy, idealistic types, but also from the dead, whose ethereal nature gives them a tendency to float above the earth unless they are weighted down. My family ate, therefore, to weigh them down to the ground and keep their feet there so they appeared as alive as the next person. Also, eating relieved postmortem anxiety. While death ends real feeling, you see, there may remain a type of phantom feeling, which approximates that state of raw and painful edginess called anxiety. This is not so surprising when one considers the experience of amputees who almost always report continuing pain in the lost limb. In death, what is lost is the whole of us, however, and that is what makes the phantom pain so terrible. Luckily, eating tends to deaden postmortem anxiety and, so, my family had yet another purpose to this activity.

Our dining room, though, was a daytime room. I often spent afternoons there, playing alone on the floor with toy horses and cowboys. Or I read the *Cyclopedia*. On summer days my sister and I played Monopoly at the table, where she regularly defeated me. She was in high school by then, but her advantage was more than that. She had a knack for Monopoly. I bought what I landed on. She bought Boardwalk, Park Place, the railroads, and then added hotels. She was lethal, and if she had been alive, I believe she would have been right in the middle of the real estate boom in the '70's. But she was dead, as I have said, and that, of course, made all the difference in her life.

At night we moved to the living-room end. My father lay back in his recliner and usually was fast asleep even before the end of *To Tell the Truth*. I oftentimes lay in the chair atop him, dozing through the remainder of the evening while my mother and sister watched their shows and chuckled. Or, to be precise, my mother watched television and my sister watched my mother. Being a child in death, my sister was only capable of experiencing the most primitive of representations. Television—two dimensions portraying three—was too abstract for her and she could only watch it by watching my mother watch it. So the evening passed, with Daddy sleeping, Mother and sister giggling, and me, pressing my face against the warm, oily cloth of my father's shirt, breathing it in.

# III. The death of my father

This disturbs me to tell, I admit. As I have said repeatedly, I don't think he was dead when I arrived. I know, really, that he was not. But the process of dying had begun and it was over before I had reached an age of sufficient understanding to perhaps intervene. He called me "Button" or the "Little Button." This was because of my nose and was the closest any one of us came to an endearment. Pet names were too inextricably bound with physical touching and, so, were not desirable in a family of the dead. What I knew of him was mostly surmise. We did not, you see, spend warming spring days sitting on an old bench beside the barn discussing his life, or mine, or anything at all. Though I often hear people repeat the lessons taught to them by a parent—"Take care of the land and it will take care of you"; "Something you don't need is dear at any price"— my father never told me anything of that sort. He was a quiet man and I generally was left to guess at what he might be thinking or the principles that governed his actions. Those few times he spoke to me, I remember.

He resembled the young John Wayne. Or, at least, he resembled the picture of John Wayne that appeared on the cover of "Put Your Arms Around Me, Honey," sheet music my mother kept in the piano bench. Like Wayne, he was tall and substantial looking. Square-jawed with thick, shiny black hair and metal gray eyes, he was a handsome man. If he were aware of these assets, however, he never let on. If anything, he seemed to treat his obvious good looks as the accident of nature it was and one he would just have to endure.

I should mention that the physical attributes of my family were not ordinarily distinguishable from those of living persons. There were certain differences, though, which I eventually came to appreciate. For one, they did not have sensations in the same way as the living. Instead, they experienced merely weight or pressure in physical contact, the same as one does when the dentist has deadened the jaw. There is some unpleasantness in this and, for that reason, they tended to avoid gratuitous touching. That tendency, necessarily, extended to touching other persons so I was raised without kissing or caresses of any sort. Nor, of course, was there any of this among the other members of my family. In truth, I never found this odd or felt deprived in any way. I adopted the practice, in fact, as my own and followed it well into my adult years.

Until I was three or four, I was able to feel my mother's touch when she held me on her lap for a few minutes each evening, as she read me to sleep. I insisted on the same story each time, "The Owl and the Pussycat," which is a poem, of course, but one that tells a story. I liked, I think, the sound of the words such as "runcible" and the incongruity of a bird and cat together for "a year and a day" and, ultimately, marrying. When I was four, however, I crawled down off my mother's lap and did not agree to be held again. Or so she often told me and others in my presence. The significance she attached to this event was never stated. At times, it seemed to be an apology for the obvious absence of physical closeness between us. At others, I detected a note of pride in the telling similar to a mother's boasting of a child's first step. My own conclusion is that, by the age of four, evidently, I had learned, like a corpse, to avoid touching other people. Perhaps, too, I was able to discern the discomfort to my mother in the close contact of lap sitting and politely declined to impose myself on her further. I had, in any event, other sources of contact that served me. I continued for a couple of years to climb into my father's recliner and sleep on his chest. He permitted this, although otherwise he never reached his hand to touch me. Even when he punished me, he preferred to use a switch or reins from a bridle to whip me, rather than his own flesh. And, too, there were the animals.

In some ways, my father appeared closer to the notion a living person might have as to how a corpse should appear. That is, he spoke very little and in a fairly monotone voice. When he talked, his arms hung at his sides, as he was not given to dramatic gestures or sudden movement. When he was in the house, he was usually asleep in his chair, and in the outdoors I often watched him standing motionless, staring intently at some project or, sometimes, at nothing at all. By contrast, my mother and sister were talkers. Their voices could be heard at a distance. They talked to each other and over each other and in a wide range of inflections. But they were, nevertheless, the ones who had already died. He was not quite there, yet.

In this way, my father was different. My mother had died because of something that had occurred. It was the same for my sister. But this was not true of him. My father died entirely of his own accord and over some time. As the years went by, he devoted less and less time to the exercise of living. Because of this, it was at last no longer second nature to him. One day, I think, he simply forgot to do it at all.

I have sometimes told friends who know nothing of my earlier experiences a different account. I have spoken of a special bond between my father and me. In these accounts, he is a complicated but uneducated man, a prairie philosopher who found some comfort in having one special sensitive child (this is me, in my telling) who alone had any understanding of the profundities swirling within him. I have joked with casual lovers that all of my good traits came from my father and the bad ones from my mother. My father was kind and I try to be, I say. He submerged his needs to those of others and I don't like to impose my will. He had taste, discretion. He was reflective, a thinker. We both loved animals. It is absurd now that I see it on paper.

There were the animals, yes. He kept our farm alive with them. He was a cattleman and we kept cattle. There was a horse or two, a dog, sometimes more, and a few feeder pigs. Daddy brought home two fantail pigeons, built them a house high atop a pole, and they were soon a dozen. We had a big and mean white goose and an old Muscovy duck. White Rock chickens and bantams. A king snake in the granary and a possum family in the barn. He brought cottontail bunnies from the fields in summer. In a home movie, I stood with cupped hands, gently holding a bit of fur toward the camera—a baby jackrabbit and the expression on my face was a curious mixture of utter delight and some darker notion not readily recognizable.

My father did not speak to me of the animals. I knew he cared deeply about them because my mother had told me that. She told me the day he refused to let city hunters shoot quail and pheasant on our farm. "Daddy thinks those little birds are cute," she said. "He can't stand the thought of anyone shooting them." That same day was the day he released the baby raccoon he had been tending. He had brought it home from the field a couple of weeks before. It clung to the bib of his overalls and hissed at anyone else who came near. Daddy put him in a large homemade crate we had used for a series of baby rabbits and took care of him. He fed him scraps from the table. Sometimes there was extra gravy, and Daddy would laugh at the little coon's efforts to wash the gravy before he ate it, staring in befuddlement at his empty paws. Once he put a box turtle in the crate and let the raccoon spend most of half an hour futilely washing the turtle, which withdrew into its shell at any attempt to grab its legs or head. At last, when it had grown enough to make its way alone, Daddy took his pet to the field after the noon meal. The following day my mother told me: Daddy had turned the little raccoon loose, made one round on the tractor, and then found the baby dead, shot through the neck. The hunters he had previously turned away needed something to shoot, she said he had said, and, in spite or thoughtlessly, had picked Daddy's baby raccoon.

By example or shared blood, I followed my father. Like him, I gathered creatures close around me. At times I cared for wild babies, too, mostly jackrabbits or cottontails, raising them up until they could be returned to the field where they had been found. Day to day my companions were my small black dog, Chimpy, and Penny, a stubborn half-Shetland mare that had been given to my father by a neighbor. Every morning Chimpy waited outside for me. My mother said he looked like a worn-out dust mop and was twice as dirty. She would not let him inside the house and pushed him away with the toe of her shoe if he tried to come in anyway. So we met on the back steps each morning and, from there, would make our rounds.

First, to the henhouse to gather eggs from the fierce and unwilling setting hens, then to the end of the lane to post any letters. By the middle of the morning, it was time to catch old Penny. Chimpy would follow along behind us as I rode the mare through the pasture or on the sandy roads near our farm. Penny was my Indian pony in the pasture, Chimpy my tribe. We scanned the horizon from atop a bluff as we looked down on the encampment of settlers. Then, at my signal, we descended in savage fury to capture the settlers' ponies and burn their camp. Or I was the cavalry captain with Chimpy, my troops, alerted to trouble by smoke rising in the distance. I rode my thoroughbred mount to the cliff above the settlers' encampment. The Apaches had circled them and a battle was raging. At my signal, we descended valiantly into the fray and drove away the marauding Indians. On other, gentler days, we discovered hidden gold mines or lost tribes, or rode in phantom parades. In the afternoons the three of us would rest awhile in a sunny spot near the pond. Penny would graze on the wiry buffalo grass and Chimpy would nap, his chin resting on my foot. In these particulars, we three could not have been so different from farm children and their pets elsewhere. What was singular was the exchange. Far from a mere passing of happy times together, our days were classrooms with Chimpy and Penny the teachers and me the student.

From them, by necessity, I learned most of what I knew of living beings, at least until I reached the age of ready commerce with the world outside my family. Even then, because of my earlier direction, I continued to follow their lead in forming associations and feelings in my living self. Surely, the first clear notion of love I could entertain came from Chimpy. His was a wordless adoration, a constant companionship. Chimpy's love was not altogether different from its human counterpart, yet in certain respects it was not the same either. It was unilateral in its definition; he demanded nothing of me but to be close by and to be looked at from time to time. I was his joy, his central thought, and it was enough for him that I simply be. There was no quid pro quo, no trade-off, nor any of the conditions I have occasionally found under the table in times since. His love was a given, a first premise, a Quinean core belief. It would not be reevaluated short of cataclysm. When I was three, I made a leash of a piece of twine and a harness of a wide rubber band, the type my mother used to bind packages of sweet corn for the freezer. I carefully removed the leash from Chimpy at the end of the day, but I forgot the rubber band. When my father discovered it a day or two later, it had cut almost an inch into Chimpy's chest. Chimpy survived but bore a permanent scar. He did not wag his tail any less after that and he still followed close by.

For her part, the mare helped even out my perspective. She barely concealed her equine contempt for me. Our relationship was one of games. I had my advantages and she had hers. I had the reins, the bit, the catalpa beans I used to sting her rump; she had her Shetland wits, brute strength, and a stubborn will to oppose me. We both liked to use the element of surprise. So most days Penny would gallop into battle with me, bear me up and down the country roads, and even stand for hours tied to a post, if I pleased. But every so often, she would take the bit in her teeth and move across the pasture in an unalterable course toward the low-hanging limbs of the mulberry trees. I was scraped to the ground or forced to jump from her bare back. She, being only half a Shetland, was too tall for me to remount without a step or a box, and even with that managed to shift away just as I was ready to climb up. After some consideration, I began leading Penny to the nearest grassy patch on these occasions. There, I would let her nibble and think she had bested me. Then, when she was well into her feeding, I threw myself across her muscular neck, startling her into raising it and sliding me onto her back. The satisfaction I felt in outsmarting her was immense. I have since stood toe to toe with corporate golden boys whose wits were less than that old horse.

But these are things that I can tell you readily, that you can understand on the usual terms. What passed between us that was most consequential is not so easily told. The creatures let me near, you see, let me touch them. I felt the red fox squirrel's shoulder muscles strain to loosen my grasp, and the cottontail's warm breath as it nuzzled deeper beneath my jacket. I laid my cheek against Penny's short, coarse hair laden with acrid sweat and felt the power of her muscles and size. I untangled Chimpy's long, silky coat and spread it over his scrawny ribs and backbone. What life I touched, in those early years, was mostly theirs. This is not so now, of course, though a handshake, a pat, or even the passionate embrace of another human being does not always put one in contact with anything living. Such connection is, I have found, sporadic and unexpected. We hoard our life as though every other were a preda-tor who would steal it away. The animals were more trusting. What they possessed was always there to be touched and given. Even now, in the middle of the city, I sometimes long for them. I have Maggie, of course. My horse-dog, with her massive head and short stiff coat. She is my compromise, I laugh.

My father died finally, I think, in the summer of 1960 when I was ten. At least, the last time I know he may have been alive was that spring. It was the day they were coming for the cattle. The farm had been sold, a house purchased in the nearby town. He found a small pasture near the city limits to keep Penny, but there was nothing to do but sell the cattle. The trucks would come that day to take them.

I had been looking for him with my own concern. I had become attached to a dead cottonwood tree that lay on its side in our pasture, just outside the corral gate. As was usual with dead cottonwoods, the tree was stark white with streaks of gray, its wood smooth and polished. This one was an especially fine specimen with great sprawling branches that looked like gigantic antlers, its points reaching skyward. Where the branches joined were small hollows, and in these I had placed bits of paper with secret notes to myself and others. On the wood itself I had carved various symbols, mean-ingful only to me and, probably, only at the time I had actually inscribed them. I called the tree my "treasure tree" and I did not want to leave it. My parents had dismissed my pleas not to leave the farm at all. My mother, especially, had long sought to move to the confinement, the closeness of town, and would not consider remaining where we were. As an alternative, I had determined I would ask my father to move my tree with us. I don't know what he would have responded. In the end, I didn't ask him after all.

I found him by the willow pen, an enclosure just off the corral with a single large willow tree. We usually kept feeder pigs there each summer, and their rooting and wallowing had destroyed all of the vegetation except that one tree. He was standing at the fence, one foot resting on a cross post, his arms separated and hanging over the top of the fence itself. The cows were in the pen. He had gathered them there because the pen had the easiest access to the only cattle chute, an old wooden structure just off the barn. He stood silently staring at the animals in the pen. I waited for him to turn toward me. I did not tug at my father or speak to gain his attention. That was something he gave or not.

I waited for almost an hour. After the first few minutes, I sat down with my back braced against the old chute. Chimpy lay nearby, close enough for an occasional pat from me but far enough away to stretch out and nap in the sunshine. To pass the time, I picked blades of fescue and made whistles and stared into the sapphire blue sky until my eyes were blinded to anything else. But he never turned. "Your daddy hates to lose those cows," my mother told me later.

My mother was always telling me what my father thought or felt or had said. It was rare that I would have any direct account from him on anything at all. Once, before we left the farm for good, my father and I were riding the county highway in his pickup truck. He was leaning forward, as he always did, with both arms resting atop the steering wheel. As was usual, he had not spoken since leaving home some fifteen miles before. Then he cleared his throat. This was the signal he was about to say something. He looked at me. "Did you ever wonder why you're you and I'm me?" he asked. I nodded, startled, and tried to think of something that would result in more from him. It was no matter. He had said what he had to say and that was that.

It must seem odd to you, given the want of conversation between us, that I say now I knew my father was alive. Without my mother's reports to confirm what I suspected, I probably would not have known. Her words gave strength to the intuitions that sometimes came to me that my father still lived, intuitions that, otherwise, would have remained beyond articulation. As I have said, I could not stand to one side and observe my life, nor had I been taught yet the differences between corpses and living persons. The life I sometimes sensed in my father was a sort of immediate knowing, more akin to instinct than to reason. The closest phenomenon I have since observed is, perhaps, that of species recognition. A few years back, I found a baby wood duck lost on a city street near my house. I took him home, fed him, gave him daily swims in the bathtub, and when he was feathered, released him on the little pond below the house. For a time, he would come willingly to me when I whistled, flying in to eat crackers from my hand and to be close to the only parent he had ever known. But, gradually, he accustomed himself to living with the other ducks, all mallards, that inhabited the pond. After a while he stopped coming to me (although to this day he will whistle a response to mine). This little creature's entire experience had been with human beings and mallards. Yet when I later acquired another young male wood duck and released it on the pond, my little wood duck was the only one to approach it. He swam around the nervous newcomer twice, whistling softly. Then he turned and led it back to his own feeding group. What can explain this except that he recognized his own kind; that he knew somehow that he himself was reflected in that other?

Similarly, I must have sensed a part of myself in my father, something that was not in my mother or sister or even my pets. Not continuously, as I have explained, but sporadic and, in every instance, accompanied by my intense embarrassment. In one case, the experience would be very similar to puttering about in a room and then suddenly realizing you are not alone. You are embarrassed and your mind races back over the preceding minutes to catalog the ways in which you have revealed yourself. That is what occurred in the pickup truck when my father's remark so clearly put another living being, a self, next to me.

The other times were more akin to intimate encounters. Intimacy was, as I have told you, missing from my life with corpses. Physical intimacy, yes, but also emotional intimacy. Both capacities to feel are eliminated in death, although there is a substitute of sorts for intimacy among the dead. It is proximity. This accounts for the fact that we bury our dead collectively in cemeteries and that couples and relatives express the desire to be buried side by side. In our family no one was buried yet, so we achieved this proximity by other means. There were the evenings watching television I have already described. Too, we took car trips, all of us brought together in the confines of the automobile, wherein we might travel thousands of miles over the diverse terrain of the Great Plains or, perhaps, just thirty miles to the county seat. In the latter case, the same effect was achieved as the lengthier trip because we not only drove the short distance to the city, but two of us often sat together in the car for hours at a time waiting on the others to finish their errands.

The occasional intimacy I experienced with my father was fundamentally different. Because it was always unexpected and, when it came, something so rarely felt, it was a startling, disconcerting event. The intensity of this feeling always came to the surface as embarrassment. I suppose that if I had learned a range of feelings as an ordinary child might, perhaps the feeling would have been something different. Embarrassment and shame were the most intense feelings in my limited repertoire, however, and that was naturally what presented itself.

That was the feeling, at least, that curled across me one Saturday morning when my father was leaving to sell roof tar. It was 1959 and times were hard on the farm. My father had taken a job "running" gas wells to pick up extra cash. After a time that job was given to a younger man whose family had lived in the county longer. Daddy had turned then to selling a new variety of roof tar, a product he found in a *Successful Farming* advertisement soliciting salesmen. He had begun it in late fall, after the wheat was in, but now it was January and he had shown little success. He had already approached all of our neighbors and the likely prospects in town. On this day, my mother told me, he was going to drive across the county to some of her family to see if he could sell something there.

He was standing at the kitchen table, stuffing product flyers into the tooled leather notebook my grandparents had brought me from Mexico. On one side of the notebook was the Aztec calendar and on the other, the tossing head of a stallion. Handles could be pulled up for carrying. Daddy was dressed in the suit and topcoat he wore to church, with ordinary laced shoes having replaced his usual boots. I watched him prepare, both of us silent. As he started to leave, he looked in my direction and I asked if I might go, too. He muttered, "No," without even parting his lips and turned away. I saw inside him, an unfamiliar view, a shock that was quickly swept away by overpowering shame and embarrassment by the intimacy of this inadvertent contact. He gave up selling roof tar a few months later and, somehow, we managed to get by until we finally left the farm altogether.

# IV. The discovery and rescue

The discovery of my life with a family of the dead followed hard on the heels of our move to town. It is more difficult to keep secrets in a city setting, even

one so small as the little farming community where my
parents had bought us a house. Also, my parents had
recently taken up with fundamentalist religion and, as
it happened, this led directly to my discovery.

Shortly after our move to town, going to church or
doing the Lord's work began to take up much of our time.
There, on Wednesday evenings, we attended prayer
meeting at the preacher's house. We sat around a
Formica-topped dining table and made up lists of people
to pray for, most of whom were new residents who had
not yet picked a church. We memorized Bible verses
and, on some Wednesdays, split into groups that then
canvassed houses to witness for the Lord. Sundays were
likewise full. Following the usual morning services, we
would reconvene at an old folks' home or a hospital
ward to conduct another meeting there. In the evenings
the preacher met with the children for youth group
and then we attended Sunday evening services. The
latter differed from the morning services in the content
of the sermons. Perhaps in recognition that he needed
to keep everyone awake, the preacher selected the
most appealing topics for the evenings. The second
coming of Christ and the symbols in Revelations were
common themes.

I do not think it was accidental that this finding of
religion followed the death of my father so closely. Like
draws like and fundamentalism is essentially a religion
of death. Its basic tenets decry life on earth as an evil

hindrance to be overcome on the way to true life after death in the presence of the Almighty Father. What one may do to ease the pain of living beings or to raise the standards and aspirations of others is of no consequence. By grace are ye saved and by grace alone. This was a place my parents, dead as they were, could be accommodated and comfortable. I do not begrudge them the path they took. It is not necessarily a simple task to live life after one has died.

At that time, however, I was unaware of these aspects of my situation. Instead, as a child will do, I had followed my parents' lead and had wholeheartedly embraced fundamentalism. This led me to the witnessing I mentioned and that led me, finally, to Winfield Evan Stark.

Mr. Stark was an older man, a widower, who lived alone in a little house directly across the street from ours. His home had actually been the city's electric department at one time, and when the building became available, he bought it and converted it into a comfortable dwelling for a bachelor. All I knew of him, at first, was that he was an atheist. Actually, he was not an atheist but an agnostic, he later explained. This was not a distinction with a difference to fundamentalists, but it was a matter of some importance to Mr. Stark. He was very particular about details.

I had heard my parents discussing Mr. Stark well before I ever met him. They would see him through the window, working in his yard, and make some comment.

Invariably the topic was his atheism and the disturbing possibilities that presented. Death limits one's perspective and my mother could see in the events and people around her only those parts that pertained to her personally. She began to believe that Mr. Stark was the devil himself, placed in proximity to her to threaten her fundamentalist beliefs. This theory became a firm conviction when she learned he had once been issued a car tag with the only numbers being "666." This coincidence was thought to have resulted from the intervention of an overly pious matron, Lucille McEwen, whose son was the county assessor. Whatever its origin, it delighted the churchgoing townspeople in whose midst Mr. Stark lived. They did not like him very much. He was a disbeliever and, worse, he was an educated one. Mr. Stark knew these things, I am certain, though he never acknowledged any concern over them. Without complaint, he dutifully placed the unfortunate tag on his red Lancer and drove the car for a year. When the year was up, however, he reserved the number "8" for himself, ensuring he would never be issued "666" again.

I first spoke to him one day as he was weeding a flower bed to one side of his house. He worked his yard daily, some in the morning and some in the late afternoons. He was a trim, active man with only the slightest suggestion of a paunch. He kept his graying hair closely trimmed in a modified crew cut and wore a tie every day, though he did shed his coat when doing the yard work. It was said he had been an FBI agent and that experience accounted for the exceptional neatness that seemed to encircle his existence. He never confirmed this to me, however, and I later learned that there were exceptions to his seeming tidiness. He was pleasant enough when I approached him and, I was glad to see, he did not resemble at all the demon my mother had come to believe he was. My purpose gave me some amount of courage. He was, you see, a prize. Bringing him around, getting him to our church even one time, would seal my own redemption, I was certain. I did not understand then that the transformation that comes when life touches life is almost always mutual. Still, I made certain to approach him outdoors where I could make an easy escape, if necessary.

Mr. Stark was amused at my childish attempts at proselytizing. He told me, politely, that he did not wish to attend our church but that he could possibly be persuaded to change his mind if I could convince him there was any good reason to go. He was a shrewd man, Mr. Stark. Filled with hope, I told my parents what I had done. For a moment they were silent. "Maybe the Lord wants to reach him this way. 'A child shall lead them,'" my mother finally said. My father said nothing.

Thereafter, several days a week I crossed the street and followed Mr. Stark around his yard, setting forth the best arguments I had. "The Bible says to go to church. Hebrews 10:25," I told him one day. He was tending his roses—ten bushes that bordered the lawn and were divided in the middle by the straight walk to the front door.

"*Hmm*. It does, does it?" He spoke without looking at me, his eyes intent on each bush as we moved down the row. Each was the same height, the same width, and the same variety—Mister Lincoln hybrid—displaying the deep red blooms he favored.

"Yes. So if you don't go, you're not doing what God told you to."

Mr. Stark glanced at me, acknowledging my statement with a tight smile, then squatted to clip a yellowed leaf from low on one bush's center cane. "I see. If *God* tells you something, you certainly ought to do it. Is that what you're telling me?"

I nodded enthusiastically, sidestepping to stay by him when he abruptly stood and continued his slow march down his row of roses.

"Of course, that assumes . . ." He glanced at me once more, then seemed to change direction. "No. No, I can't abide spending time unnecessarily with a bunch of hypocrites."

I seized the opportunity. "That's why you should go with *me*. We don't have any of those in our church." This was true. People who went so far as to preach our religion were the type of people likely to practice it as well.

He stopped a moment and looked off, considering my point. "Well, let me ask you this," he said finally. "If

I were to go to church, though, shouldn't I go to the church where my son and his family go?"

"You could," I spoke slowly, a little disappointed. I hadn't anticipated this turn.

He pressed his advantage. "What do you think my grandchildren would think if their grandfather went off by himself to some stranger's church?"

"What people think is chaff in the wind," I answered, this unexpected pronouncement making him smile. "You should only go to their church if they preach what's right there," I told him, earnestly explaining that his life after death would depend on how well he chose.

"Uh-huh. That is a consideration." He turned again to the roses, expertly clip-clipping three dead stubs in a few seconds. "I'll give it some thought," he promised, and I waited, hoping he would give in but he didn't— not that day or any other.

There did come a day, though, that Mr. Stark finally dealt with me directly. His wife was why he was an agnostic, he told me. At least, she was one of the reasons. She had died five years before and death had not been easy.

"She went through more pain than I can tell you. She died eaten up with cancer," he said, adding that, within a year, his forty-year-old daughter had died of breast cancer, enduring the same agonizing, protracted death as her mother. "They were both *good, kind* people." He had to look away then. He was trembling with anger and disbelief.

He told me these things one day as we sat in his tiny living room, the only public area of his house. He had begun to invite me inside for our conversations when the summer and fall had passed and the weather had become too cold for yard work. Sometimes, on these inside days, Mr. Stark would have refreshments—store-bought cookies or hot lemonade. While we talked, he would sit on one side, I on the other, of a massive rosewood desk piled high with books. Books were all about the room. They were on bookshelves that lined three walls, with a small window in the middle of one. They were in chairs and on the floor beside chairs. The contrast of the clutter inside his house with the neatly clipped shrubs and velvet lawn outside had been a revelation to me. Some thing was everywhere a space existed. His furniture consisted only of the desk, a few antique chairs, and a small sofa. But in the confines of his small house, they all sat arm to arm and back to back. Piled on top of these, where no books were, were photographs, framed certificates, inscribed paperweights, and a hundred other mementos of Mr. Stark's life until then. I see now that this jumble of things should not have surprised me. After his wife's death, Mr. Stark had simply moved all of his belongings from his larger house—the one they had shared—to this much smaller one. The crowding was to be expected.

The truth took the life out of our controversy. I tried to answer the implications of what had happened to Mr. Stark, his wife, and daughter. But, quite naturally, my response was limited by my age and experience. My only argument was the one I had heard given often— that there must be some unknown reason, a good purpose, for these deaths. That Mr. Stark should simply have faith that this was so. To do this, he replied, would mean arbitrarily giving up logic and reason. Why suspend these in this instance and not in all others? No good had come from the deaths of his wife and daughter, only pain for him and his family, not to mention the excruciating pain before death suffered by these women. Nor could there be any reasonable contention that either or both of these exceptional souls had deserved such an end. I could not answer him.

Once I thought I had surely persuaded him to come to church with me. I had shamelessly put it on a personal basis—would he please come to help me win one of the "membership" contests the church often conducted for the children? To help his little friend might be a good-enough reason, he acknowledged, and promised to think about it. But when Sunday arrived, he did not come.

After a time I knew, I suppose, that he was intractable. I did not stop coming to see him. Our conversations had expanded beyond their initial scope into a variety of areas entertaining to the both of us. I still began them with some pro forma effort to get Mr. Stark to church, but then our conversations took some other

turn. He asked me if I had read of the Lipizzan stallions.
I had not. He selected one of his many books and
turned to a picture of the arena in Vienna where the
horses perform. While I studied the photograph of
the magnificent white horses at work in the ring,
Mr. Stark told me of their rigorous training, the incred-
ible feats they come to master. How the Nazis tried to
steal them, but General Patton outsmarted them and
saved the beautiful animals for Austria. My favorite
part was his account of the special bond between each
horse and its rider. "Each has its own soul," he told me
gravely. "And each rider must be carefully trained to
find that soul and preserve it. Otherwise, if he fails, the
Lipizzan might as well be an old plow horse."

Mr. Stark did not approve of much that was old
or decrepit. He often remarked on his abhorrence of
elderly drivers. At the time our conversations began, he
was sixty-two years old. All drivers should turn in their
licenses at age sixty-five, he often told me. He was
certainly going to do that when he turned sixty-five.
As one grew older, one's ability to react diminished.
Worse, one's ability to know that also diminished.
He would not be some old duffer holding up traffic on
the highway or running up on curbs. No, while he still
had his wits about him, he would voluntarily relinquish
his driving privileges. That was the only reasonable
and proper thing to do.

What would I do with my grown-up life, he asked me. I was going to be a missionary. He laughed and said, Maybe so. But had I thought about working with the Foreign Service, the diplomatic corps, perhaps? That way, he explained, I could still travel to foreign lands and I could preach to the government people who probably needed saving more than anyone. He opened an atlas and we considered where I might want to go. He suggested Greece, and I thought not. But he pressed this, explaining to me first its importance to modern law and civilization. We talked, too, of the Greek philosophers, especially Plato. We spent several weeks working our way through the "Myth of the Cave," Plato's account of coming into the light of true knowledge and understanding, something that Mr. Stark thought I might want to know. He called the one that made it out "the cicada," after the buzzing insects that periodically emerge from beneath the ground and climb up trees to split their shells and hatch.

"Some are down there in the dark as long as seventeen years," he told me. "Then they finally come up to the light, get up that tree, and see all there is to see on this big prairie."

"Plato's cave bugs!" I said, and he laughed.

"An apt name for them," he agreed.

He would be pleased, I suppose, at the international aspects of my life now. My profession sometimes requires dealings with foreigners and their countries. And I have often traveled to some foreign location for pleasure, as well. Last spring, for instance, I signed up for an ornithologist-led expedition to the Amazonian rain forest—an outing essentially put together for well-off Americans and Europeans willing to pay for such things. Mr. Stark had never talked to me much of the Central and South Americas. Still, on several occasions, he spoke with respect of the Mayan and Aztec cultures and the mystery of their disappearance. Thus, tramping through the stifling wetness of the rain forest, I some-times thought of Mr. Stark and what wonderful feelings my trip would have effected in him. I have found, you see, that this is one of the ways I am able to have some of those feelings for myself. It is a kind of reflected glory. One may not be able to generate heat like a furnace. But if you stand close enough, it will warm you anyway.

Mr. Stark knew, I think, even before I did. At the very least, we reached that recognition together over the first two years of our acquaintance. And in the end, it was not one shocking moment of realization, but a final, unspoken acceptance we shared that had been built on a hundred brief moments of insight.

Only one time before my rescue, however, did Mr. Stark make any statement to me regarding my unique circumstances. And, even then, I am certain he had not intended to speak. It was the July day I found Chimpy in the ditch outside town. He had been missing for almost two weeks. In the beginning my father told me that he was probably running with the other dogs that roamed the town. That he would come back when he was ready. Later Daddy told me that something must have happened to him. Each morning as I left the house, I still looked for him anyway. Finally, I had found him. He was a half mile from the city limits—well past the pasture where we had kept Penny before finally selling her to one of the neighbors. He was lying in one of the deep unmown ditches along the graveled road that ran through the center of town.

He lay on his side, the empty eye socket that had been hit by the bullet facing upward. His carcass was drying out now, well past the bloating stage. I had carefully brushed off the sticks that clung to his coat and carried him back to the house. I lay him on the steps and went to fetch a soft tea towel in which to bury him. No, my mother said. She took the towel and told me to put him in the truck bed. "Your daddy will haul it off." I was leaving to tell Herbert Thompson, the town's lone peace officer, that my dog had been murdered when she finally, reluctantly, told me. "No one murdered Chimpy." I waited without speaking. "He was so dirty and always whining to come in. You have other things to do now. He wasn't any good to anyone anymore. I told your daddy he should get rid of him."

When I had crossed the street to Mr. Stark's house and told him, I began suddenly to weep. Not the crying of pain and indignation that follows a whipping, but the low and keening cry of mourning. It was then that Mr. Stark, startled by my tears and, perhaps, a little angry for my sake, had impulsively spoken. He reached out his arm to comfort me. "My child, what did you expect?" he whispered softly, and almost to himself, "You are living with dead people."

As I recall, my conversations with Mr. Stark continued for a year after that—nearly three years in all—when my parents decided I should not spend any more time with him. My mother told me one morning at breakfast that I was not to go there again. She and my father did not believe I would ever convert him, she said. It could even be that I was at risk to become possessed by whatever it was that had possessed him. I did not press them to change their minds and I don't know still if that could have altered any of what followed. I reasoned that I was busy with school and would not have seen Mr. Stark as often anyway, and I thought that when it got closer to the religious holidays, I could persuade them to let me talk to him again. That was where my upbringing betrayed me. How could I have thought that my moratorium on action could ensure forbearance on the part of another being? That Mr. Stark would sit silently on the shelf where I had placed him only in my mind? Those are altogether reasonable assumptions when in the presence of dead people, however, and as a child of corpses, those are the ones I made.

Thus, it was on the day after Halloween, November 1, 1963, that Mr. Stark undertook my rescue. He decided to do so after I had not crossed the street to his house for almost six weeks. He had fretted about the consequences of interfering, he told me later, though he had never imagined, nor could have, what transpired as a result. He cared about me, about my soul, he said, and he was afraid I might slip back into the "cave" unless he acted. But he had no understanding—could have none—of the fragile structure within which my strange family survived. And when he crossed the street to confront them with the truth he knew, he did so without knowing at all what that might mean.

On that day in November, I was in school and attending a special assembly in the auditorium. A hypnotist traveling from school to school was performing that day, just as he had about the same time the year before. He had stood on the spotlighted stage surrounded by seven or eight folding chairs and asked for volunteers, especially those with bad habits they wanted to be rid of or those with faulty memories they wanted refreshed. I instinctively pulled back from this call to take the stage and let one's inner thoughts be touched, but the chairs had quickly filled with eager others. Donna Ferris, who had asthma and chewed her fingernails, and James Turnby, one of the boys living at the foster home in town, were among them. The hypnotist began his soporific suggestions. For a time all of the volunteers appeared to be

trance-bound. Donna was given a posthypnotic suggestion that her nails would taste like bar soap and another
student was made to bark like a dog the first time he
heard the word "macaroni." One by one, the volunteers
"awakened" from their trances and, as previously
instructed, left the stage. Only James was left. The hypnotist, unaware of James's orphaned status, was taking
him back in time to his earliest childhood memories. The
rest of us sitting in the darkened auditorium squirmed,
partly from embarrassment and partly in fascination.
Finally, James recalled his fourth Christmas. He received
a wooden train set, he said, and a large kickball. The tree
was decorated with tinsel and electric lights. Was he
really awake and just making this up? His mother wore a
purple dress with polka dots. He seemed very excited and
happy. Time was running short and the hypnotist began
the steps to awaken James. When he awoke, the family
he was remembering, made up or not, would be gone.
Before he could do this, I felt a hand on my arm. It was
Mrs. Brewer from the principal's office and she signaled
me silently to come with her.

She led me to the large glass doors at the school's
front entrance. We looked toward the drive in front,
where Sheriff Thompson sat in his "cherry top,"
a '54 beige Ford with its single red light on the roof.
"They need to see you at home," she said cryptically.
"The sheriff will take you." I did not question her. Had
I known, after all, that this day would come to pass?

Sheriff Thompson, likewise, did not volunteer further information. We rode silently the few blocks to my house. As he started to turn onto our street, however, he suddenly blurted, "Now, everything is going to be fine. Don't you worry. I'll stay right with you. Okay?" I nodded without speaking and turned to look down the street. The doors were opened, I noticed. Every door to our house that I could see was wide open, the screen doors, too, the latter held at right angles to the house by chairs or sawhorses. Several men in dark uniforms— the state troopers—stood about, and I saw the station wagon from Preston's funeral home backed up our sidewalk to the front steps of the house. The troopers' two patrol cars were parked on either side, on the lawn itself. Mr. Stark was talking to a woman I did not recognize, and a dozen or so more of our neighbors were watching from their own front yards.

Mr. Stark reached me first. He thought it best I not go inside; it would upset me too much. He had forgotten, apparently, that being very upset was one of those inconveniences from which my family had long ago freed me. I walked into the house, the sheriff following close behind, and realized at once why the doors were open. The stench was staggering. The smell became increasingly stronger until I reached the kitchen. I did not need to go farther. There, sitting on the floor, were my mother and sister. My sister was leaning back against the oven door and my mother sat, her back against the refrigerator, facing my sister. They were dressed in familiar clothes and my mother's hand still held the morning's paper, opened to the comics. All around them was the food—food of every sort and in varying stages of decay, piled on counters, on the table, and even on the floor. For my mother and sister, things had changed as well. They were still dead, of course. But now there could be no mistaking that fact. All the outward appearances of life, the flesh, the hair, the substance, were gone. They sat now, skeletons and nothing more. Their bones were smooth and gray white, with the patina that only comes from long years of exposure to the elements. I thought of my treasure tree. "How long have they been like this?" Sheriff Thompson asked in a strangely patronizing tone, and I started to smile.

My father was found a few hours later, his body still intact in the remains of his overturned pickup truck. It was supposed he had fallen asleep and left the road, or perhaps suffered a heart attack. However, the coincidence of this occurrence with the discovery of the others was inevitably viewed with suspicion. Some of that naturally came to focus on Mr. Stark, who had been the one to call the sheriff. There might have been ruinous results had the nation's attention not been suddenly redirected by the assassination of President Kennedy a few weeks later.

• ◆ • ◆ • ◆ • •

AND SO THAT IS IT. I have set down such details and information as I have. There is no more. Oh, the consequences. But how can I be the one to tell of those? I eventually lost the religion altogether, of course. It is difficult to both think and hold such beliefs, and I don't consider now that I have that much of my concentration to spare. What I have I use to keep from being dead, which is, after all, almost second nature to me still. I need only to be left to myself sufficiently, to be allowed to summon again from time to time those instincts of life I do possess. And now, having written it all down, I would like very much to just sit here for a while longer. Here, with Maggie, and I can rest my hand on her warm head.

*THE END*

# THE REMAINS

# 1.

THAT IS THE ACCOUNT I
wrote. It was the one demanded of me here—in this very
cemetery—ten years ago, during the graveside services for
the recently departed Mr. Stark, the same body who is departed once more, although whether *recently* no one knows.

Evan says that "Granddad wouldn't have been missed
at all, except that Lucille McEwen died," because it was
only when they started marking off that site that his
grandfather's grave was seen to be half over on hers. So
they dug him up to cure his trespass on his old foe and he
was not there. Today they are set to dig again at Laurel's
close-cropped buffalo grass, adding to the defacement left
by their first effort, the half loaf of lime-streaked clods

I saw when I arrived yesterday. Then as now, I parked my car over here, on Laurel's far north drive. I overtook the grave gradually, winding my way through the fifteen rows between this side and that until I knelt and reached my hand to touch the slick Colorado granite of Mr. Stark's headstone. It was not the gesture of sentiment that it surely seemed to be to those watching so carefully, but only my getting as near his grave as I could. I came close to listen. I was expecting a message from him, a communication as clear and direct as Mr. Stark gave me on the day of his funeral.

He had passed unexpectedly, although in the way that each of us secretly wishes—well groomed and fully dressed, dropping gracefully to the sidewalk not two doors from Preston's, the local funeral home and ambulance service. He was ninety-four and I, forty-three. That was one thing of which I was reminded at his burial, but it was something else encountered there, quite unexpected and nearly pushed in my face, that forced me to offer the details of my life with corpses. Funerals! It is a dangerous folly we indulge. Staying one's distance is always the safer thing to do.

His family took his body, displaying it in the entry hall of the Methodist Church—theirs, not his—and the narrow pine boards creaked beneath the weight of the passing queue, the same sound I heard as a child when my Sunday school classmate was displayed, run over by the V-ridged wheel of her father's Case 500. Oh, yes, I was a proper Methodist before the other—before my dead family found the real religion in fundamentalism—and I sang "Jesus Loves Me" and "I'm Going to Let It Shine," and, once, "I'm a Sunflower from the Sunflower State," although I do not remember the Christian reference for the last. A square-boned woman from Arkansas, June Barger, was our Methodist minister for those three years, remaining hidden from the small me except for rare days my mother permitted me to stay for the full service. Those times, the soft round of Miss Junie's large face beneath her straight bush of gray hair hung above the pulpit like a rising moon and her soothing monotone floated out over the intermittent creak of folding wooden seats until I was as still as my crushed friend. The Methodists do not make death their central tenet, perhaps, but they are well versed in its etiquette.

I recall that I stood at the very last of the mourning line and for a reason. There, I could easily step, unnoticed, farther away from Mr. Stark's open coffin than was the practice of those preceding me who were nearer and better able to cast shivering glances at the waxen face of his corpse, to come so close to the wiry hairs quite still on his folded hands that the tickling of their touch could almost be felt. Too dangerous, I knew, and I stayed back, safe but for what later occurred without my cooperation. I almost escaped, in fact, my fingers on the car's chrome door handle when Evan, the daughter's son who had been a year or two ahead of me in school, touched my shoulder.

"Granddad would have appreciated your being here," he said, and I nodded. But then, "Do you know the way to the cemetery?" he asked, and so I was trapped into going to the very place I had determined to avoid. I had already begun to develop quite a fear of lying, you see, suspecting it could be the one deadly deed to finish me.

Cemeteries are filled with corpses, of course, and people suppose that the bodies are confined to locked boxes and buried under two feet or more of suffocating soil to protect them and to honor them, but that is not so. Their interment seeks to protect *us*, the living, from them. From their resurrection among other events—you recall what an enormous amount has been made of one such—else my family would not be the exception but the rule. I think that each of us surmises this without saying so directly and that accounts for the stories: the suggestion, for instance, that Christ was extraordinary in rising up and, also, the legends of vampires and zombies, specters and the like, the walking dead, all of them. Anyway, as I was saying before, I went to the cemetery unwillingly, planning as I did how I would remain distant, outside the fence if it were possible. As it turned out, it was not.

*Laurel Cemetery.* It is not called after the town but has a name peculiar to it. The day of the funeral, our procession drove there, headlights blazing, for a mile on the highway, other cars pulling to the side of the road while we passed. (That is still done in the countryside out of respect, I am certain, but I envied them and wanted to join them.) After a mile the hearse turned left onto the quartz gravel road for another mile until the six-acre square of the graveyard was in full view, its field-wire fence enclosing it. While the rest of us pulled to either side of the road, Mr. Stark was escorted inside through the double gates, which were directly beneath the arch of black iron that held the letters LAUREL.

The graveside service was short enough, although having the Lord's Prayer spoken over him was probably the final straw for Mr. Stark, who was being made to endure indignities to his principles sufficient to make him turn over before he was even in the grave. Then, the precise moment when the man concluded "deliver us from evil," I heard the first thump. Actually, the very first of it was a faint hiss so that I thought it might only be something next to me and no one else, which would explain why I alone looked to find the source of the sound. On the prairie, it is not unheard of to find diamondback rattlers in lightly trafficked pasture, even in April if the weather is sufficiently warm, as it had been. And the wind, as is usual on a warm, dry day in Kansas, was steady and many sounds are often laid off to it when they are in fact something less benign. After the hiss, I heard a thump. I looked toward the flap of the funeral tent that covered us, as if the wind had flipped the sharp knock from the deep green canvas when, quite clearly, the noise came from below my ears and not above. A bosomy woman with tight gray curls was at my shoulder and I turned my face to hers, widening my eyes in polite inquiry. I did not whisper any words, not because of the ritual, but because manners here discourage speaking unless spoken to, making conversations a rarity, as you might imagine. But she gave no response except to look me once over. Then, as now, I was a curiosity to these local faithful.

Then it began in earnest. *Thump. Thump, thump. THUMP!* Surely, I thought, some weak soul will break ranks and run in terror from beneath the tent and the braver of us will follow after. It was not so. No one but me turned or blinked, and it was not as if the others were distraught with grief, so taken in tears and sorrow that the incidentals of the world were pushed from sense. This was, you remember, the funeral of a ninety-four-year-old man and it is somewhere around eighty-five that eyebrows begin to be raised in mild concern that a man has outstayed his welcome and risks committing a sort of existential faux pas. No, it was not that at all. They did not hear. I heard and they did not. But, then, the message was for me.

I was the one, after all, who had proposed that it be delivered in precisely this manner, having done so on my last visit to Mr. Stark when I found him in bed, laid up with one or another of the elderly's endless succession of short maladies. There were no greetings or other niceties. Kansans are quick to the point and he asked his question at once—"Will you not tell of the corpses?"—and an argument of sorts ensued during which I recall most the feeling of foolishness at being in a contest with this old, frail man. But he was up to it and pressed me hard to tell the truth that was a burden I had carried for years, shifting it like an overfilled backpack one way then another when it caused fatigue. Still, I demurred and he scolded me.

"Truth is not your possession, child, to share or hide away at your pleasure," he chided, but his stilted words did not strike their mark at once. I only thought how he had become increasingly Platonic and German, seeming, I mean, to speak always in absolutes and capitalized nouns.

"The risk is too much, the truth too little, perhaps," I argued, but he would have none of my misgivings and raised his age-crooked fingers in a dismissive wave, his voice rising with them.

"Do you want to save yourself or not?"

"I don't want to make things worse."

His hands dropped heavily to the bedcover and he fell back against his pillow. When he spoke again, I could barely hear him. "You don't have any way to decide that."

"What I mean is that we shouldn't always say every thing we know to be true," I said.

"I know what you mean. Of course, you don't tell Mrs. Amerine that she has on an exceptionally ugly dress today. That's one woman, one dress. You can know about that. But something that affects so many . . ." He searched for the words to explain, then sighed, exasperated. "You can never know enough to justify the lie. That's all."

His concern was reaching a fever pitch and I was uncomfortable in the presence of such intensity. That was what prompted my foolish provocation that, if he were right, if telling were the proper route for me to take, he would surely know when he passed and he could send me a message from the grave. *I will never have to tell*, I thought. Yet it was not two years before Mr. Stark told me in the manner I had suggested. There can be no doubt of it.

Still, reason fell solidly on my side, against the rash telling of truths—grave truths, if you will—that could shatter lives, perhaps even my own. I was already so very close to dying. You can understand, can't you, my reluctance? Why should *I* be the one to unveil these mysteries, to say aloud what had for centuries been so carefully unsaid except in the abstractions and complexities of art? What would be the consequences? That is why I did what I did, offering Abraham's goat instead of Isaac, saving myself but without knowing for what span and what part of my life after was a grace undeserved.

WELL, THAT MUCH, at least, is finished if not answered, my half deed—the book in my lap—a surprise gift from Evan after dinner last evening. "Like I told you, they said . . . *said* they found it down in Granddad's grave." He rolled his eyes toward his wife, Carol, who ignored him and kept her own eyes fixed on my face. She took the slender volume from Evan's hand and passed it to me.

"Here. I can't believe Evan didn't show it to you first thing."

I looked at the book. It was as he had described it. The red cover was unmarked, pristine: My Life with Corpses in shining gold letters, my name beneath, unfaded. Ruffle the pages and they bear the same quality, raising a powdery scent of new paper in a new book as yet unread, nothing to identify an owner or if there has ever been one.

"Lawrence and Donnie found it. They—"

"Said they found it," Evan interrupted. "You know. The guys you met today. The grave diggers."

"Cemetery workers," Carol gently corrected him. "There was a little space around it, as if it were its own little grave. Or a message in a bottle."

Evan snorted and dropped into the chair across from us. He looked toward me, trying to invite me to share his disdain but revealing instead his fervent hope that I could explain everything. It is a measure of how different he finds me still. He thinks I know all he knows plus things he does not; people often mistake the unconventional for the profound—thinking an odd perspective is a larger view rather than one that is simply different. Sometimes, of course, they are right, but what explanation I could give Evan was nothing likely to ease his mind—that Carol had stated, if only by accident, what I knew to be true. The book was most certainly my message from Mr. Stark. My account told the Truth but not all of it, addressed only a part, not the whole I promised Mr. Stark, and he has sent it back to me for correction. The impossibility of it, this untouched book buried beneath several feet of lime hard-pack, only emphasizes his point.

Anyway, Evan's understanding is not my foremost concern just now, given my own transgressions, which are to this point merely confessed and not redeemed. Well, I attend to that now. I am not so foolish as to risk disobeying an order received from beyond the grave not once, but twice, so I am writing this to you as fast as I can—whatever wrong I have done, I am about to put right.

# 2.

MY PRESENT CIRCUMSTANCES. You must know some part of them, I suppose, in order to assess the rest. All those years of reason, I believed other-wise. I vouched for the independence of ideas, the efficacy of blind evaluation. No more. Well, I suppose I do still be-lieve in these things in some abstract, theoretical way. In the way that I believe a million monkeys will eventually peck out Dante's *Inferno* on their collective typewriters, given infinity in which to do so. But in my finite exis-tence, I no longer look to logic as the sole guidepost of my intentions and I want to know the mouth speaking. I am always on my guard and I advise you to be just as wary.

I don't live here in Kansas anymore but *away*, in Oxford, Mississippi. These last few years, I have lived alone. Otherwise, my account must change with the setting inasmuch as in Kansas I am the child of corpses, whereas in Oxford I am something else, my history stopping in both cases at the state line. Too, they are quite different places. Here, the dry gusts pick up and blow away the weak and the unclean and dead things. In Oxford what dies decays in its place and the microorganisms of the unclean form cities and elect their governments unmolested. And there is the matter of the sky, which in Kansas is particularly blue and big. One day in my childhood, I lay within it at its deepest blue and uninterrupted by clouds. I was on buffalo grass that had been cropped close by grazing cattle, and when I turned my head so that the dry blades scratched my cheek, I could see the herd across the pasture. Beyond it was a low hedge of sand plums, then the gravel road, then the bare furrows of the Moores' field, planted to maize, another field lying fallow, and then a rise into dark elms that set the limit of my vision, but I knew well enough what they concealed—the Lederer house, a two-story white frame, abandoned in the late '30s and full of weak, treacherous floors and bold ghosts in the years since.

The Oxford sky, on the other hand, is mostly a theory, its blue mere conjecture behind what is visible—a lush green canopy of oaks and sweet gums, tulip magnolias, and native pines, all of them partway to having their own canopy of creeping kudzu while yet another layer lies beneath, tangled and unruly with fragrant honeysuckle, dogwood, and privet. I thought this primeval nature would save me, that I was guided to it and, if I were patient, the very same force would do what was necessary to redeem me. See. That is what often happens when logic is out of it and intuition left alone. Superstition and mysticism come right in because we must have our answers. We feel we are entitled to an explanation and no less so, if reason fails us—"God does not exist," I mean, is not an explanation; it is merely a denial and one by those who keep throwing out their own reasonable beliefs every fifty years or so. Our turn to the sixth sense has some merit. Without intuition, the world is reduced to 4 = 4. And yet without logic, 4 equals whatever you want it to; every notion is true but trivial. What gives the truth and when? It is really our central difficulty.

Oh, I was saved after all, but I do not say that with the relief of the fabled Presbyterian who was "glad *that* is over." Being saved is a repeatable event, not an everlasting condition. You have only to consider my rescue from a family of corpses to observe how quickly such falls away, overtaken by what I mentioned earlier, those special attributes and deficiencies, I mean, that my peculiar upbringing had produced in me.

EVERYONE HAD THE BEST of intentions. Sheriff Thompson was the first to take charge of me, a child unnaturally composed in the face of what he would thereafter describe as "the dangdest god-awful mess" he ever encountered during his thirty-six-year career in law enforcement. He sat me on the back stairs off the kitchen while he worked, his job being to watch while the county coroner examined, measured, and photographed the bodies of my mother and sister, and Floyd Preston, the undertaker, wrapped their remains in plastic shrouds to take them away.

Three hours passed altogether. Halfway through, the state troopers who had found my father came in to use the bathroom and the telephone, then left again. Sheriff Thompson stayed all the while by the kitchen door, moving only to let the others pass or to flick lint from his pressed khakis, although two or three times he did lean back and look kindly at me. At the last, he accompanied each body on its gurney as it was rolled out the door and down the sidewalk to Floyd's flesh-colored DeSoto station wagon, which was ambulance or hearse as the situation required, and waved it on its way. When he returned to the house, he came to the stairs and knelt before me. "Floyd's going by the mortuary to pick up your daddy. Then he's takin' 'em all out to Laurel."

I shook my head. I knew the cemetery because I had ridden and walked the road with Penny and Chimpy, but I doubted my parents, given their special circumstances, had made any arrangements for a plot.

"Don't worry about it. Ol' Floyd told me. He's got a spot he can put your folks. Real nice and respectful. By some old-timey family hasn't been around maybe fifty years." He went to the kitchen and brought back two IGA sacks from those my mother kept wedged between the refrigerator and stove.

"Get what you need," he said. "I don't imagine you'll be coming back here."

I took the bags from his extended hand and climbed the stairs to my room, filling one sack with a few clothes and the other with the contents of my bottom dresser drawer, the place I kept those belongings that required special protection: a pressed four-leaf clover from the farm, a few photographs—including one of my parents when they were younger and still alive—my Bible, two books that Mr. Stark had given me, and a little paper box containing the mummified remains of my pet chameleon from the state fair several years before, along with the safety-pin-and-thread leash that I had used to anchor him to the window screen where he had died when we had an unexpected early freeze. I carried both sacks downstairs and to the sheriff's car, stopping on the way to get a pillow from the sofa— a small square one, covered with velvet that was printed to look like a leopard's skin. Then we left.

I would not tell you anything whatsoever of what came after—during, I mean, the next three years—did it not bear on later events, and I tell you only that part. I have forgiven those who needed it, myself included, and regard many of the events of my sudden transition to a life with the living to be of personal interest, of no use to others except as the sort of titillating detail that feeds the taste we have for such, just as it is to the taste of dogs to go searching for a cache of cat excrement.

That is what Aunt Bert called this sort of information, in fact—"cat poop"—and she became well acquainted with the demand for it following the day she brought me home with her. Without fail, reporters called or drove by or came onto the farm every day during the next few weeks, joined in these intrusions by a like number of those who had not even that professional excuse but were simply gawking. The questions were ever the same: Does he talk? Can he dress himself? Does he sleep in a coffin at night? Were they frightened that I might kill them in their sleep? What did I think of modern appliances? For a farm woman, Aunt Bert was unusually adept at pleasantly thwarting this inquisition, but, as I said, there is a certain hunger we have and denying it food only increases it. So the frustration was growing, and I don't know when it would have ended or where it would have led had the presidential assassination not redirected the attention of the entire nation and given it an ample source of sustenance for some time thereafter.

WELL, I SPEAK AS IF these circumstances ended then, but they are with me still. I am still the corpses' child, and as the fallen woman cannot atone by merely behaving herself in the future but must also lead the church choir, that curious past requires me now to be less controversial than most, *extra ordinary* as it were. Even now I permit those at the fence to believe, for instance, that I am here the day long solely on Evan Crews's behalf, to supervise the redigging for his grandfather, rather than to write this account that will give lie to their most-valued certitudes. It is an excuse that satisfies them despite the improbability of it— requiring as it does that someone who is not even a member of the family drive over a thousand miles to do what could be hired here, and at minimum wage.

It is half-true, I suppose. I am writing here and not the preferred somewhere else as a favor to Evan. "You don't want to turn around and drive right back," he objected this morning when I said Annie and I were going home. "It would be a great help to me if you would stay on while they dig," he said, and thereby neatly trapped me the same as the day of his grandfather's funeral. No one brought up in Kansas, you see, can comfortably refuse work on grounds of mere personal preference, and so here I am, stuck within the bounds of Laurel once more.

The reason that the diggers have returned at all is that during the day and a half it took me to drive here, Evan decided he had solved the mystery of his grandfather's disappearance. Guessing that the coffin had been placed on the other side of the monument for some forgotten reason, he confirmed the presence of a coffin there by using a metal detector, then a probe. He has failed, however, to convince Carol that Mr. Stark is the body in it. "The woman they were moving him for was his worst enemy in the world. Friday is ten years to the day that we buried him," she stated as if it were a syllogism. "And what about the book?"

Evan, who is county engineer and, in any event, methodical and thorough by nature as well as profession, rose to her challenge. By the time I came to Laurel at noon yesterday, he had already obtained authority for an exhumation to make matters "absolutely certain" as well as rehired Lawrence and Donnie for the job. Ordinarily, such a rapid progression from idea to execution would impress me greatly, but in this case, I am fairly certain that the most difficult obstacle to digging up graves in a country cemetery outside a declining farm town is probably obtaining the shovel to do so. The accomplishment is further lessened by the fact that although this is the second day of work, no actual digging has yet taken place.

Not fifteen minutes after Evan left us yesterday, Lawrence and Donnie abandoned their rig without ever starting the backhoe and strode from that side of the cemetery to this. Lawrence, the big one with the beer belly and strawberry nose, led the way with the wiry, little buttless fellow—Donnie—following behind. Lawrence rapped on the glass by my face and I turned on the key and lowered the window.

"It needs a new sprocket. Prob'ly to get one . . . it's hard to tell . . . prob'ly have to go on into Pratt," he said, turning to look toward the backhoe, still perched on its trailer, and I resisted the impulse to quiz him as to how he had come to bring a sprocketless backhoe to do a job and why it was that such condition would only be discovered here and now.

"Uh-huh," I nodded, giving the desired approval to their departure, and they were released, the rest of the morning and half of the afternoon passing before the two of them returned to complete the day's work with a purposeful display of installing their new part. As I said, that was yesterday afternoon. This morning they have actually started the backhoe, apparently to unload it, although at the moment it is still on the trailer.

BUT I WAS TELLING you of Aunt Bert. She wasn't my aunt, of course, because any living relatives of either of my parents—there were only a few—were unwilling to associate themselves with this unseemly ruckus. Bert and her husband, Everett, were from Walnut Station, north near the county line, "good folks" according to Sheriff Thompson—people who took in homeless children as readily as my father had brought home orphaned animals. He had called her almost as soon as we walked into his office.

"Bert, I got a boy here you might want to drop by. Take a look," and within the hour she was there looking.

"Okay" was all she said, and she took me and my grocery sacks out the door with her. She motioned me toward the passenger door of a pale green GMC pickup truck and

I climbed in, closing the hollow door with a grinding creak, while Bert hoisted my bags into the truck's bed and secured them under the corner of a fully stocked carpenter's toolbox. My chameleon box was thereby crushed and the photo of my parents creased, but both were also saved from flying out during the half-hour trip to what was the least-settled part of the county and over ungraded dirt roads that had hardened into a pastiche of snaking ruts and mud rills where they had not fallen away in jagged clumps altogether. Throughout, I braced myself against the springing seat with both hands pressed up to the thin felt that lined the truck's roof while Bert endlessly shifted and steered when she wasn't twirling the radio dial between swap programs. We did not talk. Bert was nearly deaf and the callithump of the road, together with the resonating blend of radio and wind in the truck's cab, precluded conversation in any event. When we were finally parked in the Branscom farmyard, however, Bert cut the motor and turned right to me.

"You *do* know that you are not a boy?"

I nodded. I knew I was not a boy, although I *had been* a boy until that very moment. It was only my mother's well-meant charade, to provide the requisite son, and my father had acquiesced.

At that, Bert sighed and puckered her lips tightly. We sat silent for a minute more, then she sighed again and looked me straight in the eye. "Well, from here on out, you're a *girl*. All right?"

Again I nodded. Being boy or girl had so far meant little to me: I wore trousers; my hair was cut short; I peed standing up. My body had shown more effect, I guess, cooperating in the pretense of maleness by not yet developing curves and I did not menstruate. And there was one other notable difference, although it came from without, I mean from other people, not my parents. I missed being instructed in certain requirements about males and females, all of which seem to come down to a peculiar American version of walking two steps behind, head bowed.

I admit that the biggest reason I did not expect much to change with my gender was that my family had accustomed me to nothing changing much, as well as taught me to keep a purposeful distance from others. That muted the effects of any environmental alterations I might encounter, although I could never duplicate *their* accomplishments in this regard. They had an advantage, you see, being possessed of the ancient skill called *surgeria*, a protective shifting that can be made to take oneself a half step out of the causal plane's way. It's quite commonplace among the dead—a sort of metaphysical disengaging of the clutch. It is a handy practice that unfortunately eludes the rest of us, the living, who are forced to remain where we are, unavoidably affected by whatever is there with us, necessarily cooking in the ontological soup, night and day, for both good and ill.

In any event, whatever concern I did have or might have had was quickly overridden by one more pressing.

Until that day, you see, *I* was the unwelcome intrusion of bumptious life among corpses. At the Branscoms', I was the cigar-store Indian, and uncomfortably susceptible to upending as well. There were four of them altogether. Bert and her husband, Everett, were a matched pair—farmer and farmer's wife with the same muscular square bodies, wrapped in the same papery sun-browned skin, their eyes in permanent squints, and their jaws set for hard work. She was bigger, though—nearly twice the size of Everett—and cleaner, always wearing soft cotton housedresses made loose and faded by washing, her hair netted and kept tightly curled by twice-a-year home permanents. There were also two daughters, Lois and Linda. They were fifteen and fourteen, respectively, and harmless girls, really—most notably possessed of bubbled hair and middling intellect, with no greater task in life than to simply bide their time until they could leave the farm for a job and their own apartment in Wichita.

All of them together were uncommonly loud. Everett and the girls shouted to be heard by deaf Bert, who, inexplicably, shouted back, although when I think of them now, I don't *hear* but rather *see* them, their arms waving, then down, mouths open, then shut—discontinuous brief images that flash in slow motion before me, as if I were witnessing their lives illuminated by strobe. I know that merely an hour among them exhausted me and that it was the precise wearing down I have since endured in lengthy visits to countries where English is not the native language.

MY LIFE WITH CORPSES

That is, everything I said required a struggle and what they said was beyond my ability to understand.

"It must be so hard to lose your whole family just like that," Bert offered the first day, while she was showing me to my corner bed in the girls' room. "Your little heart must hurt something awful. But you know what? It will get better. I promise you."

She patted my shoulder and pulled me toward her in a brief one-arm hug, then left me to unpack, and I looked after her, bewildered, wondering why she had said what she did. I had not so much as thought of my dead family since leaving the sheriff's office and, as for the other, could not imagine what a heart would feel like, if one were to feel it, and yet she had seemed so certain. For nearly a half hour after, I sat on my new bed to think this puzzle through, making myself very still, leaning back against the cast-iron headboard, resting my head between its rails while I held the pillow in my lap. I barely breathed while I tried to detect any overlooked sensation within me that belonged to my heart. There was, however, nothing of the sort. In fact, I could not feel my heart at all and reasonably concluded, therefore, that it could not possibly be in pain.

Supper that evening was even more discomfiting, bringing all of us at once to the kitchen, where we pulled up chairs to a marbled red Formica tabletop that put us shoulder to shoulder, even with Bert at the stove. The table was singular in its spareness, however, since there was too much of all other. The food began it, Bert piling high each of our plates until they were invisible and barely adequate to transport their load—butter beans, snap beans, and creamed corn wedged next to a two-inch slab of meat loaf and mashed potatoes in a mound sufficient to hold a quarter cup of brown gravy. Corn muffins and a serving bowl of orange-carrot gelatin already on the table extended the meal even beyond the plates, and this sur-feit of food was matched in kind by a profusion of sound and movement. The telephone rang. Someone came to the door. Linda left the table to get the milk, Lois shifted her chair off of the metal floor seam, and everyone talked at once, Everett telling me stories about the girls, talking over Lois, who argued with Linda, then asked for more potatoes from Bert, before interrupting Everett's account to correct him.

"That wasn't me. Linda was the one who caught her tongue, and it was the barbed-wire fence by the garden, not the trellis." She elbowed Linda, who, long accustomed to her older sister's management, readily affirmed Lois's story.

"Yes, yes, yes. She's right. It wasn't her. It was me!"

I ate silently, continuously, dazed by the pandemo-nium and their ceaseless expressions of feeling, which seemed to me not only overdone, but also unprovoked. When, at last, there was a single moment that the discor-dant rhythm of the uproars converged in one brief beat of total silence, Linda pounced on that as if it were fresh kill.

"Mama, I love this so much!" she exclaimed, then reached across the table to tap my hand—"Don't you just *love* it?"—causing me to jerk back and spill a forkful of corn on the tabletop.

The others raised their faces to me then, expectant, but I said nothing. I was ignorant of the unseen sensation she had described as well as what produced it. Only when Aunt Bert leaned over the table to look at my plate— "You still got some. Don't you like it?"—that I saw Linda had been talking about nothing more than the *meat loaf*. My own efforts to make sense of the matter would never have brought me there, doomed for the same reason that I was confused at all.

I was much like the celebrated finch, you see, the one kept alone and in total silence from before it pipped its shell until it was grown to full feather. To the investigators' surprise, the finch still sang despite the imposed solitude, but that is not to say there were no consequences. The little bird's songs were only faint copies of proper finch songs. Having never heard the songs of others, that is, its own were incomplete and often confused, breaking up at unpredictable intervals as if they were radio tunes borne on a weak signal. In the same way, while I had a certain talent for sensation and emotion that is innate to the living, it did not exist in the same measure. That is to say, it is not that I didn't feel and the Branscoms did, but rather that I did not feel *what* they did.

There seemed little reason, moreover, to think that these differences would ever diminish. I did not return to school. At first it was impractical for me to do so, and later it seemed the most convenient arrangement for everyone. Instead, I gathered eggs, hoed the garden, and helped Bert clean house and cook. Sometimes I drove the truck for Everett when he changed fields or held a piece steady while he welded a repair. At night I helped Lois and Linda with their homework and after a time did it all for them. The rest of the day, which was most of it, however, I was left to myself.

I used the time well, I think, that first year rereading the books Mr. Stark gave me along with everything the Branscoms had in their house, which was Everett's collection of Zane Grey novels, ten years of *Reader's Digest*, *Saturday Evening Post*, *National Geographic*, and *Capper's Weekly* in addition to the King James and Douay versions of the Holy Bible, the latter having been handed down to him from Everett's Irish grandmother. One day, while dust-mopping the floors, I found *Lady Chatterley's Lover* wedged under the right rear leg of Aunt Bert's dresser to level it and read that, too, putting in its place Grey's *Wild Horse Mesa*—which I had already read and which contained the same number of pages.

Other times I walked the roads and fields nearby, tramping over more than three entire sections and along four miles of Peace Creek, which angled through both. I ended up most often south at the T, where the road dead-ended into a line of tall arching cottonwoods that shaded the deep sand beneath. It was sea sand—silky and the color of creamy hot chocolate, good to bury toes and draw pictures in with a stick or track the meanderings of red velvet ants, and it was there I found a stray shepherd-collie bitch and brought her home. I named her Esther for the biblical queen, but Bert considered it sinful to give a mongrel a name from the word of God, so we all called her Lady instead. Or, *I* did, since she was always with me and no one else, following me wherever I went days and sleeping curled next to me in the trailer at night.

I had forgotten that part, that I often spent the nights alone as well, leaving the room I shared with the girls to sleep outdoors in a small utility trailer that Everett left parked south of the granary, although not, as you may be thinking, for the quiet. Buzzing cicadas and bullfrogs croaking and the mystery of intermittent snapping and rustling that might be either wind or animals or the unthinkable made the outdoors as noisy as inside. But I slept better there just because of those fractal night sounds— their harmony enveloping and narcotic, and wholly unintentional. Like the ebb and flow of the tide, I mean, or a pulse beating or, more nearly, a collective respiration. And, too, as I said, I had watchful company.

But I was telling you about the days. After the T, I next favored sitting on the Branscom back porch, which was situated on the west side of the house and, therefore, cool in the morning but otherwise baked toasty warm by the sun on even the most frigid post-Christmas days of winter. It was no more than a smooth rectangle, really, three steps up of poured concrete and not altogether pleasant—a seat there cost enduring the wind that blew unchecked around the house's corner hot and dry or cold and sharp according to the season and that sometimes abated, swirling in this direction, then that, but never stopped. That is the nature of Kansas wind, you know, rising with the sun to come in mighty gusts, and it was up to blowing my thick hair into a tangled mop then whipping the corded strands to sting my face and not the sort of gentle little breeze, I mean, that might flip your newspaper off the veranda settee.

Oh, like everything and everyone, it has both its good points and bad. This morning the wind has reached its stride and is wrapped around me so well that hardly any of the fence people have given me a glance in the last hour. We are less visible each to the other, the wind inserted between us so that I might as easily be alone and deep within the pink swirls of a giant deserted conch shell listening to the deafening rhythm of its long-departed sea. The sea, you know, is all that could ever match the wind's gift for solitude, and that, I suppose, accounts for the special loneliness possible on these windblown Great Plains, which are no more than the ocean's bottom for some while absent the water.

But that is what I was about to tell you and what seemed to me for a long while unaccountable. During the several years I lived with the Branscoms, I mean, I was mostly alone so my life should have been altered only in small respects, by a few inconsequential details, and yet I was changed. Not the change of years, although when my body suddenly and belatedly permitted puberty, the process, once begun, was uncomfortably rapid. In the course of a few months, painful pea-sized breast buds developed into full, round breasts, I began to menstruate, and the timber of my voice lost the soft, low tone familiar to my own ear to become stronger and more melodic. Still, when Linda asked me about my newfound maturity—"Are you excited?"—I said that I was, although, in truth, what I felt was the same as always, that being nothing much.

*That* was the change most profound—when I began to feel more *something* and less nothing. It did not arrive full-blown but after a subtle progression barely detectable for some while, then mildly perturbing in the way of a sleeping leg coming to wake. Yet its occurrence at all, being something substantial from very little cause, was a puzzle to me. Of course, it is clear enough to me now that I learned these feelings from the Branscoms, something they gave without intending and that I received without knowing. Had I merely given a little more consideration to that transaction, I might have guessed right then all about everything and saved myself a good part of my future troubles, but I did not. We do not. It is all with us all the time, you know, and the proof of it is that when we have the least insight, we can always look back and, for all those many years before, see the same truth repeating and repeating, imploring us to turn our eyes to it, to only look and we will see.

# 3.

THE FIRST CONVINCINGLY new feeling that I recall did not come to me at the time one might expect—spring when the sap is rising—but in November during the shirtsleeve days of Indian summer, the last respite from morning frost before winter. I was a few yards beyond the driveway heading north toward the bridge over Peace Creek when Lady, a step ahead of me, let loose a screech and wheeled back into my shins. She was yip-yapping and I rudely cursed her to shut up, but she ignored me and instead moved in a wide stiff-legged circle in the road. That was the only reason I saw it in time—a thick-bodied diamondback that had come up from the ditch to sun on the warm gravel and lay coiled, twitching its tail less than six feet away from me. I didn't hear any rattles before then, and I could not have heard anything after because my heart was beating with such force that my ears were throbbing and my breath was merely gasps of cold air sucked in noisy bursts through clenched teeth. I backed away one step at a time, facing the snake, its tongue flicking continuously to gauge my retreat.

When I was safely back in the driveway, I dropped to the ground cross-legged, cupping my hands over my mouth and taking deep breaths. Lady came creeping on her belly, wriggling closer until she could reach her slender muzzle across my thigh, pressing against me and looking up to see my face. She was ready to take her punishment for disobeying my earlier order of silence, but, instead, I wrapped my arms around her and pulled her to me. I felt my heart beating, not from fear, but in a way I had not felt before. Each pulse was pleasantly full and strong, warming the space around it. The muscles in my face changed, too, becoming relaxed and enlivened at once, so that I could not stop smiling. "Good girl!" I praised Lady. "Good *girl!*" I could not hold her close enough. It was a powerful feeling—and good—but I had never felt this way and didn't know what to make of it.

Later, when I told Everett about Lady's bravery, he kindly provided me with the proper name for my experience. "Well, she's just an ugly ol' mutt but I guess you were grateful that she was there," he said.

"Grateful." I calibrated it against the complex of sensations that I'd felt. It was a process I followed for every such event for some years after, feeling something, finding the name of it, then putting one with the other in just the manner of Wittgenstein's scorned linguist hanging names on rocks and chairs.

Well, of course, it is not always so simple. There are some number of emotions that can never be named—those that do not permit complete description or that, perhaps, never repeat, a fact I learned in the same winter but after the season had come full force and settled in. It was February, I think. I know that the day was bitter cold and everything was brown and white from a dusting of snow earlier in the week. I was out walking again, this time south toward the cottonwoods. I was almost to the T, the wind's sting about to turn me back, when a pickup truck came speeding up from the east, then nose-dived into an abrupt stop. Two men jumped out and went to the back of the truck, one lifting a brown tarp draped over a large box so that the other could unlatch a small hinged door whereupon three giant deerhounds bounded from the crate to the ground in one leap and, in the next, cleared the fence to the pasture, converging there with open-jawed snarls on a small coyote.

Well, I couldn't see *then* what it was. I only saw the coarse gray tangle of furry bodies, spinning and lurching, and heard the coyote's caterwaul, then the dogs' deep, grunting growls as they tore it apart. After less than a minute, the dogs sat back, panting, docile, pink tongues glistening and hanging from the sides of their mouths. They looked back and forth between their prey and their masters in the pickup. One of the men must have called or whistled because the three dogs suddenly rose as one and returned to the truck, which turned and drove off in the direction it had come.

From a distance, the remains looked like crumpled tar paper. I went closer a few steps. That was when I saw it was a coyote, the triangular head thrown back on its crown exposing a delicate jaw, its patch of white-gray fur seeming to be suspended above and disconnected from the carcass below, dark and wet with blood where it lay. I don't think I have ever had that same feeling again, the one I felt then. The sensation was wholly silent and began low before moving up and tightening, as though powerful fingers had taken hold of my gut and were grabbing up all that they could hold. I don't have a name for it even now, but I do remember feeling it and, also, that I vomited.

EVAN WAS HERE a moment ago—Carol, too—and he was a little annoyed to find not even the first dirt clod overturned. I explained to him what Lawrence told me, which is that he doesn't have enough space for the back-hoe and "can't get a good angle on it," forcing him to dig around the outside by hand except that he hasn't done that yet either.

"You know. Actually, I don't really care. I already know he's down there."

"You don't *know*, Evan. It could be someone else."

"Carol, common sense tells me it's him, so I know. I also know that doesn't carry much weight with you. That common sense isn't as exciting as nonsense."

"I have as much sense as you do, Evan Crews, if that's what you're trying to say. Just because I don't claim to know everything or think I'm a rocket scientist because I read *Scientific American* once or twice a year. If that."

Both looked toward me then, but I am staying out of it even if I do have an opinion. I have to admit that Carol is on firmer ground, but her logic seems more an excuse for believing what is more interesting, as Evan says, and she seems well possessed of the necessary talent for constructing an entire edifice on a square foot of foundation. On the other hand, were either of them to have seen what I have, there would be no limiting their hypotheses.

At least, in their case, the conjecture will be found true or false. There is so much that stays just a hypothesis, no more, time being far from sufficient to allow a proper investigation of all our mysteries, our hope only that events prove them one way or the other without our efforts. At the Branscoms', that happened as I woke to a wider variety of emotion, thinking that a seed of sensation had sprouted within me that would grow and blossom over time in an orderly fashion. That view was rather abruptly proved false and replaced by the understanding that what I had so far was a mere leak that one large push could break open into a flood.

THAT PUSH CAME my sixteenth spring, in April, which was the month that the farmers brought the livestock back to summer pasture. I was aboard Princess Grace, a half-thoroughbred made fat from the winter wheat and unruly from lack of riding. She belonged to our neighbor Virgil Gagnebin, who told Everett that he was afraid she was going sour so Everett volunteered me to ride her back to shape.

I had walked over after morning chores and Virgil was already tightening the cinch on the big mare, who stood ground-tied, her head hanging, eyes drooping sleepily. I re-membered her then from the Pioneer Days parade the pre-vious summer—the docile, diffident horse clopping along behind the clown who handed out bubblegum. All the same, she had stood out from the usual palominos and quar-ter horses favored in the area by practically everyone but Virgil—"If you say salt, Virgil can't help saying pepper" was how Bert explained the difference in his preferences.

Virgil lifted his chin to me. "She's almost ready. I got this here saddle at a farm sale over by Greensburg back in February. Whaddya think?" He stroked his prize, a West-ern stock saddle that was hand-tooled everywhere but the glossy seat. Engraved silver medallions anchored leather strips, three on each side, with one tying a lariat at the left front, just below the saddlehorn. "S'your rodeo show saddle," he said. "Only time it was used."

"If it's okay, I'd just as soon ride her bareback," I told him. "I'm not really used to a saddle."

"Well, I *guess* you could," he pondered. "I don't know. You say you're not used to a saddle but Gracie, she *is* used to one." Then, deciding between us, he stepped in and taking the cinch strap in hand, raised his knee sharply against the mare's stomach. Gracie let go her breath in a rasping huff and Virgil pulled the cinch three inches tighter. He laughed and winked at me, then reached to hold the stirrup steady and motioned me to mount. "Tell you what, why don't we leave it on today? She's just off the wheat, you know. Next time, you do what you want."

I lifted my left foot to the stirrup and Virgil gave me a push up and onto the hard polish of the seat. Gracie was seventeen hands at least, and seated atop the saddle my knee came even with Virgil's head. I took the reins and pressed them against Gracie's neck to turn her toward the road.

"Give her a workout, now," Virgil called after me. "She can take it." That was the reason, I recall, that I did not go south to the Branscoms' but headed north onto a straight shot of nearly four miles of dirt road that ended at Highway 4 and just past the railroad tracks.

The saddle was a nuisance, creaking with every move-ment. A few minutes rubbing by its stiff leather chafed so much that I squeezed my legs in to lift my crotch forward off the hard seat. It started that moment, Gracie beginning to trot then, her legs striking the road, then bouncing up again as lightly as pebbles on taut canvas.

"Whoa, now," I commanded her, and tightened the reins. Her step faltered and she nearly stopped, but then she abruptly shifted instead into the faster rocking pace of a gaited canter.

"No! Whoa!" I drew the reins shorter, irritated with the mare both for her disobedience and for making my heart skip a beat. Gracie responded with a burst across the intersection in full gallop, throwing me roughly back on the saddle. I pulled the reins again and again she shot forward, nearly unseating me this time when my torso jerked back and up onto the cantle. Now she was in a flat-out run.

Her behavior stunned me. It was as if I had let go of a brick and, instead of dropping to the ground, it had flown straight up and hit me in the face. I tried to think what to do but I could barely stay aboard Gracie; the volume of what was going on *right now* did not allow for thinking. I grabbed the saddle horn to pull myself forward. Her arched neck filled my view; Gracie's eyes opened wide and her head held high, pulsing forward against both wind and reins in determined striving. I moved with her as best I could, my head following hers, my legs gripping the saddle, pressing the stirrup leathers so hard into her flesh that with each pounding stroke, the skin of her shoulder muscles rolled back over them and tapped my knees. Her long mane was switching wildly above her neck while my own flew into my face, stinging my cheeks and whipping my eyes until they teared.

The feeling began as no more than a hard balled fist pushing against my chest, then spread slowly and steadily like a stain, and with a certain weight to it that made it a comfort rather than a burden. Then, when the entire space between my belly button and breasts was covered, the feeling moved into my head, where, inexplicably, it pressed out rather than in, and it was as though the push and pull were lifting me above Gracie's saddle, where I floated weightlessly, accompanying rather than riding the stampeding animal below.

This state, whether it was thrill, surprise, fright, or some catalytic concoction of the lot, expanded in me without resistance. There was no time for fighting it even had I wanted to mute what was altogether agreeable. Every part of me was taken up with the feeling of it and, still, it was pressing farther and farther out, moving me to limits I did not know. Finally some other part of me, more interested perhaps in my long-term survival, made me raise myself up and squint to see the road ahead. There, only fifty feet before the north highway, the morning Illinois Central freight train was approaching slowly from the west.

Gracie was going so fast I was almost certain we could beat the train, but I knew she would never run into the side of the clattering cars, or even cross in front of them. When she got close enough, the noise would spook her and she would stop or turn or rear or fall. The danger was that she would do one of those at racing speed and that I had no idea which it might be. I reached my hands to the bit rings and drew them back so hard I thought the reins would snap. A drop of spittle splashed back on my hand from Gracie's open mouth and there were faint waves of wet and foam on her neck, but she went faster still, her nostrils flared and her neck bent double by the straining reins.

Now, all pleasing sensation was replaced by nauseating panic. I dropped the reins, lowered my body close to hers, and grabbed the horn to hold on.

At the moment the reins fell loose, Gracie abruptly slowed, dropping through her gaits from gallop to canter to a soft trot as smoothly as shifting gears in a car. I turned her around carefully and took her back to Virgil, who was sorry he had forgotten to mention that in her earlier years, Gracie was raced at the county fairgrounds.

"Right there at the end, real close to the finish line when they want them to go all out, they pull back on the reins as hard as they can. They train 'em to know the signal, see?" I did.

SOMETHING I SAW HERE in Laurel earlier today reminded me of those very times. I saw that coyote, or rather I mean to say that I saw *a* coyote, and it made me think of that earlier one if only for a second. Perhaps an hour ago I went to retrieve Annie, who was off on her own in the northeast corner, sticking her nose down into one after another of a succession of huge clumps of switch grass, deaf to my calls to her, a pretense exposed when I stopped calling and crumpled a cellophane candy wrapper in my pocket and her head jerked up to look at me before burying itself back in another bundle of grass. Dog psychology, you know, is simpler than most. Anyway, I walked over to get her, snapped on the lead, and turned to go back and it was there. The coyote, I mean, standing near a cluster of lilac bushes and looking at me. I started to get the feeling, that same hard pain I had felt the day the dogs killed it, until I instructed myself that it could not be the same animal and the feeling went away, leaving only my appreciation of the unlikelihood of a coyote appearing in a place where there were people nearby and the digging apparatus and all. That was when I saw that there *were* no people and no digging equipment but only the coyote on the prairie that extended to the horizon in all directions. And the grass. It was not clipped anymore but tall—as tall as my shoulders in places—bending and rippling in sequence when the wind hit it. A few seconds later, the gravestones and machine and the fence people were returned, and for a moment I could see all of it together, but then the coyote and grass faded and I couldn't.

I was reminded, too, of events that followed my first writing about corpses. That account also stirred puzzling visions, even nowhere near a cemetery. Still, I have given the matter some consideration and I don't think it is reason for concern. Then, as now, it was only for a while until I was able to mute what I saw and make it leave.

The mastery of that skill—*muting,* I mean—was facilitated by my corpse upbringing and became a necessity with the changes at the Branscoms'. It was essential to keep my new emotions, once they found their footing in me, from overtaking me altogether and that commotion otherwise interfering with my thinking. I was about to mention that, in fact. You misunderstand me if you believe I am claiming that living requires letting one's feelings run rampant because, no, it does not. That course can bring its own death problems. Muting was even more important to me, therefore, when I understood there was some delicate barrier behind which feeling is generated and held, a maidenhead of emotion, which, once breached, is gone forever. Despite my efforts to mute them, however, the feelings that came began to gather a certain momentum. Before spring was finished, what I had once been able to observe as individual, discrete occurrences became a continuous, surging stream of undelimited feeling carrying me along with it as fast as Gracie. I was always feeling something and, often, more than one thing. The feelings did not have to agree. In any event, as June arrived and harvest with it, I was no less full and ripe than the wheat.

It was to be a different harvest in many ways. Mid-May, Everett had slipped in the chute while loading cattle and cracked his tailbone. He could not sit comfortably at the kitchen table, let alone on the iron seat of a rocking combine through twelve-hour days of cutting. However, the *Farmers' Almanac* forecast that the Kansas brood of seventeen-year cicadas was due to hatch in early June, and Everett would not be convinced the insects were not the locusts of the plague, posing no threat to his crops. He declared that the wheat needed cutting as soon as it was ready, which left him no choice but to hire custom cutters. It was a dark day for Everett because he and the neighboring farmers were still talking about the looting done by an Oklahoma crew the year before. Lois and Linda, on the other hand, were giddy with anticipation, a reaction I only understood on June 11 when the custom crew finally arrived and I saw that it was composed of two older men with all the rest teenage boys.

We surveyed the lot of them that first day, looking from the kitchen window to where they displayed themselves for us, propped up against the trucks, feigning indifference. They had begun work more than a month before in Texas, cutting their way north through the plains as the wheat ripened, and were already baked nut brown, their muscles evident beneath sleeveless denim snap-button shirts with the tails hanging out and the snaps unsnapped. So they were all in very fine condition, but one of them, Eddie Soul, was unquestionably the pick of the litter. There was no fair way to proceed except to draw straws for him, and when I won Linda rolled her eyes and Lois sighed with exasperation. "He'll be wasted," Lois said.

It was true I lacked Lois's range of experience, which is perhaps an amusing subject for another occasion, but not relevant here. I was not an innocent, however. I had, after all, been a farm girl—and boy—and was not a stranger to sexual facts. When the first pair of testicles you have ever seen belongs to a Hereford bull, you know, it tends to put all the others in perspective. Too, I was blessed with just enough of my father's good looks and my mother's curving figure, and those are sufficient with men for some long while.

In any event, for each of the ten days his crew was in the area, Eddie and I were together an hour or more, and one rainy day we spent the entire afternoon in an empty granary, listening to KOMA on Eddie's transistor, eating soda crackers and Colby cheese and drinking Arriba wine. Each meeting was a story, sweet and complete and, most certainly, filled with intense sensations, yet I remember only a few odd details: His skin smelled of castile soap and his breath of Dentyne, which I considered to be a gallantry inasmuch as, days, Eddie chewed Red Man with the rest of the crew. He told me he was part Cherokee on his mother's side, that he was going to join the air force when he turned eighteen, and that he always took care to wear his boots with the proper length jeans—long enough to kick up a little trail of dust behind him when he walked.

When he came to say good-bye, he cupped my face in his hands and just looked at me smiling for a long time. "You're a funny one, you know that?" he said, and then he pressed his full lips against mine, at first softly, then passionately harder, thrilling me and, later, Lois and Linda as well when I recounted the event for them in detail. Apparently, at some time Eddie and I also went so far as to have intercourse, although I don't recall doing that at all. Eddie was seventeen, as I said, a teenage boy—and actual sex with a boy of those years is often barely noticeable, let alone memorable. But I must have because the cutters, Eddie with them, left the county on June 20, and by the second week in July, I had gone more than a week past the date of my normal period.

"How could you be so stupid?" the girls demanded, refusing to believe what I told you—that I didn't know that we had done anything—although it was true. At least, I did not claim it was only once, and that I had *that* dignity is still a matter of some pride.

That was Sunday and on Wednesday afternoon Lois went with me to the drugstore and Doc Greer's office in the back. He smiled at both of us when he came in and patted Lois's shoulder. He hammered my knees with a rubber hatchet and shone a scoped light into each of my ears.

"How old are you?"

"Sixteen."

"Sixteen. You look good and healthy to me. What can I do for you?"

I looked at Lois, who spoke for me. "She's late."

Dr. Greer's brows and mouth shifted by fractions of an inch. "How late?"

"A couple of weeks," I told him.

He sighed and shook his head. "Oh Lord," he said under his breath, and left the room.

A half hour passed before he returned, but when he did, he was cheerful and friendly again. He was holding a syringe and asked me to drop my jeans and lean over the examination table. After two tries, he found the mass of fat he needed and dispensed the shot. Then he handed Lois a small envelope. "Give her half of these tonight before bedtime and the rest in the morning before breakfast." Then to me: "Okay. These'll take care of you. You should get your period in a few days."

"I'm not pregnant then?"

"Now, listen to what I'm telling you. This time you got lucky. It'll be different the next time, so don't be letting any more boys in your pants."

Two mornings later I was wakened by cramping pain so severe that I had drawn my knees up against my chest in my sleep and could not unlock myself until I had lain there, breathing deeply, for several minutes more. I willed myself to get up and, bent double, leaned against the hallway wall all the way to the bathroom. I dropped onto the toilet seat just inside, barely down when I passed a bloody rushing glob, a mass of thick bloody clots that filled the bowl. No more came, but I sat hunched over my knees for a long while, waiting for the pain and cramps to go away. Finally, I wiped myself clean and stood up, then turned immediately to vomit a foamy flesh-colored liquid, gold mucus, and blood into the toilet with the rest. This sequence repeated three times more before evening, although the blood became more fluid, the clots fewer each time. The following day I began to menstruate in the usual manner, continuing for three days, and I have never missed a period since.

After that, I returned to sleep nights in the little trailer, and it was as if I had wakened sober after a weekend drunk. The first night was oddly still. The buzzing cicadas had come and mostly gone; the moon was dark and the Milky Way directly above stood out from the inky sky. I stared at it for several hours without feeling. Or perhaps I *was* feeling something, but only some variety of loneliness that can easily be confused with a void of feeling by one as inexperienced as I was in these matters. I wasn't thinking either, although I might well have thought I was delivered from evil. Yet twice I caught myself trying to summon back all the disturbing, unpredictable sensations that had filled me so completely in the days and weeks before this night when I was suddenly returned to feeling nothing much whatsoever. I stopped that at once, of course. I had been feeling almost happy, and when you are as ignorant as I was about the nature of what was about, that is a dangerous state to inhabit—whistling in the dark, as it were.

I slept in the trailer every night thereafter, Lady curled next to me, until two weeks later when I woke up, surprised by Mr. Stark standing over us, silhouetted against the early sun, his arms crossed like a stalwart Pawnee chieftain and his legs wide apart to brace against the wind. His tie was flapping back over his shoulder and rippling the fringes of his neatly cropped hair.

"How did you know I was here?" I asked him, but he never told me.

"Let's get your things together," he said, holding his hand out to help me up while he picked up a large suitcase with the other. I was fully packed in less than an hour and had put everything in his car, including the sack of mementos I had brought with me and left untouched in the back of my closet. It would be best not to take Lady, he advised.

"Don't worry about her. She can sleep in our room," Linda promised, and I have always told myself that is what happened. Still, when Mr. Stark was driving me away, I looked back and saw Lady trotting away from the farm in the opposite direction, down the road toward the T where I first found her, so I don't know. If I had ever spoken to Linda again, perhaps I would have asked. As for me, I was returned to Sheriff Thompson's office and I stayed with the sheriff and his wife until it could be determined what should be done with me.

You may have noticed already that Mr. Stark has come to my aid more than once. That is true and I am duly grateful. Nevertheless, I would not want you to think him a safety net that does not fail, the wise old Merlin who knows all. He has never known all that I know of the corpses, never saw what I came to see. Otherwise, he could have undertaken this account himself rather than imposing it on me. And, furthermore, proceeding thus blindly, his work has risked unknown consequences he might have thought better of had he known. When he came for me at the Branscoms', he found me changed in unexpected ways. I was no longer a boy and I had grown older, more knowledgeable. There is no denying that the life I possessed had quickened, although the greater portion of pain to pleasure darkened me and put the reins on my burgeoning feeling.

And although my own reading and the girls' homework were sufficient to prepare me for college, Mr. Stark's arrangements were what sent me, a few weeks later, to enter the university at barely sixteen. I am not saying it brought me less good than if I had gone a different way—such counterfactuals are necessarily indeterminate—only that his choice was blind in ways he did not appreciate. Well, what matters now is that it was done and with significant effect. It was at the university, that is, that I first saw that there is more to the problem than one child and one family. There are other corpses.

## 4.

IT IS 12:06. AT PRECISELY noon Lawrence and Donnie stopped what they were doing and broke for lunch. They moved their pickup over by the east fence, to a spot under a sixty-foot incense cedar, the only shade tree in Laurel Cemetery without graves directly beneath it, and at this moment they are sitting on the tailgate gobbling bologna-and-margarine sandwiches and pickled eggs and drinking slushy RC Colas.

Earlier Lawrence walked over to invite me to join them. "We got enough for a half dozen. You'd be doin' us a favor. It'll just go to waste."

"Thanks. Maybe later," I told him, and watched his lumbering gait back to the truck. In the brief moment he was here, I thought I saw a pink-purple spot near his waistline at the same time I felt an acute pain in that location in my own body. My surmise is that he is in the early stages of pancreatitis and would do better to avoid soda pops and pork fat himself, although, of course, I did not say that to Lawrence. Instead, I have renewed my determination to close out any more of these visions, to mute them as far as I am able.

As I told you earlier, I have had to cultivate that skill of inhibition, which in recent years has served to prevent unwanted seeing, although its first adversary was no more than unfamiliar and unruly feelings. That was certainly the case at sixteen, when I arrived to begin my college studies. I was barely acquainted with my own emotions and it was best they be kept in check. In fact, if I had not already possessed some talent for doing so, I might not have borne the surprises that awaited me, the most notable of which was the existence of other corpses.

There are, you see, more corpses in academia than anywhere else you might name, and that was my conclusion after even a short time there. And it was at the university, too, that I met Jeanne Napoleon while she was dying in a manner I had not previously known. Since then, I have named it: I call it *Donovan's death* after the fictional tycoon whose brain was kept alive in a vat, his eyes floating nearby. That is what is peculiar to this death—the brain is the last to go, deluding one into thinking she is in the wellspring of life at its fullest while all the time she is only the flame of a candle burning more brightly at the end. I once suspected that Donovan's malady was the real source of my own eventual weakness, but now I think not. There are so many ways to die.

I met Napoleon the first day of classes, a Thursday, and before half past eight I sat with twenty or more others around three long tables pushed together to form a Gothic U. Napoleon said nothing when she entered a few minutes late, sufficient to impress her professorial rank upon us, wearing sunglasses, men's trousers, and a thin mouse-brown gabardine coat that went almost to her ankles. She threw the coat in soft folds across a neglected chair and handed a stack of mimeographed sheets to the boy at the corner of our table. The faint smell of ether was passed in silence from hand to hand while she crossed her arms and held herself, pacing a small rectangle in front of the dormer windows that extended from ceiling to floor of our third-story classroom. She was tall, not rangy, but substantial in the way of farm women, with a healthy child's face and thick, willful hair. Her green-blue eyes were uncommon, glowing against dark rims, a wolf's eyes looking out from black night, and if anyone dared to look into them, there was seen her mind pacing, too, which just then watched some idea through the windows' panes, intently as if it were on the hunt, ignoring us altogether. Yet the last student had no more than touched the syllabus when she turned and strode to the center of the room, removing the lectern and silently sliding back on the smooth wood of the desktop. She pulled her legs into her and under, sitting yoga fashion to face us. "I am Professor Napoleon," she said, and I was in love.

She called roll, asking each the preferred manner of address. "Oz," I replied, and for the first time, she turned her wolf's eyes on mine.

"The Wizard?" she said matter-of-factly, and frowned when there was tittering. "Or *a* wizard, for that matter." She pushed herself off the table, walking again to the windows, staring out at the top branches of a Dutch elm, then turned toward me, studying my face as if she were searching for something there, in the way that a mother looks over her child—the same intense, immodest, proprietary scrutiny.

"It's from my last name—Oscar," I lied.

She let the matter go but turned her chin up as if to let the substance of my claim pass by her, and her half smile was enough to say she knew it was false. Once more, I felt pass over me an unfamiliar sensation, akin to a rising panic, as well as the desire to gaze upon her that could not be satisfied despite my gaping at her the entire class time of seventy-five minutes. She could not have, in her condition, given me life, but it is wholly accurate to say, I think, that she single-handedly amplified what life I possessed, turned up its volume, so to speak. The contradiction of something does not negate, you know, but underscores.

Napoleon was already a person of note, or more accurately, about to be noted. She was thirty-five, eight years past her doctoral dissertation at the University of Chicago, and soon to present a paper that would bring her to the forefront for good. That was two years away, but already she gathered the regard. She moved through dimly lit institutional halls with long legs, sure strides, oblivious to the envious, lustful stares of her colleagues. They deferred to her long before her achievement merited it.

I did not feel the same carnal lust for her that I had once for Eddie Soul. I simply revered her in an explosion of passionate regard previously unknown to me, and I was, therefore, totally unaware of the consequences. I knew nothing, saw nothing apart from the ideality of my happy circumstance. Plato was right again: the ideal is real, not the other. And it is not that one cannot lust after a corpse. There is a certain calmness, assuredness—not to mention consistency—to the unchanging form. Deterioration is halted, the body now a mere projection of what it was when last organically alive. It was no matter. If there were anything present that could have told me I loved a corpse in the making, I did not see it then.

Too, there were distractions. Common death was everywhere. Bonnie McLeod died that first November, choking on a bite of sandwich—whole wheat and Winchester's bologna. Bonnie's roommate found her sitting on her bed in the half-light common to dormitory rooms atop one of the matching, plaid spreads they bought together the first week of school, her back leaning comfortably against the wall, her face fixed, not in agony but an odd look, closer to surprise. We others saw nothing more than Bonnie on a gurney, covered in a hospital sheet, rolled down the dingy cork-tile hall, and out of the dorm. In short time she was returned to Sublette in the western reaches of Kansas. None of us attended the funeral.

Less than two weeks later, my roommate's mother was felled by a stroke at the age of fifty-five. In my teenage wisdom, I consoled Mogie, "At least she had a long, full life." Death was also in the newspaper and on CBS *News* in the daily body count from Vietnam. In the dormitory lounge at 5:30 each day, a few of us girls sat on Coke-stained cushions and stared at the television, our fingers twirling long hair while we watched a soldier in his last moments, mortally wounded and being carried from right to left across the screen, one arm hanging loose, the other secured across the body to hold in guts, the blood never fresh, but dark and gelatinous, covering the arm down to the elbow where it split into three forks and ran between his fingers. I don't watch the news anymore. I know better now. And the assassinations. I almost forgot.

So death was very much with us then, although our attitude was not fear but loathful resignation. I mean to say that death was no longer an occurrence that left us thunderstruck but more an unavoidable condition of our lives, a stinking penance hanging on us like the rotting carcass hung around a dog's neck to cure his chicken killing. As a corrective measure, however, neither seems ever to have worked particularly well.

Still, the greatest distraction was my discovery that there were corpses other than my family. The first I recognized was an older secretary in the graduate school (where I found the work-study job for what money I needed beyond room and board, that having been provided by Mr. Stark). I suspected her right away because of the way she moved and was, coincidentally, right. There is no sure pattern, really. None at all. It was just that Mrs. Guyll's movement caught the eye. She flowed rather than walked, pressing forward silently, without effort, her body insinuating itself from desk to door like snowmelt finding its channel. And she looked the part, her hair pure silver, set in hard waves and pulled into a tight bun, her face powdery white except for electric blue eyes and red lipstick.

I liked my job there, filing the new applications or transcripts from the hundreds of foreigners who wanted to do graduate study at the university and searching for the old ones, a significant number of which had been lost. While I worked, Mrs. Guyll tended her delicate duties. She typed memoranda, in triplicate, for the dean, a single memo occupying hours because she always started over rather than unsatisfactorily correct an error on four different pages. She answered the telephone and took messages. She took a bathroom break "to freshen up" at 2:00 P.M. and a coffee break at 3:30 P.M. during which she left her desk to sit on the stuffed love seat in the waiting area, eat home-baked pfeffernüssen, sip tea, and talk about herself.

"We are going to drive to Canada," she announced in early September. "I'm hoping we'll make it to Prince Edward Island this year." Every day during the weeks after, she brought pictures or bits of information about what she and her husband would see if they made it to the island. "I've always wanted to see it," she said with such wistfulness that when her October vacation day arrived, I wanted it for her with as much fervency as she wanted it for herself, but they didn't make it that year, or the next, or any year I was at the university. One day the dean told me that Mrs. Guyll had expressed this same wish each of the years she had been his secretary, going on seventeen years.

"I don't think they're ever going to make it," he said, and I am fairly certain now that it was exactly that unproductive wishing that killed her. Well, what I am saying is that ideas and notions are not mere ephemera without shape or substance but, rather, at the most primitive level, constructed of the same matter as, say, Mount McKinley. They have their effects in the world unless blocked, in which case they can turn back like a deflected bullet and wound us, sometimes mortally. Oh, there is no use in thinking about it, because it is not as if we can avoid the risk. Wishes just occur, like weeds in our garden of ideas, each a criticism of what is and capable of generating a dozen others like it. Mrs. Guyll was an unfortunate casualty is all.

I told no one but took care to keep my distance from Mrs. Guyll, and I looked for another job. Within a few weeks, I had found one in the campus library, where, each weekday afternoon, I spent several hours alone in the stacks searching for books that had been returned but, apparently, wrongly shelved. I am certain that I would have done nothing more than that had I only known of this one corpse, no matter the surprise. But within a few weeks, I had met yet another, and I soon knew that it did not stop there.

In the face of these discoveries, my class under Napoleon—Ethical Issues in Contemporary Society— was my sure respite and I arranged my time around it. She was already writing *The Morality of War,* so the subject came up more than once. Her own view, however, remained unclear and she refused to answer questions to that end.

"Philosophy is not the study of what someone else thinks, but how to think oneself" was her only response. Given the attitudes of the times, most of us assumed that she was devising some ingenious argument destroying any justification for the Vietnam War and perhaps all other such scourges as well. But, as I said, she kept close counsel and no one really knew.

Outside class I found other ways to be near her and, indeed, that was how I saw the second corpse—when I was in Rhatigan Hall, a previously condemned building that served to house the philosophy department. It was a small one-department structure that had been rescued from impending implosion when the statehood centennial celebrations generated a surge of preservationism, although whatever money was forthcoming to put philosophers in better quarters had not yet arrived. Still, it remained standing, if precariously, its Prague gray blocks arranged in the style of a German castle with a large third-story turret set to one side. That was Napoleon's office. The narrow stairs leading to the third floor led no place but her door, and I often loitered in the second-floor hall below, where there was plenty to soothe the unease of being alone. Pink, green, and yellow pages of graduate school descriptions, fellowship competitions, and announcements of visiting speakers were tacked together and over each other on a corkboard. Frosted-glass panels in faculty doors displayed cartoons from the *New Yorker*, clippings of perceived absurdities and profound sayings, self-satisfaction hanging over it all like a fluffy white prairie cloud. I read them all—several times—but by midterm I merely sat on the dulled linoleum, my back against the wall, knees up. I was comfortable enough—being alone doesn't cause me the unease so much as being itself, and I withdrew from that into my own head, where I constructed fantasy worlds, imagining untrue scenarios and my part in them, all the while I waited for a glimpse of Napoleon. Not to be with her, but to watch her being. Do you understand?

It was exactly there in that hall that I saw him—Kenneth Butler, the aesthetics professor. As he came sufficiently close to me—less than ten feet, I would say—my perception of him encountered a "hard space" in the sensory continuum. As my attention met its edge, it glided across too rapidly, as if I were driving across a patch of black ice and I had to bring my attention back into control and back to where Butler was before I saw him again at all. This sensation drew my notice, but it was only later that I realized such can be a feature of the corpse presence. Then I did not see what he was and, in any event, corpse identification is not bird-watching but rather a judgment reached over time and repeat encounters. How simple it would be if the dead could be picked out by this feature or that! I tell you, it is not like that. I warn you.

He moved right toward me, as if in recognition, then stopped and looked down where I sat. "Tired of the world?" He squinted his eyes at me in what may have been his only gesture of amity. I shook my head.

"Just waiting."

"Oh." He shifted uncertainly, as if my merely sitting there obstructed his progress, although his office was in the other direction, away from where I was. "For Godot?" He sounded the t to pronounce the name phonetically, a conceit of his based on the belief it was pretentious to use foreign pronunciations when speaking English, and laughed at his own joke with a half-choked snort. It was no difference to me. I did not comprehend the reference.

"No. Napoleon," I said, and he nodded weakly, ambling off toward his office. I first suspected his condition after that, when he had gone and I felt the momentary world-weariness and an unpleasant sensation of breathing moldy air that sometimes accompanies a meeting with one who is dead. But the same sense can also come when the other is very much alive and trying to pull the last of your life out of you. I did not want to jump to conclusions because—especially because—I did not want it to be true. Still, I signed up for Butler's aesthetics course the following semester with no better intention than to try to know for certain.

The remaining weeks of the first semester rendered that effort unnecessary. Mere suspicion proved sufficient to open my eyes. In short order, I saw that the university was home to a passel of corpses and the rare day was one in which I saw none. For the most part, they were distributed evenly among the different departments and administrative offices, although there was a virtual coven in the business school and my statistics professor, Mr. Jones, was so clearly a corpse that I wondered that the other students did not see it. They called him "Flasher" Jones because of his habit of wearing his long coat in the classroom but never noticed the bulging pockets filled with pieces of iron to weigh him to the ground. There were so many others—the baker who made the cookies we devoured daily in the student union and who brought the hot pans bare-handed from the oven, the nearly famous chair of the anthropology department, teaching his class of five hundred one day a week, then mysteriously disappearing from view until ten minutes before class the next week, not to mention the housemother of our dormitory whose stage makeup did not always cover the grayed flesh just in front of her ears.

So I saw corpses everywhere and, yes, Butler was one of them, his revealing moment not long in coming that next semester. He had the habit of being late to our class, and one day he carried it a few minutes too far, allowing the students to invoke the "twenty-minute" rule whereunder we were permitted to leave without penalty. In our rush to go—we could see him coming outside the building—I left my jacket under the chair and had to return. When I did, he was there, lecturing to the empty classroom as if the class were in place, attentive and taking notes. He did not mark my entry into the room or my quick departure after I had retrieved the coat, and the following class he continued on from the point he had apparently reached in his solitary lecture. None of the other students so much as noticed the unexplained gap, demonstrating an overly common apathy that is lethal in its own way. I dropped the course before midterm.

Perhaps I should have seen Napoleon's precarious condition as well, but in the midst of all these dead, you can understand that the death of my beloved, not yet a corpse and full of rare and fine ideas, was the last of my thoughts. What captured me were her mind and her unsurpassed talent for thinking. Her field of expertise included logic but also ethics and religions. Philosophy of religions, that is, since she freely acknowledged her own atheism.

I asked her, "What if you die and there *is* a God?"

She only laughed. "I've always been willing to admit I've made a mistake," she said.

That is a quality the rest of us would do well to culti-vate, or maybe I am talking to myself again, which is often the case when giving advice to others. My mistakes might have cost me less dearly if I had readily owned to them, but I find it difficult to change course once committed to it. Still, that doggedness passed down from my pioneer an-cestors is also the will that keeps me on course despite ob-stacles or discomfort.

It helps me, too, when I need to keep my fears in check, as here and as in every month and year of my pe-culiar life. It is always the way with such things that we let inside—once they are there they mingle casually with the rest of us and we find it difficult to say who is who. Or we grow attached to them like some bothersome neighbor who is always dropping in, hanging around and borrowing things, until one day their life is no longer separate from but a distinct element of our own. Of course, it is clear that we should be doing something like spring-cleaning at intervals, but there is a problem of sorts. We are loath to cut away parts of ourselves—even the bad ones. It feels like a small suicide or self-mutilation. So the best is to stop these fears at the door lest they become in you like heart-worms in a dog, threading their way through the heart so intimately that, in the end, to kill the worms you must sacrifice the animal as well.

Napoleon. Another reason I missed her increasing deadness, I think, was that she was physically very robust. Her ancestry was German and Russian and, as everyone knows, those people live practically forever. Each day she walked from home to the campus and back again, and it didn't matter that in Kansas such must include walking in stifling heat and stinging, bitter cold, not to mention "fat rain," the kind with big, soft drops coming so fast and heavy that nothing can prevent them from reaching your skin. And no matter which of these conditions, there was always a stiff wind inevitably blowing in the direction opposite the one you were going. She also walked just to walk, around the campus in the middle of the day or to almost anywhere at all in the evenings and on weekends. It was considered an oddity then, some years before anyone thought to run on purpose to be out of breath. I saw her myself many times, walking her purposeful walk, eyes fixed at some distant point on the sidewalk, her lips moving in solitary conversation. If the reputation of her intellect had not preceded her, we might all have thought her mad.

Few did, though most could never really understand what it is like to have a mind like hers, to be not merely bright but very-smart-indeed, to have what those in academia like to label a "first-rate" mind. That is a special one. What is the name of that victorious king in 1066? The lesser mind says, "It starts with a W" and within a minute has used some pedagogical tool to extract "William the Conqueror," and that is really all that is needed. However, one like Napoleon's sees matters differently. "William the Conqueror" her brain retrieves in less than a second, followed by details about the Norman conqueror's life and loves, the decisive importance of horses to his campaign, and the image of the dress the queen wore on page 135 of the fifth-grade history book and that the buttons appear as if they are tiny seashells like the ones her grandfather collected with her on the one trip ever to a beach, the Gulf of Mexico in 1940 near Brownsville, where she first ate tacos, twelve of them at one sitting! It goes on and on, mere memory of facts proceeding to complex connections and theories, until another part of the mind has had enough and screams, "Stop! Stop!" over the din of synapse firings at ever-increasing velocity. *Stop! Stop!* But it doesn't stop and she is always thinking, recalling many things at once if let go, or analyzing to their unsubstantiated limits what others happily accept as unquestionable truths.

So that was Napoleon's mind and it is the sort that can achieve great ends but frequently does not. Instead, it is often left to direct itself and, therefore, is a dangerous mind to have. Let go, it takes over, taking more attention and resources than the rest of the body has to spare. That is how Donovan's death begins, the mind pulling everything in, striving toward complete life for itself with nothing to damper it. At the very last, perhaps, the victim sees the truth, that she is stranded there in her head cut off from the body that has sustained her and faced with a desperate, nearly impossible return to the body for sustenance. That was what happened to Napoleon, and I suppose there were signs to see if I had only known. Then, however, she seemed to me more alive than any of us.

I had been working in the library almost four months when I happened upon her library hideaway. I was on the third floor in the Gottshall annex, built as a memorial wing for the aviation manufacturer's son and sometimes referred to as the "bookend" for its ad hoc relationship to the rest of the library, itself a mossy arts and crafts structure, whereas the annex jutted out to one side of it and was a Bauhaus glass tower brightly reflecting back the Kansas sky. To get there required coming to the far northeast corner of any of the library's four floors, then passing through several doors and a four-story walk-through. It was not someplace one would be without intention, and that was exactly the quality that brought me there with some frequency.

On the day I found Napoleon, I had come to poke around the Emerald City, a room that Betty Gottshall herself designed and that contained the Gottshall's collection of books, documents, and other items pertaining to *The Wizard of Oz*. Betty had made certain the purpose was clear. Forest green club chairs sat atop plush emerald green carpet, and green tweed covered the walls. In the center of the room stood a polished wood replica of one of the apple-throwing trees in the magic forest, encircled by a padded bench and containing in its crotch the prize of the Gottshall collection—one of the five pairs of ruby slippers Judy Garland wore as Dorothy, the shoes safely sealed in a Plexiglas box.

Bookshelves and display cases sat on every wall, but in the far corner of the Emerald City there was space for a single unmarked door. I knew that it stayed locked and so noticed at once when I saw the door slightly ajar, pulling it open to find a small conference room. It was well furnished with a long polished mahogany table and four padded chairs. Daylight was more than sufficient to light the entire room—the east wall was entirely glass and, unlike the outer room, the walls were off-white, save the presence of a double chalkboard that was, of course, green.

Napoleon sat at the table, her back toward me, and she was writing in a loose-leaf notebook. Her long body sprawled between two chairs, and she was dressed comfortably in jeans and a black loose-fitting shirt with a fisherman's collar. Her feet were bare, moccasins dropped under one chair.

I watched her for maybe thirty seconds before speaking. I couldn't help myself. Her intense concentration on the problem at hand was mesmerizing; she seemed so admirably pure to me, as if she were engaged in an enterprise of spirit where Reason and Truth were her only concerns and with no space for the petty matters that occupied the rest of us.

"Is this yours?" I asked finally.

Napoleon turned around suddenly then, although less startled than interrupted. She stood up and stretched. "Oz in Oz?" She smiled at me. "Are you ever going to tell me how you came by that name?" she asked, then turned in a circle, sweeping her arm around the room. "Yes . . . for a while anyway. It's nice. I can leave everything." She held up a key and motioned toward the far end of the room, where piles of books and journals sat neatly stacked, small tabs extending from each to mark what she had found there. That she had looked at them at all indicated she was well into the paper because it was her habit to work through a problem herself first, then check others to see if they had thought of anything she had not.

"You're about finished?"

She shrugged and sat back down, reaching for the notebook, and I was thereby dismissed. I hesitated only a moment before leaving her, closing the door behind me. That is all there was to it, except that if I had been asked then to give a definition of what it was to be alive, I would have described her in that moment. And yet, as I told you, she was already close to death. It is not the form, you see, but the content, and that simple truth has taken me years.

After that, I modeled myself on Napoleon. I wore, within the limits of my money and imagination, what she did—men's slacks with too-small shirts stretched over little-girl breasts and under oversize jackets. My legs were as long as hers and it was easy for me to copy her long strides and purposive walk. I cut my own thick hair to the same chin length and went without makeup save the one exception Napoleon made—lipstick, in an odd red-brown raisin shade—and, of course, the opaque cream I used to cover the narrow red scar that split my face. (An accident I suffered during my years with the Branscoms and of no particular importance.) I declined to join the philosophy club or any other identifiable group, save the Collegiate Young Democrats, which was not really a group but two prelaw students and me. And, in accordance with persistent rumors claiming Napoleon had an absent lover, I found my own off-campus hidden love—Peter Wirth, a boy my age who had dropped out of college after the first month and since become a local radio personality. He was intentionally and agreeably mysterious—slender in that manner that suggests dissipation and unconventional sex, always dressing in black and using only his stage name— "Rabbit Rock"—so that no one knew him. What's more, he was fortuitously sterile due to childhood mumps that went down on him, although I can't say whether that prompted his choice of "Rabbit." So he served my purposes and I preserved his secrets, needing only to make certain that others knew I spent time alone with him at what were considered inappropriate hours and places. That was what I structured in emulation of her.

We were not the same, of course. I knew about the corpses that roamed the campus and surrounding city and she did not. I have fretted over not telling her, putting her on guard as I was and, perhaps, changing what happened. I don't know and will never. The fact is that I said nothing and less than two years later, in August 1968, she died.

# 5.

NINETEEN SIXTY-EIGHT. IN
many ways, it is as if it is the only year that ever existed,
that was "in itself." Even then, while I was in its days, that
was how it seemed and I have always thought of that year
by the name *Pueblo* because that ship began and ended it,
being seized by North Korea in January and only released
in December. The assassinations, begun the previous summer with George Lincoln Rockwell, the American Nazi,
continued. On April 4, Martin Luther King Jr., then in
June, Bobby Kennedy. Still, there was more to it than
that. Czechoslovakia was crushed; students marched and
rioted in Paris, Prague, and Peoria. It was the year Jackie
Kennedy married Aristotle Onassis and Richard Nixon

was elected president. The latter occurred in November, *Pueblo*, but Napoleon was already dead by then.

That spring I had finally told Mogie about the corpses at the university, not only their existence but, also, that it seemed as if they were purposely staying close to me. I told her, in part, out of selfish concern for myself. I was drawn again and again to the corpse side to share its view of things, to watch those living persons moving about in two-dimensional space. It was, I knew, a comfortable, familiar perspective—that bemused watching with an ever-so-slight disapproval of all those living others, breathless, flush-cheeked, and so very unaware. I must be careful of it, even now.

My concern was a burden I was glad to share, but the main reason I told Mogie was because I thought she was my friend. It was a relation of some importance to me. Whereas other students—Mogie included—seemed to have a host of ready friends, I had only her. I preferred it that way, really, regarding the rest of those I knew as mere acquaintances, curious people who found my celebrated history interesting or found it useful to say they knew me. I knew very little about friendship, of course, but I thought that friends, at the least, must truly know who the other is, so I told her.

I should clarify that Mogie had always known about the corpses who had raised me—anyone who could read knew. She found that situation intriguing, although not so strange as to be beyond her ken. She herself was the

child of a family inclined to lunacy of the dirt-clod variety I have already mentioned and had warned me from
the beginning against being alone with any of her siblings
who might come to visit. But as for the corpses at the university, she was as stunned as I had been.

"Oh my god! Oh my god!" she kept repeating when I
told her, then pressed me for all the specifics of my sightings
and thoughts about them. She did not hesitate for a second
to believe all that I asserted, a seeming faith that I mistak-
enly assumed to be a compliment. "We have to tell Dave."

"Who's that?"

"You remember. Dave Schrag. Dark hair, walks
hunched over. Physics major. He is *so smart*." Mogie
waited for my assent and when I said nothing, declared,
"Well, I'm going to tell him."

"You just now promised me you wouldn't tell anyone!"

"I did not promise," Mogie insisted before, a moment
later, allowing, "Oh, yeah, I did promise. Well, I shouldn't
have promised and, anyway, it doesn't matter now. I'm
going to call him to meet us at the Cellar." And she did.

Mogie's vehement denials of inconvenient facts soon
became as familiar to me as her subsequent remembrance
of them. At first these lapses seemed only to indicate that
she was scatterbrained, a forgivable offense, but the regularity of their occurrence soon required another explanation: Mogie felt, rather than thought. Statements were
true as long as they did not give rise to uncomfortable feelings that prompted Mogie to abandon them in favor of

their contraries. I learned that my stern look was sufficient to keep her course corrected but found out, too, that measure only worked while we were together. Given her disposition, Mogie's beliefs were most generally aligned with those of the last person with whom she had spoken.

Anyway, we did go to meet Dave at the Cellar, a pub and dance hall three blocks from campus. I had tagged along with Mogie there before on "Ladies' Night" to eat popcorn and drink cheap beer while we waited to be asked to dance. Before each of these excursions, in our dormitory room, Mogie took the lead in preparing us and was adamant about what needed attention.

"As long as your hair and face look good," Mogie advised me, "it doesn't matter what you're wearing. You could go naked." It was some years later before I appreciated the fact that if we had gone naked, it wouldn't have mattered about our face or hair either.

When we arrived, Dave was already there, standing just inside the door, but he was not alone. Standing next to him was another student, a boy I already knew from the Young Democrats.

"Do not say anything!" I whispered to Mogie when I saw them.

"Oh my god! Who is that?"

"Ronald Davidson," I said. "He's in . . ."

"He looks just like Samuel Beckett," Mogie declared, although he most assuredly did not. Ronald was a sturdy, curly-haired, Scandinavian farm boy who did not resemble in the least the spare Irish author and playwright. But Mogie's theater class was performing cuttings from Beckett's work that semester and, as I said, that was how her mind worked.

"Remember. Nothing," I said again, but Mogie looked back at me with a blank expression. She had already forgotten why we had come in the first place.

The four of us gathered in one of the high-backed lacquered pine booths toward the back and drank two pitchers of beer, downing shredded ham sandwiches on fresh rye, fries, deep-fried dill pickle slices, and fried cheese as well. We sat there for two hours and discussed the important issues that needed our considering. It was, remember, 1968, a time when college students felt compelled to support, remedy, abolish, or comment upon any and all situations brought to their attention. I was thankful that the subject of corpses on our very campus was never raised that day or any other, but the meeting did begin a routine of sorts, and nearly every week thereafter, the four of us met on Friday afternoons at the Cellar. Well, after a while Mogie tired of what was, after all, mostly thinking and stopped coming. After that, it was just Ronald, Dave, and I.

Oh, I know what you will think, how you are going to judge me. During this year of encapsulation and protection, death a backdrop, you say, I was mistaken to ignore the most important questions—what is it to be alive, dead? How does one fan the flames of life and keep the ever-present corpse at bay? But I did. It was some time yet before it occurred to me to consider these matters as to me. Why should it be otherwise? Raised by the dead, I was left to myself to master the art of living, and it can take a long while done that way.

In 1968 life in me persevered in spite of me—a thorn plant growing on hot, dry sand. I hid it in my head and, instead, constructed an existence sustained by my intellectual love of Napoleon, life itself as a theory, i.e., one that is assumed like the first premise of a logical proof. See how dangerous philosophy is? I know that now. Still, in the end, it is the only path to the Truth. The danger is this: pure thinking leads us into our heads and away from everything "extrinsic," as we philosophers say. Away from the imprecise musings of other people, away from what we see with our own eyes, or feel. Away from our hearts. It is a trip that must be taken, but no one tells us that it would be well to mark the trail and never go as far as the road can go, because after the long journey to thought, we must find the way back to our hearts or die.

Napoleon was trying to make that return journey, I am fairly certain, but, as it happened, that is also one of the reasons she died. Her death occurred rather suddenly, if not at the Democratic National Convention held in Chicago, August 1968, then shortly thereafter and as a direct consequence. I was there when it happened. Ronald and I had come as Young Democrat representatives and had booked rooms at a small hotel in the Loop, the closest we could get to party headquarters at the Conrad Hilton two blocks over on Michigan Avenue. Napoleon was not far away. She was just south, staying in the Gothic faculty club on the compatibly dark campus of the University of Chicago, where, at last, she would present her paper on war to the summer convocation of the Central Philosophical Assembly. Yes, it was a coincidence and, yet, one that seemed to indicate that orchestration was going on at another level—like Nixon being in Dallas the day Kennedy was shot. Napoleon giving her analysis of the morality of war, I mean, at the same time and place that thousands of politicians, delegate-citizens, students, and, through television, almost everyone else were engaged in combat in the very same place and over the very same issue. Well, the others were not proceeding with the same pristine detachment as Napoleon but with the urgency of those who have something of value at stake right now. So things were not the same for everyone, you see, and that was why we could not agree.

Napoleon read her paper to the philosophical assembly on Monday afternoon. It was, of course, written precisely, the reasoning impeccable, and its conclusion was startling at the time. War does not belong in the realm of morality at all, she said, but that of law. So to ask "Is War Moral?" is to ask nonsense in the same way as to ask whether a window is on key. A category mistake, pure and simple. That is to say that decisions about going to war and who should go were legal questions to be decided in the legitimate courts of the country in question. She had mooted the objections of an entire generation.

It might surprise you to know that there was a stir. But the times were different; our concerns of a different shape. I should say that, in a gathering of philosophers, a "stir" is defined as the intellectual rush occurring when someone presents those professional thinkers with a thought they had not thought, and it is the sort of event that keeps them struggling, their equivalent of the one perfect golf shot that returns golfers to the course for a thousand slices. Well, that would have been all, I suppose, had this been the usual gathering of midwestern analytic philosophers, but the appeal of the Continent was already invading and there was a young and overly ambitious professor present from the University of Pennsylvania who recognized the existing dialectic between the position of the protestors at the convention and that of Napoleon, creating the possibility of synthesis, which I suppose is best described as a sort of Hegelian nirvana.

"You need to take your paper to the people," he told her. "Dellinger and I were at Stanford together. I know he'll let you speak."

He was right and so Napoleon came to be in Grant Park two days later, mounting the podium immediately after Allen Ginsberg, to tell three thousand youthful members of the Mobilization that they had made a category mistake. As it happened, Ronald and I were in the park, having followed William S. Burroughs there—at a safe distance, of course—and I saw her at the bottom of the stage steps, pulling off her usual dark blazer because of the heat, leaving her in long pants and a clinging tank sweater.

"Look, Joni Mitchell!" Ronald gasped when he saw her, but in twenty minutes he and the crowd knew differently. By then, Napoleon had both explained and proved to those gathered, in terms understandable by a fifth grader, why their objections to the war had to be made on legal grounds, if at all. Then she took her notes and left, convinced, I am certain, that her job was complete, the irrational, irrelevant battles between police and students over. Of course, she was entirely wrong and I wondered whether she had even bothered to study Plato's "Myth of the Cave," or perhaps she had simply forgotten because the truth did not change anything there either and, worse, the truth tellers were killed. In Chicago that night, the truth teller wasn't killed, but died. I think you will agree that, in the end, both are pretty much the same.

She probably did not actually see the violent evening and the irrational acts that followed her dissemination of the truth. I only ventured from the safety of the hotel once myself, walking three blocks before being stopped by two Chicago police, shoulder to shoulder, completely blocking my way. Tear gas was beginning to roll in and a slender girl in moccasins held out a damp washcloth to me. "Here. Breathe through this," she said with such urgency that I obeyed instantly, and then she took her cloth and disappeared, apparently following a kind of Aquarian justice that allowed only one breath per person. I went back to the hotel and knew nothing more until the television news reports began to appear, and even then I knew only what I was told, that being that there was no retreat of the protestors, no diminution of the threat felt by the Establishment, in this case the police, nor any move toward rational order at all. Instead, everything went on as before—more violent and more chaotic, if anything—as if Napoleon had never thought anything about anything or shared it with us, as if she had held her hand up to stop a swinging door and the door, unfazed, had passed right through it. The nothingness was fatal.

Let me say that, ordinarily, such an assault on one's view of things is quite survivable, although distressing, but that is only because of what circumstances are ordinary. Given the right facts, being hit on the head by an apple can be fatal and, apparently, Napoleon was struck at an inopportune time. That is why I feel certain that she was making the transition from mind to heart, a move that requires a most delicate transference from one part of us to another, in any event.

For Napoleon it was more so, because she had taken the whole road to mind, and to do that, one must let go of the heart altogether. There is a problem in that, it seems, because it is not for nothing that we have the heart. We can survive awhile without it and some, like Napoleon, have been tempted to do so. As far as I know, only one of those has succeeded. You see, if you can arrive at the place in mind that she did, you are as close to being a god as you will ever be, seemingly immortal because it appears there is nothing to die. However, our minds are generated by an organic engine and, thus, need fuel. When the need for sustenance arises—and that need must be met or extinction—how to get back? Neither the neurologists nor the cardiologists have yet given us the physiological requirements of making the jump, but it seems obvious enough that an unstable, unprotected stretch across some undetermined neuronic gap must form some part—that time when the hands of one safe haven must be let go and the swinging bar of the other grasped, not a time for jostling or tremors because the abyss below holds catastrophe, be it nihilism, fanaticism, or death itself. For Napoleon, jarred at the critical moment, the outcome was death.

CAROL CAME OUT awhile ago and kindly brought club sandwiches and real potato salad, a thermos of coffee, and a hamburger for Annie, then sat with us while Annie and I ate our lunch together.

"I told them to leave off the pickle," she said, and I told her that it would have been fine, that Annie liked everything except pinto beans. "Well, I thought it might not be healthy for her," she explained further.

"Yeah. Your tummy doesn't work as well as it used to, does it?" I reached down to scratch Annie, who was motionless while I persisted, turning her eyes up to see where the hand had gone when I stopped, then flopping heavily on her side to nap.

"How long have you had her?"

"Oh, eight years. Since she was a puppy. I've had four of them—Chloe, then Blanche, Maggie, and now Annie. She's getting on though." I was more than willing to go on, to compare my dogs' very distinct personalities and share some stories about them, but caught myself when I glanced up at Carol looking past me to where the digging was.

"Well, I guess I better get back to work," I said. "Thanks again for the lunch, Carol. You didn't have to do that."

"What? Oh, sure. I need to get back, too." She picked up the sack she had used for the food and checked around for litter. She started away from us, then turned. "May I ask you something?"

I nodded but looked at her directly from the bottom of my eyes, eyebrows raised, chin down—a posture I have found helpful, limiting the scope of what another is willing to inquire from you.

"Last night when you saw the book. You didn't really say anything but . . . I could tell you were surprised. Right?"

"That he gave it to me? Yes. I guess so." I measured my words, uncertain where she was heading.

"No. I mean you seemed . . . Well, I was just wondering . . ." She looked down at the ground then at me, smiling.

"*What?*"

"Well, you know, what *you* thought. You didn't say anything. You must have an idea. Especially, I would think, since . . ." She stopped at the hard look I gave her. I didn't mean to do it but was glad in any event. "All I am asking is what did you think about it?"

"The book?"

"Right."

"Nothing, really," I hedged, although it was the correct answer to her literal question, which concerned what I *did* think about it last night rather than what I have thought about it since. There is one little puzzle, you see. I noticed it flipping through the book this morning. The account published ten years ago contained an error—"perjorative" for "pejorative," I remember it quite clearly and how annoyed I was—and this one does not. Still, I saw no reason to tell Carol. "I guess I'd want to talk to Lawrence and Donnie. You know. Whether there was a chance someone could be playing a joke or something like that. What do you think?"

I regretted the question as soon as it was out because Carol seized the invitation and walked back to me, suddenly enthused. "Well. I've been reading this book by this guy who is an electrical scientist or something like that. He's gone all over the world measuring the energy fields and—well, you would just have to read the book—but,

anyway, one of the things that he has found is that wherever there are cemeteries the energy is a lot greater." She
paused, nodding, waiting for some response.

I reached down to scratch Annie. "That's . . . well,
there's so much we don't know."

"I know. It really makes you think. You know. Maybe
the energies of this place attracted energies from your
book and it coalesced there in the grave. There's just so
much that doesn't make sense otherwise. Did I tell you
that this week is the week we buried Evan's grandfather
ten years ago?"

"Yeah. Evan mentioned it, I think."

"Well. There you have it. I mean, that is too much of
a coincidence to be a coincidence."

You see? It is exactly that propensity of which I spoke
before, the talent for mighty conclusions with minuscule
foundation, for traveling three hundred miles on a gallon
of gas, and I hope you can understand how disturbing this
entire conversation was to my philosophically trained
mind. It was as if I had been brought to the door of a room
with furniture wildly skewed and boxes of clutter sitting
about, some half-emptied on the floor, and asked what
would bring it all together. There was no good place to
start and the whole enterprise was daunting. In my earlier
years, I might have rolled up my sleeves and dug in. Today
I decided the room was not my responsibility and simply
walked in the other direction.

MY LIFE WITH CORPSES

"We may never know for sure."

"I know." Carol sighed. "That's the hard part. Well, listen. I'll stop bothering you. Evan really appreciates your doing this," she said. "Me, too."

"It's no problem. Really. I've got my computer, you know, the cell phone . . . Annie for protection. From . . . whatever."

"And I've been meaning to tell you that if there is anything we can help you with here, let me know. I know it must be hard being so far away."

"Away?"

"Your family and all. So if you'd like us to include them when we bring the flowers on Memorial Day, we'd be more than happy."

"I don't think . . ."

"It's nothing. Really. We always have too many flowers anyway. My aunt raises peonies, over by Valley Center. The Oscars, right?"

"Oscar. Yes."

"They're not very far from Evan's aunt." She was standing near her car by then, one hand holding her keys and the other pointing across the cemetery. I looked where she indicated, south to the far reaches of Laurel, past where the diggers were digging, past the Shanlines' plot. There was nothing there, only the lilac bushes, a large cedar, and the fence, but I had learned my lesson and asked nothing more.

"Thanks," I said. "I'll keep that in mind." And now that Carol has told me where they are, perhaps I *will* visit the graves of my parents and sister, although not, I think, at this moment.

FOLLOWING THE CONVENTION, Napoleon did not return to campus until the second week of the fall semester. I don't know where she was, but I stopped by to see her when she was back in her office. She seemed different to me, restless and preoccupied, anxious for our conversation to end. While we talked, she fidgeted with the papers on her desk, rarely looking up. Even when she did, I could never get in her full view, her eyes never meeting mine but seeming instead to look at something a fraction to one side of me.

At first, I thought she might merely be indulging in a kind of pique over the failure of her argument to change everything. I admit feeling some contempt for her because, even then, I knew that events are not individual with causes and effects, but part of a moving glacier that one rides atop or is crushed beneath. I had already observed the indifference of people's acts to what is true, whereas Napoleon seemed to think that truth had a kind of power that could not be resisted. Well, perhaps truth cannot be resisted, but the work is not done in the time we might think. The truth eventually has an effect, that is, but only at the proper time.

Gradually, however, I understood that she was gone. Corpse recognition can be like chicken sexing in that way. There are no definite physical indications but repeated exposure eventually develops a sort of intuition, if one is trying to know, and in the months afterward, I noticed too many changes not otherwise explainable. The first of these appeared in me more often than her, as if I were the litmus paper reflecting what she was. I stopped taking her classes, for one thing, and I didn't go to her office any-more. After a while I began to dread even our occasional encounters on campus. "Oz! Why 'Oz'?" she asked every time, never looking at me or giving me time to answer, if I had wanted to, which I did not. She looked straight ahead, laughed, patted me on the shoulder, and walked past. It wasn't until my senior year that I smelled the mold.

I almost left philosophy then, when I first saw what had happened to Napoleon, I mean. I did not take any classes in the subject in the spring of 1969 and avoided Rhatigan Hall. But I was already enough of a philosopher to be driven to make sense of things, and after a while that led me to a theory about Napoleon's death and, with that, enough consolation that I could move ahead. My hypoth-esis was that her death was brought on by the loss of her lover or, perhaps, the nonexistence of the lover no one had ever seen. This lack of love, I surmised, had caused Napoleon to die. Oh, I knew that I loved her, that people in general loved her and thought she was very clever, in-deed. But "love in general" is being loved at a distance, and only a few intermediate calculations show it is not love at all, but a form of tourism. It is very like those purple-hazed distant mountains, which never look the same upon arrival. They may still be very pretty, mysterious, enchanting, full of surprises, but the grandeur is lost. In a person, that loss is never forgiven. (All right, it is not much different to be loved in particular, but I am speaking of what I thought then, what I knew then, not what these intervening years have shown me regardless of whether I wanted to know.)

I do want to say this about theories and why we bother to construct them at all since nothing relies on a theory to proceed. We seem perpetually determined to eliminate the possibility of surprise. It is, of course, a yearning doubly comical. For one thing, it is odd to give this level of concern to future events when so very few of us even have any notion of what is happening right now. For another, our goal could use some examining. Only the dead are un-surprised. Still, in the end, we are saved by our lack of faith in our own surmises. Theory or no, no one really believes anything until he sees it, and a lucky few of us can avoid commitment even then.

Anyway, however Napoleon's death had come about, it seemed of no moment to her career. She was given tenure, having presented such a well-received paper, one published in the *Journal of Philosophy*, cataloged in the *Readers' Guide*, and assigned in classes on contemporary ethical issues in universities everywhere. Over the next two years, she wrote five more papers as well, all published, although none was anything more than a variation of her one on war.

I continued to visit the Emerald City, never seeing Napoleon there again until one day late in May 1970 just before my graduation. The door to the small conference room was open and when I looked in, she was there. She was not sprawled as before but rather sitting neatly upright, one arm propping her up, her feet tucked under the chair. On the table in front of her was a bound pad, on which she was doodling. She saw me as soon as I came to the door and looked puzzled, as if she didn't know who I was. Then, suddenly, she smiled. "Oz in Oz?" she said, and I nodded. "Are you . . . ," she began, but I interrupted her.

"No," I said, and I left, walking directly back to the walk-through to the main library, through its stacks and lobby and out the front door. I got all the way back to the dormitory and the door to my room, in fact, before I cried.

Following graduation, I took a summer job at the Pratt newspaper not far from where Ronald was spending his summer on his family's farm before going off to law school. Mogie married the boy she happened to be dating when school ended and moved to Chicago. Dave was admitted to the doctoral program in physics at KU but then he had to leave for Vietnam.

The military draft had resumed in December 1969. A lottery system was developed to give the appearance of fairness while its principal effect was to underscore the extreme difficulty of intentional randomness. Each birthday was written on a slip of paper, put in its own capsule, and dropped into a drum located at the offices of the National Selective Service in Washington, D.C. The first birthday drawn was September 14, and everyone born on that day and eligible for the draft was given the priority 1. September 14 was Dave's birthday. He took the news well and the campus newspaper did an article about him. "I've never won anything before," he said, and in the photograph he threw his arms open wide, one foot extended out in a kick, a man who was embracing his good fortune. It is clear enough from this that he had to die, and it is not important how because there is no ranking that makes sense. But there is always an order of sorts, and when one is thrust into the limelight as Dave was, events have to play themselves out with a sense of the dramatic. Dave needed to die so that the campus newspaper could run a follow-up article that began, "David Schrag, who on hearing his birth date was priority 1 in the draft lottery, said, 'I've never won anything,' won a second—and last—time today as the U.S. Army awarded him its Medal of Freedom posthumously. Pvt. Schrag and 10 others in his unit were killed in an ambush near Ngoc Linh last month. He was 22 years old and is survived by his parents and an older brother, all of Medicine Lodge." I have noticed this special dramatic order and I am going to have to think about it some day soon. What explains it? Yes, everything has some order, but this obvious order is the exception. It stands out from the mundane events surrounding it and forces us to look. We see connections, for once, and it is a rare experience, one suggestive of conclusions. It is John Wisdom's carefully tended flowering plot in the wilderness, hinting at a gardener where none ever appears.

# 6.

WE DO NOT EASILY GRASP
the extremity of the situation. We are like those farmers
and townspeople standing over there by the fence, who
are merely waiting for something to happen. Everything
seems more manageable that way, you know—as a spectacle, no more, then over and back to normal life. But that
is not the way that it is. It is too benign a surmise to posit
only corpses wandering amongst us, although I grant that
to be a disquieting thing to know, not the least of which
because corpses remind us of our own destiny of endless
nothingness. (Oh, I know all about the idea of immortal
being through recycling—our bodies biodegrading into

food for some pawpaw tree whose fruit is eaten by a raccoon—however, I cannot say that I know of anyone who is particularly reassured by that prospect.) There is so much more than that, so it should not surprise you that it occupies us without our knowing it and despite our intentions. It is our constant struggle, a contest, a war. Did I say that already? Well, I know that I have not said that it is fought on every front. It is as much a war within as without, and that is the hardest so far to understand.

I'm getting a little ahead of myself in the telling. The summer after my college graduation I knew none of this. That was 1970, the summer I was supposed to wed Rabbit Rock but declined, electing instead to live with my old friend Ronald Davidson, the Kansas farm boy who had plans to be a lawyer and, then—we all were certain—governor. You may believe that, at the very least, I examined every aspect of him, his mind and body, to be sure he was very much alive, but there was really no time to do so, given that I had lingered with Rabbit until the preceding December, when I was obliged to begin plans for a June wedding or not. And so I failed to notice altogether Ronald's peculiar malady, that being that he was susceptible to a condition that not only promised to kill him but threatened my life as well.

Of course, decency required that before going off to live with another, I sever my ties with Rabbit, which I did, in fact, do while he was on the air, a quarter to midnight the week after Christmas.

"You'll never find anyone else who will love you the way I do" was all that Rabbit said, repeating what seems to be a universal sentiment among men being left behind, and I gave back to him my engagement ring in its little velvet box.

For a while after, I worried that I had ended our betrothal for less than noble reasons—because of the way he dressed, because he had dropped out of college, because his name was Rabbit—but the truth is worse. I had proceeded to the separation of our hearts in the realm of pure intellect, reasoning as Napoleon had taught me from A to B without error.

Let me explain. In accordance with my theory of Napoleon's death, I gave high value to Rabbit's love and its part in preserving me. However, Ronald also came to love me and was conveniently attending the same graduate school. QED I didn't need Rabbit anymore and I dumped him. There is a practical advantage, you see, to having been raised by corpses—sentimentality is never an obstacle to doing the prudent thing.

Well, as it happened, I was mistaken about nearly all of it, not only the source of Napoleon's demise but all my suppositions concerning Ronald as well. For one thing, he has not become governor and it seems rather unlikely to ever happen, although a fair number of corpses have risen to great heights in things political. And as for his fervent love and regard for me, that was an error in judgment of some proportion. When someone is totally taken with you, so overwhelmed with love for the extraordinary person that you are, it is wise to consider the possibility—no, *probability*—that there has been a mistake of identity, most especially where you have not previously noticed your having these special admired qualities.

Oh, our life together began well enough, but the difficulty was not long in coming, beginning some few weeks after the New Year, and lacking any subtlety whatsoever, testimony to the strength of life and the sheer power that death must exercise over it to get anything done at all. If you doubt that, then you may have listened to one too many eulogies in which the "fragile gift of life" is centerpiece—all quite wrong. Have you never tried to dispose of a tick? And I can think of no better demonstration than the frozen flies that were lying in mass graves along the windowsills of the Lederer house when the drying remains of Mr. Lederer were discovered some weeks after his death. After letting the mortician attend to scooping up the body, several townswomen cranked up the heat and set to work cleaning. By the time the lower rooms had reached a mere fifty-five degrees, the first low buzz could be heard, and with a few degrees more, the ladies were forced to turn their attention to vacuuming up the horde of supposed fly corpses before it was too late, but there were too many, and at the last the women were flinging themselves one way then another, vacuum wands swinging high over their heads, as they tried to suck in the life of hundreds of living flies who had never been defeated by death in the first place, all appearances to the contrary. No, life is a mighty opponent; I think it is reasonable to say we might never die at all but for our substantial and willing cooperation.

The trouble began at 8:30 on a Sunday evening, the Sunday before the first week of the second semester and an hour or so before our usual bedtime. I was reading on the sofa and the sound of material ripping disturbed me. I walked across the room and into our bedroom and saw Ronald putting a foot-long strip of masking tape up the wall at the head of the bed, dividing it in equal parts. Shorter strips were already in place at each corner so that the bed would remain perfectly centered on the tape.

"I can't sleep with someone constantly poking and pulling at me," he explained, but what he meant was that he did not want to be touched at all. During the nights that followed, even my slightest transgressions across the tape were met with swift punishment—at first merely deep sighs of exasperation, replaced in short time by sharp jerks away from any inadvertent contact, then intimidating spins to glare at me in the dark. Within two weeks he had kicked me, striking my errant foot with such force that it broke a bone. (Well, as Ronald pointed out, it was "only a hairline fracture," not even requiring a cast.) I began, you surely understand, to have trouble falling asleep. I lay awake, thinking, until Ronald's breathing changed from nose to mouth, from nearly silent, mere respiration to the strong, steady white noise of ocean tide. I didn't sleep until he slept and that was how I learned that when he finally did, his hand crept to my side of the tape and closed itself tightly around my wrist. I had no intention of waking him, so I learned to fall asleep in his grasp.

At nearly the same time, his previously affable demeanor became dark and sour, saturating the space around him so that his presence in our apartment was sufficient to taint all of it. He left early each morning, but a sizable trace of him still lingered, the remains of his having walked through and the way that he did it, his wide shoulders rolled forward to make his arms threatening wings, his full lips sucked tightly into the sharp Nordic angles of his cheeks as if he were holding his breath. We don't just go from here to there with no effect, you know. Simply standing to stretch involves a thousand interactions of those atoms we claim as ours and the rest, I mean, all of the atoms of all of the other. That makes thousands of catalytic events in each second, really—remarkable when you remember that our skin is constantly shedding as well. There was no way to contain him, although I did what I could. While he was gone, I opened the door to new air and the early morning sunshine.

I had no notion of what drove these acts, no thought beyond the discomfort and unpleasantness of the individual instances. The ordinary assessments of observant friends and armchair psychologists—"He's under a lot of stress"; "He's feeling inadequate"; "He's a jerk"—all seemed to falter at one point or another, and I did not consider any that were other than ordinary.

I understood the true nature of Ronald's condition only after the fact, at a time when I was able to observe similar workings in a number of others, those where the same protracted, painful struggle preceded resignation to an imminent and certain death. Ronald was in *death throes* and such are common, although not for those succumbing to age or wasting illness, who have taken a long journey, sliding toward death at a gentle angle. Rather, death throes are the unhappy fate of the stronger among us, like Ronald, someone taken a little off guard, perhaps, but who possesses the energy to fight against a wound that is, nonetheless, fatal.

He thrashed about in desperation and anger, and it was a pitiful sight to see, but I am not telling you of death throes as a voyeur or simply to relate the drama. What you need to know and what I did not is that they are a danger to others as well, often resulting in death to not one, but two. Such occurs more often toward the end, when the stricken one panics and grabs for someone close in a vain attempt to rescue himself.

In this latter stage, there can be minor differences of style. All may sit on the bench, heads in their hands, shoulders slumped. Or they float facedown in the water, the ocean's swells moving their bodies in graceful glides over the sea. But as you get within arm's reach, one's arm shoots out to grab hold and never let go, pulling you down to the bench, too, or under the water, as the case may be. His eyes are wild with fear that you will escape him and, so, his salvation. If he has an advantage of muscle and size, he will use it to keep you with him. Another, however, will never reach out but hold you just the same with a constant, unrelenting refusal to be saved. You lift up his head; it falls limply to his hands once more. You try to pull him from the water, and he becomes a dead, flat weight, a halibut on its side being pulled to the top. And before you know it, your efforts to save him have drained you as well.

With Ronald, all that protected me was my instinctive withdrawal from his reach, an avoidance that was made easier by the demands of law school, which dictated that most of Ronald's time at home be spent sleeping or studying. His office was the basement boiler room, a few steps from the inside door of our apartment, and he arose every day at 5:00 A.M. to study at his desk before leaving for school at 7:30 A.M., as well as after dinner until ten or eleven, all done, of course, with the sort of serious and purposeful air that men adopt to lend extra importance to their activities that when examined more closely are usually fairly ordinary.

I am not saying that there was nothing to admire. He did not go down easily. I see that now. He struggled to save himself, by means that would never have occurred to others more timid, less determined. In our second year, he thought to acquire weaponry, apparently believing he could fight off death as if it were some ill-intentioned intruder. His requirements were specific—never-shot or new guns in their original cases and at least .38 caliber—and to this end, he perused the monthly editions of *Guns &*

*Ammo*, checked the Nashville classifieds every morning and afternoon, and, when the opportunity arose, attended gun shows. He bought five guns that year—a .38 Smith & Wesson, an AK-47 assault rifle, a Beretta 9 mm pistol, a nickel-plated .45 revolver, and a 30-30 Winchester deer rifle. On the drive back to Kansas for the summer, we stopped off in Oklahoma to pick up another one, a Shilen rifle, custom-made for him with a fiberglass stock and specially wrought barrel.

Also, toward the end of that year, Ronald began to put his life in order in the way that people do when they know the end is coming. If he had restricted that task to himself, he might have made better of it, fighting only against time and the principle of entropy, which in the space of one day can undo what is accomplished in the day before. His scope was much wider than that, however, and included putting me in order as well.

I could hear him coming each afternoon. He had a certain gait as he descended the sloping drive to our door, and it made him scuff the toe of one foot, so that there was a three-beat step-*sh*-step noise as he approached. He walked head down all the way into the living room, then sighed as in surrender to the task he set for himself each day at that time, that being his walk through the four rooms of our apartment to conduct a sort of inspection and find the things that infuriated him most.

He was not predictable. I will give him that. I never knew what inadequacy of arrangement might catch his attention, although had I known, I suppose it would have ruined the entire exercise. One day, for instance, the kitchen table might not be squared sufficiently to the kitchen counter; on another, the bedroom lamp not placed in the position affording optimum lighting. Ronald's toothbrush was to be placed in one corner of the medicine cabinet, the bristles facing away from the door. If it had been moved by some accidental jostling, the entire contents of that shelf were raked into the sink to make the point. Postage stamps were to be glue-side up in the drawer so that those surfaces would not be contaminated by the other contents. Or perhaps it was that they were to be glue-side down so that anyone opening the drawer would not contaminate them with human bacteria falling from above. I don't remember and, fortunately, I can now obtain self-adhesive stamps in a roll, although with Ronald long gone, there seems no compelling reason to be concerned. Nevertheless, having such strictures on one's sanitation is somewhat like being reared a Roman Catholic or a Baptist—once all those ideas are put in your head, they are there and no amount of rational thinking will ever wipe them completely clean.

I'M SORRY. I NEEDED a few moments to recollect where I was before Lawrence interrupted me once more to tell me that he needs a hydraulic hose and I told him, fine, go get it, but he insisted I walk back to the grave with him, over to where he and Donnie are working. "If you see it, you can explain to Mr. Crews and I won't have to," he said.

I didn't see anything at first. The digging has removed a sizable portion of soil already, entirely sufficient it seems for safely covering a box and a dead person, but Laurel requires more than most—at least three feet—because "there's too many critters hereabouts that like to burrow." Then we both looked into the open grave, and I saw Mr. Stark's coffin sitting half down in the dirt, its curved top in plain view.

"Oh, you've got it uncovered," I said.

"You jokin' or somethin'?"

I looked back into the grave and now there was no coffin, only dirt. "Yeah," I said, and stared into the hole, watching the view in front of my eyes change from dirt to curved casket top and back again.

"We're almost there. Two feet or so down. But what it is, see, is it's been hard clay most all the way. Broke a tooth. Second one, 'cause one wiggly one came off first thing. Root, prob'ly. Two gone's too many. Now, the line. I told you that." He sighed and shook his head. "I'm goin' to have to go back over to Pratt."

I looked up at Lawrence, nodding to whatever he had said, having heard it without listening, and something else happened, too. He removed his cap to wipe grit and sweat from his face, his forehead pearly white and clean where the cap had been, the *before* to the *after* of the rest of his face that shows red creased skin and splotches of burst spider veins extending beyond his nose to his cheeks. I wondered what he was thinking. Well, no, I think I was going to wonder when I *knew* what it was, that he would like to go back in town to have a cold beer at Dud's Pool Hall and let young Donnie finish this wearing task.

Well, thinking about it now, this last could have been intuition or, more likely, simply a reasonable assumption under the circumstances, although it came to me differently than those usually do, feeling as if one moment I didn't know it and the next I did, in the same way that it happens when someone speaks to you and tells you something you didn't know before.

As for the casket, I don't know but I am not yet admitting that my ability to mute these visions is irretrievably lost. The sight of the coffin was so brief and unlikely that I am certain there are any number of reasonable explanations for it. I do not apologize for this default to reason in the face of uncertainty as, in general, I have found it well advised to make my choices that way and hope for the best.

Anyway, by the beginning of our third and last year at Vanderbilt, Ronald had reached what Sartre and his ilk called "nausea." Ronald was not feeling *that*, of course, on account of an important distinction that they never told you about in all of those abstruse lectures on existentialism. One near to being a corpse is incapable of feeling something as complicated as nausea, or at least the kind that Sartre said pointed toward death. I, myself, have only felt it one time and not for myself, but for Blanche, my dog just before Maggie. Her stomach had swollen tight as a basketball with bloat, and she was lying on the vet's steel table looking at me. Her tongue turned a shade of blue and her eyes glazed and I knew that she was dying. I felt it then, so strongly that I had to leave the room for just a minute or I would have vomited. No, one has to be aware and paying attention to feel that nausea, and Ronald was no longer capable of such interaction with what was around him. He was, instead, at the point where survival is the only goal, and so everything must be seen in that light—will it help me live or not? If not, it is nothing to me. If so, I must have it. He was at last straws and I was the only savior in sight.

That was why, in his last moments, what distance I had kept no longer afforded me protection and he began pulling me down with him. I wasn't sleeping with him at all anymore, understand, having fallen into the habit of watching television late at night, falling asleep on the Hollywood sofa in our living room. After watching the news and the *Tonight Show* monologue, I set the channel on public broadcast, using headphones so as not to disturb Ronald, and in that way acquired a significant amount of incidental knowledge while both waking and sleeping— principles of flower arrangement, for instance, the tortuous history of the Italian peninsula from the Etruscans through the Médicis, and, from some series I never determined, the ability to count to ten in Japanese.

Nevertheless, in early October I woke one morning unable to move. I mean that my eyes opened, but the rest of me stayed sleeping on the sofa. I am not reporting that I tried to lift myself and failed. I could not have done that, because the source of such effort was itself still sleeping. I mean what I said and no more: my eyes opened and the rest of me stayed sleeping. Ronald had left more than an hour before because I could see the clock on my desk and it was already nine o'clock. I was to be in class by nine thirty, but soon the clock read "9:05" and I had not moved. Then I began to hear my breathing both out and in, a flat, rasping noise against the fabric of the sofa pillow, and it was so bothersome that I adjusted my face away and turned on my back. For a moment I lay that way hesitant to try to rise, but I made it up and to class.

After that, I sometimes woke unable to move just the same as that first day and other times was able to rise at once. I never knew which way it would be, so my first moment of each day was the feeling of simple dread, which is no more than the fear that something that one cannot perceive does nevertheless exist. The dread rises in that moment before the inevitable knowing. It is walking a board blindfolded, not knowing whether it is a bridge or a gangplank, only knowing that when all the walking is done, the question will be settled.

This suffering seems of little matter to me now, however. I was being injured, yes, but Ronald was the one who was dying. If only I had possessed the characteristics and qualities of a normal person, I would have had resources to help him and perhaps he could have survived. I have never known for certain what set him toward his doom, although the wound may have come from his family, farmers in near western Kansas and very much like Ronald—robust, big-boned, and neat to the point of obsession. The family, as you know, is the usual suspect in our malformations up to the age of thirty. After that time, I think we must admit our own responsibility for any that endure, but it is altogether possible that the family will kill you off before then and, so, that could have been the case with Ronald.

He had an older brother, Carl, who was the golden firstborn with admirable grace and the usual good looks. Carl had been valedictorian, of course, and prom king, an officer at Boys State, and winner of IGA's "Don't Be a Litter Bug" poster contest. He received top honors in extemporaneous speaking three years running and played George Gibbs in *Our Town* and Tom in *The Glass Menagerie*. Ronald did not expect to exceed his brother's accomplishments, but if he ever hoped to match them, he learned soon enough that goal was as elusive as the greyhound's rabbit—a teasing lure forever ten feet away.

Having such a brother, though, is no more than a burden, and death throes are suffered by the *strong*. A mortal wound to such a specimen is one that cuts deep, slicing to the bone and perhaps breaking it, and in Ronald's family, there was only one person who could have inflicted that degree of injury. That was his father, Bertram Davidson, and I should tell you that I don't like to think of him much for fear that the mere idea of him in my head might leave behind damaging debris, but perhaps this will suffice to describe him:

One summer's weekend, we were about to sit down to dinner when Mrs. Davidson, a truly gentle woman, pointed out the plate-glass window to a two-inch hole by the hydrant.

"You'll never guess what we have. A mother ground squirrel and three little ones," she said, then sighed. "I guess I'll have to go around to the neighbors, get a cage trap to move them."

"Don't waste gas for that," Bertram said. "I'll take care of it." And right then he went to the closet and got his shotgun. He walked to the little hole the rodents had made, pointed the barrel straight down, and pulled the trigger. The ground around the barrel exploded upward in a gritty cloud and, in that, the mother ground squirrel with her babies. They lay writhing on the ground, their legs sprawled and other parts torn completely off and scattered on the lawn nearby. Bertram returned to the house, put away the gun, and sat down to dinner, satisfied.

So I admit that I would like to blame Bertram for his son's predicament as that is the way when we find particularly loathsome individuals. We want to ascribe all our ills and those of the world to them. But I don't really think it was his fault, either. Yes, he was a kind of nullity where Ronald might have had use for something to hold him true, but that is all.

No, Ronald's throes came at a time that points more to me than his family, although I don't think I was the principal cause of them any more than they. His injury was suffered during our first months in Nashville and, given that, there is only one likely cause. It was in those months, you see, that Ronald was forced to abandon nearly all of the assumptions he held most dear, and for a man barely twenty-one, he had a great many.

"There are only two kinds of people: winners and losers" was his central tenet, and if he had left it at that, he might have made himself less vulnerable. Ronald, however, believed that generalities were for losers and, therefore, he strove to be specific.

He made his own determination, in accord with principles he never stated, of what tangible items and circumstances were necessary to being a winner and then set about acquiring them. His conclusions were quite detailed, even to the point of brand names. He subscribed to *Esquire* and the *Wall Street Journal*. He bought an Irish country hat and a Waterman fountain pen. He began smoking Alfred Dunhill cigars—Monte Cristos for two dollars each—while he sipped at Hennessy Cognac V.S.O.P., having already acquired the proper accessories: a nickel-plated cigar cutter, a Baccarat snifter, and a burl walnut humidor.

Of course, Ronald knew that he could not complete his transformation until he was out of law school and had "so much money that no one can tell you what to do." Nevertheless, his notions of what the final desired state looked like were already fixed. For one thing, he would practice law with the venerable Lowell firm in his home-town, although his principal consideration was the composition of his office, which would have a rustic country-store theme—hardwood flooring and a potbelly woodstove across from a massive rolltop desk, and he would add a private bathroom. He planned to live outside the city limits and, specifically, in the old Nivens home, a two-story vintage farm house on 160 scenic acres of good farmland not far from his family's own. He would own a golden Labrador retriever bred out of the famous Mon-tana kennel, and a grape arbor would stand between his back porch and the creek running below the house. There was more, so much more than I can tell you, because no detail had escaped his attention.

Vanderbilt Law School was a mere path between here and there to Ronald, more a distraction than a necessity, which is just as well since it was also his first encounter with the social concept of being nobody rather than some-body. That is a division observed as a mere convention in most places whereas, in the South, it is actually believed. In fact, Ronald managed only one real friend at law school and that was Hampton Carlisle, a New Englander who was out of his element as much as Ronald.

Ronald and Hamp shared classes at the law school and also spent most Saturdays together while we were in Nashville. The weekend was when Hamp came over to help Ronald smoke his cigars and drink his cognac, while the two of them luxuriated in dissecting the failings of the other students in their class and evaluating the wives of those who were married. They congratulated each other that they were not "gunners," those overzealous sorts who inhabited the library through most of each day, and kept themselves, instead, rooted firmly in the future, where they would both be the enviable ultimate winners.

As it happened, Hamp was steeped in unhappy feelings that he shared with me in hope of some good advice. He was never able to remember that I was studying philosophy, not psychology, but I needed no expertise anyway as his insecurity was the usual sort, arising from having a successful father who expected more than Hamp either could or would give and, so, only needed listening. Ronald was not privy to these exchanges, but then neither did Hamp know that after seeing Hamp off, Ronald invariably turned to me and said, "He is such a loser."

Anyway, as I mentioned earlier, a large number of these dearly held notions, Ronald's underpinnings as it were, departed in short order during those first few months in Nashville, and I think he could have survived the blows if these plans had not all unraveled so very quickly. We had been in Nashville only three weeks when he learned that the Nivens land had sold, the owners reneging on their promise to let him know of any pending sale. Then, when he called Harlan Lowell to ask about clerking, the old man was oddly distant. Over the Thanksgiving break, and after repeated inquiries by Ronald, the elder lawyer advised him that unless Ronald was in the top tier of his class, a degree from the Harvard of the South and its advantageous alliances were of little value in a Kansas county seat.

"We can't use you otherwise. We need Kansas lawyers to practice here. You need to be at KU or Washburn," Lowell said, and any hope he might meet the stated exception was dashed the end of the semester, when Ronald earned grades insufficient to put him in the upper half of the class, let alone any lesser fraction.

It was not too long after this that his dear friend Hamp had little time for him, needing to build connections with those who would be practicing in New York or, at least, New England. Ronald still had the comfort of his few material acquisitions, but by that time, I am certain that he had noticed, if only beneath consciousness, that for all his smoking fine cigars and drinking expensive brandy, he was still just Ronald Davidson, a few months older.

Well, the destruction of assumptions is familiar territory for infants and children, rarely a fatal shock to their brains, which are still malleable and receptive to notions that contradict other notions within them. It is only later, apparently due to hormonal changes beginning in puberty, that the brain hardens itself against contradictory notions. If it did not, you know, we might always be changing our minds and beliefs at the most trivial difficulty.

In any event, by Ronald's age the neural pathways devoted to his views had already thickened and branched. Thus, if they had to be discarded, they would not simply disappear but rather disassemble into something very much like tire scraps hurling in all directions against other pathways. That is what I long have thought happened; the battery came from the disassembling of beliefs at his very center, and that is why, I think, it was fatal.

In whatever manner, however, there is no doubt that Ronald suffered the fatal blow. Moreover, I did nothing to help and, in the end, took no more definite action than to run away. As it turned out, I survived but not by way of some rational plan but the sort of fortuity that places a fallen tree over a chasm one needs to cross. I deserve no credit for surviving Ronald's death throes except for sheer endurance and unjustified optimism and especially because I was very lucky. Except for some serendipity, you know, we would all succumb in short order without so much as a bubble to mark our passing.

# 7.

Donnie is heading this way. I knew that he would. At first he seemed to hide behind Lawrence but he has since decided that I am suitable company. "I told my wife, if you didn't know it, you'd think you hadn't got past eighth grade" is what he told me this morning, and I took it as the compliment he intended.

So let me tell you very quickly the two fortuities—other than keeping my distance—that permitted my survival of Ronald. The first of these was that when, following Napoleon's death, I was tempted to leave philosophy, I did not. If I had, I should have missed the healing power of Truth and I would never have been brought into the thrall of Professor Gregory Koehn, a man who was himself as near to being a corpse as can be attained without dying.

It's funny. I haven't thought about him or his own remarkable survival in some time. Gregory's condition was quite intentional, a wondrous accomplishment when you consider what it was and the requirements to maintain it. Just like Napoleon, he had abandoned the demands of his physical existence to give all of his resources to the mind. Unlike her, however, he had managed to survive and some part of that was luck. Koehn was fortunate enough, you see, to be in a department with more than a few good minds and an energetic cheerfulness approaching unfettered joie de vivre. The elevated mood was of such a degree as to smack you in the face with its happy state and especially annoyed Ronald, who, like most plains people, had been raised to believe that out-and-out happiness approached dissipation. The reason for this joy, though, was simple enough: the university had a great deal of money and paid its professors unusually well. As you must know, nothing so reduces our anxiety at the same time it nourishes our fraternal capacity as does an abundance of cash, and that is as true for the dead as the living.

Of course, the Nashville campus was rife with corpses. Thus, not only was I occupied with my own studies in philosophy; I was also trying to pick my way through the killing fields of academia without suffering the fate of Napoleon. In the academic environment, however, there is no talisman powerful enough to resist its own essential nature, and the death rate for professors, as I have said, is higher than in the general population, but that of philosophers is staggering. I laugh at those statistics trotted out every so often listing "construction" or "farming" or "mining" as the occupations most hazardous. Those are child's play when compared to being a professor of philosophy. Well, I must qualify that. What is hazardous is not simply being a philosophy professor, but being one who is, at the same time, a first-rate philosopher. That is the pinnacle of danger.

I knew corpses were somewhere in the department as early as the second week. You may recall my mention of the occasional musty odor that can be detected, the sudden wave of ennui, but there can be other signs, if you are willing to see them. For one, when inside a room with more than a single corpse nearby, you may begin to feel an unexplained breathlessness that increases to near suffocation, forcing you to abandon the premises in an effort to recover. In any event, that was the very feeling that overtook me at the first departmental symposium, a late afternoon program featuring Donald Malvey, the highly regarded linguist from Cornell. Malvey's repute crossed disciplines and the room was filled. Koehn was seated against the wall to my right, although I did not know who he was yet. Two other professors—Drs. House and Bridges—were seated across from him, and, as it turned out, they and a nearby graduate student had all recently succumbed. Together with Koehn, their number and proximity to me was more than sufficient for the effect, which began with painful pricks at my temples, before spreading across my forehead and behind my eyes. I had encountered this unpleasant state many times as a child, including those times that I did no more than sit down to a meal with my family, leading to my life's habit of standing away from the table to eat or, better yet, eating alone. I had to step away from the door and the knot of spectators there, avoiding what I knew would otherwise come— a severe pounding, oxygen-deprivation headache or worse because the simple fact is that too many corpses in a room creates a vacuum that all that is in the rest of the room must rush to fill.

It was at the sherry party after that same talk that I was introduced to Koehn. He was sitting in a small library off the main room, almost hidden by the broad, deep arms of a massive leather club chair. Three or four of the older graduate students stood nearby, including my office mate Charles Mandt, who motioned me over to meet him, pushing me through the group to stand directly in front of Koehn.

"Gregory, this is Oz. She's new."

Koehn peered up at me over his glasses, giving me a once-over with the half-openmouthed smile common to drunks. He *was* a drunk, as it turned out, but you had to know that—as his mind and tongue always served him without fail, whether he had downed a shot or a fifth. Neither did I see, in this first meeting, anything to suggest his existential frailty beyond, that is, the signs of an abused body. He was quite thin and I would say he was tall and lean, but you would think of Gary Cooper in *High Noon* when what I mean is that he was a rather beat-up stick; a long, emaciated collection of bones and skin supporting a large bearded head. Everything about him was that way, even his hair, which was slicked down and lightly grayed, above a long wolfhound face.

"Oz?" He raised one eyebrow and I nodded. "So, Charles, a new member of the collection, eh?"

I turned my eyes toward my office mate, but he only smiled and nodded. Koehn was studying my reaction. "You didn't know that you're all collectibles?"

The other students were smiling and I thought he might be making fun of me. "There's a lot I don't know," I said with an edge, and his eyes widened a little. He smiled at me and sipped at Wild Turkey whiskey, his choice over the less potent sherry the rest of us were drinking. He propped the arm with the glass on the chair and turned his head to it when he took a drink, never altering the position of the arm itself. His other arm hung loosely over the side of the chair, and when he brought it up, I saw that he was smoking a cigarette, long and thin, like him. I never saw him without a cigarette, in fact. He smoked them ceaselessly, the extinguishing of one and lighting of another serving as the only interruption.

"That's very good. Very good. Well, what I am saying, Oz, is that when you are *Dr.* Oz, and not just you, you will be a collectible. Then all of the really important people— I mean those with family pedigrees or, perhaps, a great deal of money—those people will . . . or, wait. Maybe power, too. Yes, family, money, or power—those sorts of people need to collect people like you. And, I should say, *me*, although ordinarily I shouldn't want to be the one to say that." Koehn sipped some more at his drink, licking his lips and narrowing his eyes as he brought the smoking arm upward.

"We raise the average IQ," one of the students said and laughed, and his interjection sent Gregory into a short spasm of coughs.

"No, it's not that. Well, yes. Yes, it could be that in part, but I don't think that is the principal purpose. How can we best characterize it?" He paused to reflect, looking across the room and not at us, which was the same when he talked, his talking out loud seeming to be just a mechanism for turning up the volume on what he was thinking.

"How about it's a way to keep an eye on us? Let us know who owns us?" Charles offered dryly.

Koehn fixed him with a stern look. "Condescension is the wrong pose. I'm not criticizing them. Not at all." He returned to his musing. "It has to do with aesthetics, I think. That's really all that the wealthy have left as an interest . . . wouldn't it be? Their other needs are filled. Yes, that's right. So they buy art and pretty clothes and they have pretty people at their parties. Of course, you have to be prepared. You have to know the social rules or it could be very embarrassing. That's why we're here at this charming affair. So you can learn."

"Is that why you're in philosophy?" I asked him, irritated, not knowing why. "To be a prize for some rich person?"

His eyes flashed up at me. He looked annoyed, then smiled. "Ah, you're only joking. Going to parties and doing philosophy are different activities, of course. I do the *former* to get good whiskey and expensive food and gaze upon beautiful young women."

"And the *latter?*"

"Now, I *know* you are joking. There is only one reason to ever do philosophy, but you know *that.*"

He sucked deeply on his cigarette, held the smoke for a few seconds before releasing it, then looked at me over the top of his glasses, one eyebrow lifted as if waiting for me to state the obvious. My mouth opened but nothing emerged.

"*Truth.* To search for Truth. Of course," he said, speaking so softly and sincerely, that it was more prayer than declaration.

By the second semester, I had become a part of the small cadre of students Koehn considered "his," and it was not until then that I saw what he was and the delicate balance between living and dying that he had achieved. There was no sudden moment of recognition, no specific chronology that I can recount to you. We have been over that already, haven't we? It was simply that he appeared to be exactly what he was, that being a person who had given over all his resources to his mind at the expense of his body.

I never saw him eat anything but he did drink a great deal, the amount increasing as the day proceeded. He began his intake openly after three, first Wild Turkey whiskey, then downing two gin martinis before dinner, and, during that repast, several glasses of wine—an Italian or Spanish red. Like any living organism, Koehn surely required sustenance from his body in order for his mind to continue. But he had, I think, one of those rare physiologies that is able to draw its necessary sustenance from those few substances that affect the brain directly such as cigarettes, liquor, or other drugs.

Koehn enjoyed having his favorite students to dinner, nevertheless, sitting with us at the table, although he had long before ingested all that was necessary for a day's support of his spare body. He liked to watch us, I think, and always sat back with his arm propped on the chair's, the cigarette between two fingers serving as a pointer as necessary.

After dinner Koehn moved to his favorite chair and circled back to the Wild Turkey whiskey, sipping it straight until the evening ended some time after midnight.

When I returned from these gatherings to the apartment I shared with Ronald, I did not even suppose myself to be in the same year or place. It could have been ten years earlier or later and ten thousand miles away, such was the space between. When I was with him, Ronald engaged in his assault and I must have participated in my own injury as well. But what I am saying is this, that I survived each day to return to the academic incubator and Koehn, where I could be pulled back a little, permitted at least a partial recovery.

For himself, Koehn had long before figured out what was necessary to maintain his precarious perch. And it *was* a perch. In fact, more accurate than saying he was nearly dead is to say that he had stretched the resources of mind and body to an extreme tension so that one more tug would be the snapping point and the retreat, broken, of both sides.

I don't understand the entire physiology of it to this day, but I believe that the principal quality that allowed him to maintain this tension, the one that worked to my benefit as well, was Truth itself. Gregory was scrupulously honest. Intellectually honest, I mean, in that he did not permit himself to say things or to act in ways that were not consistent with what he could rationally defend. Brought within his influence, his habit became mine. It was not enough in itself to preserve me; I do not have Koehn's gift for life up there in the mind with nothing more. But his influence was sufficient to keep me in half-truth rather than a complete lie and, thus, gave me a little more that was alive.

I should mention that Koehn's honesty was all the more to be admired because it was not a convenient one, leading him to change religious beliefs as often as others change socks. His particular problem was "evil," the same concern of Saint Augustine in the fifth century, and a host of Catholic scholars and ordinary people since, the question being "How can there be the God that the theists claim and evil in the world, too?" It was, of course, the very concern that had undone Mr. Stark's belief, but for Koehn, both a Catholic and a first-rate philosopher, the matter was far more complicated.

He admitted that he wanted to believe in God's existence, but if the premises on which he based his belief were shown untenable, Koehn felt he had no choice but to dutifully cease believing until he could refute the argument. He did scholarly battle with several respected philosophers through the journals, and if ever his arguments were refuted, Koehn refrained from attending Mass and, presumably, any other act of religious devotion until the problems were resolved.

I am aware of these details firsthand as, quite naturally, given Koehn's interest and my own time with Mr. Stark, I became absorbed in the problem of evil with them and made it the subject of my dissertation, a part of which was devoted to a refutation of Koehn's most recent theodicy. I have always regretted that choice somewhat, as it made for an unusually anxious year for Gregory. He spent less and less time in his office and more at his home, a towering stuccoed manor with Moorish arches and filled with cavernous spaces best suited for brooding. While I was writing, we met there several afternoons a week as well as at week's end, on late Friday afternoons before the others came for dinner. For two or more hours, we sat together in an unlit room, with me setting forth the newest elements of my thesis, and Gregory smoking, drinking Wild Turkey, and trying to argue his way back to church.

Sometimes we just drank. Those times were set by Koehn, who signaled his intent by pouring me whiskey and handing it to me before I was even seated. Then, touching his glass to mine as if to seal the unspoken agreement, he would sigh and sit back. "Good. This evening I need a god."

THE BUCKET IS REPAIRED, the new hydraulic line in place, and the cemetery workers are departed as of four. I am here by the grave for another look. When Donnie came over, he told me that he wanted to catch me up on how they are doing. He said that the backhoe will get them another six inches or so, then they will dig the rest by hand. Burying a coffin is one undertaking and excavating it another, and they require different protocols. He explained the various steps for each, and I can't deny that it was interesting to me. That is the usual case, that it is not the subject but the insight of the speaker. Anyway, he convinced me that there is more to exhumation than those who have never done it can possibly know.

"Lawrence is the best digger around. You know? He's the one they get to dig all the big irrigation wells around here. You have to know what you're doing," he shared. "You don't, it can be bad. Over at Iuka?"

I nodded.

"That's the worst I heard. There was some regular con-struction guys, never been in a cemetery—the guy hired 'em to dig up some guy, you know? I forget why. It was in the paper though. So these guys figure it's a quick buck, nothin' to it." Donnie's hands are up to frame the gate to the cemetery. "They take their backhoe right on in there, roll it off the cart, and fire it up. Don't check nothing to see what's what. Just dig. Bing, bang, boom! You know?"

I said that some people get in too big a hurry.

"Exactly. They dig the body up lickety-split like it was some Idaho potato or something. Man! Punched right through the lid; it was bad. Flipped like the femur or lemur or one of those over onto the operator. Right smack in his lap. I guess he 'bout had a heart attack. Family sued 'em. They ended up paying 'em something—I forget how much. But . . ."

"You have to know what you're doing," I offered.

"You got that right."

He may, of course, become a little humbler about it if they use the backhoe much further. Not because of the coffin I saw earlier, when I was standing by Lawrence, I mean, and looking into the grave while he explained his troubles or the fact that, when I stood here with Donnie, I saw it again and its lid is closer than they think and they could punch through it for all their care. Rather, I say that because of what I see now, now that I can look by myself with my full attention. Yes, it is right there where I said, the coffin, a foot or less beneath the surface. It is encased in a concrete liner and slightly askew. But as for Mr. Stark . . . well, the truth of the matter is, he is not in it.

You can understand that I am inclined to leave this place myself and were it not for Annie's steady company, I most certainly would. There is at least an hour more of daylight, however, and I need to tell you of the other piece of luck that contributed to my survival and that was Lucy Cupp.

Lucy was the editor of the Pratt newspaper and she was a *source*, possessed, that is, of a special mechanism by which she boosted the life in those around her. I worked for her summers, when I left Koehn and returned to Kansas with Ronald, who went to stay at his parents' farm a few miles outside town. I did not know then, of course, of Lucy's special gift, but I admired her a great deal, her work and her undeniable talent for knowing what was news, how to tell it, and, as importantly, how to get it arranged in six columns and fifteen pages by 11:00 A.M., printed by 2:00 P.M., and on the streets before 5:00 P.M. Only a few can do that anywhere, and, as you might guess, there was no swarming cloud of those in a town no more than a gateway to western Kansas, even if it is home to the State Fish Hatchery and the Miss Kansas Pageant.

Lucy was also my landlord from whom I rented a room for my summer's housing. We rarely saw each other at home, though. I never got to the paper as early as Lucy, who was there no later than 6:00 A.M., five days a week.

"I have to be there first," she told me. "Have you ever seen a bunch of chicks that can't see its mother? Well . . ."

She didn't finish the thought, or most of anything spoken out loud. Lucy saved her prose for the news and for the editorials she wrote, the most notable of which concerned the depletion of groundwater by the growing practice of irrigation wells, earning her the William Allen White Award along with the enmity of the Kansas Farmers Association.

"No woman should be running a newspaper, let alone spouting her views on things she knows nothing about" was the opinion of Ronald's father, and it was true she was not a woman to everyone's tastes.

She was small boned and shorter than anyone else at the *Pratt News*, but that was the only concession her body had made to being female. She had none of the usual soft layer of fat given most women but was straight, sinewy, and her veins showed Prussian blue beneath her leathery skin. Her rather obvious efforts to affirm her femaleness made things worse. She never wore jeans or slacks—more suited to the handling of smudgy newsprint, dripping photos, and rubber cement. Instead, she wore—every day—a long, straight skirt and a white cotton blouse topped with a short sweater with some sort of pink flower border at the bottom. She did not go so far as to wear stockings or heels, just white socks and tennis shoes, and her wiry gray hair was clipped so short that her bangs stuck out like a visor over her forehead. She drank coffee continuously from a paper Dixie cup with two paper handles, one hand lofting that cup, the other on one hip thrust sharply to the side against red poplin and beneath delicate pink rosebuds, and, well, it was not aesthetically pleasing.

Nevertheless, Hap Runyan, the manager of the stock-yard, presented himself at her house every Friday and Saturday, bringing steaks or, sometimes, fresh fish to grill and fried some of his special corn fritters. Lucy tossed a huge salad with fresh produce from the farmer's market. They drank Johnnie Walker before dinner, Chianti with the steaks, salad, and fritters, and ate Blue Bell ice cream with fresh strawberries and grapes for dessert. Hap usually stayed the night, although they didn't know I knew that, and he would leave at 5:00 A.M., giving Lucy a bear hug and a big smack, whispering, "Keep it in the road, Miss Rodeo." That always made me smile. I wasn't sure what he meant exactly, but I understood that it conveyed love and good tidings, as it were, and that was enough.

Yes, she had her failings, for one that the Miss Kansas Pageant absorbed her to an unnatural degree, but it is also on that account that I know that she must have been a source. Each year, during late July, the contest was staged at the Pratt Armory, and, understandably, the paper gave full coverage and printed its only supplement of the year. Weeks before, however, Lucy began combing press re-leases for information on the contestants in order to com-pile a sort of "racing sheet," listing for each what she regarded to be the determinative factors, the nature of which, as far as I know, she never shared with anyone. By the day the pageant began, Lucy was invariably able to narrow the field of thirty-two to five and, once she saw the swimsuit competition, to declare the eventual winner.

Well, every year's competition inevitably contained painful moments, and the worst I witnessed was my second summer when Miss Lucas College, with sixteen years of ballet training, forgot her routine some fifteen seconds into it and spent the following three and a half minutes leaping and twirling free-form around the stage in an apparent interpretation of a body's flailing as it falls into a bottomless pit. That, at least, is how I described it to a fellow reporter the following day. Less than ten minutes later, Lucy joined me at the paste-up table, feigning interest in the arrangement of the community social news columns.

"You could never be Miss Kansas, you know," she said, moving the Etta news to the bottom right and Davine farther up.

"I don't want to be Miss Kansas."

"Right. I can see that. Well, that's good. Because you *couldn't* . . ."

"Okay."

"Your walk is . . . Well, you need to walk like . . ."— she took a few steps back then forward again. "You know, like you're going nowhere in particular . . . just out of reach. The look is . . ."

"*What?*"

"Oh, now. You know I don't mean *that*. You're a lovely girl. Very pretty. Really. And a damn good reporter! I told you that already, didn't I? But, your eyes . . . no, it's the squint when you listen . . . He says something you don't like and *kwhap!* . . . upside the head. You see?"

I thought I gave a measured, dignified response, declaring stiffly that I had never struck anyone and that, further, I had no desire to compete for titles based on physical appearance with a particular year attached, since that too closely resembled winning the two-year-old calf competition at the 4-H fair, a victory that, I added, was always followed by being auctioned for slaughter to one of the various meatpacking plants.

Lucy turned to look at me, then, having heard what was, in fact, a kind of wounded bleating. She touched my arm and I distinctly felt it. My body suddenly relaxed and filled with *something*. She gave me some free life, you see, even if I did not understand that at the time.

"I didn't mean to upset you, dear," she said, but on the way back to her desk, she added, "I just didn't want you to waste your time thinking about it."

So Koehn and Lucy replenished some of what I was losing at Ronald's hand; without them, it might all have turned out much differently. I am grateful, although it was difficult to think of these things once I came to some understanding of the mechanisms of life and death. With that knowing, you see, came nausea, fear for what might have been, as if I had crossed a bridge, only to learn on the other side that it was on the verge of collapse.

Still, I did make it to the other side, my course finally decided for me during the semester break of the third year.

Ronald and I were in Kansas and we had been arguing over something—I don't recall what—the subjects of our arguments having become so many, they were indistinguishable. Afterward Ronald was sullen, set jawed, and went to his loading bench to fetch his Colt .45, placing a handful of extra shells in the pocket of his jeans. He picked up the Shilen rifle and a box of shells for it, too.

"Do you want to go shoot with me?" he asked, the Colt hanging loosely from his right hand.

(Oh, I remember now. I had missed watching the granary transfer. He and Bertram were trying out a new augur and I had missed seeing it.) I nodded and walked behind him to the pickup truck. He placed the Shilen between us like a third passenger, the Colt lying next to him on the seat, and we drove north for several miles, all the while enveloped in the pleasant mixer sound that rolling tires make on loose gravel.

When we came to the field he intended—sixty acres lying fallow out of a quarter section otherwise planted to maize—Ronald lifted two five-gallon buckets, each containing three small tin cans, from the pickup bed and we walked to the far edge. He turned one bucket upside down and sat its three cans on top. The same was done for the second, and then we walked, silently, back to the truck. He took the rifle out first and loaded it, walked around the truck, and sighted down its barrel at the cans. *Phwap! Ping!* All three of the cans on top of one of the buckets exploded. He turned toward me and walked past me to the tailgate and started to set the rifle down. Then he must have changed his mind, because he continued on around the truck, the long way, and put the gun back on the seat where it had been. When he came back, he walked the same long way and he was carrying the revolver.

He turned it side to side in his hand, the barrel pointing off to my left, viewing with his head tilted to see some unknown something.

"This will stop someone," he said. "A .22 just makes 'em mad." He looked at me for my response, but I did not hold his eyes, looking at the gun instead, as if I were studying it to assess the validity of his remark. In that moment, I knew full well that he could turn the barrel a distance of less than two inches—there would be no time to react— and "stop" me. He knew that, too, and savored the knowledge, sucking out of it the last pleasure he was able, taking it as a kind of substitute for the even-greater pleasure of shooting me on the spot. My intuition was to appear totally interested in the activity itself, to lend it dignity and importance, i.e., to gratify his ego a little so that the pain I had caused it otherwise did not become unbearable. It was also important that I be as little like myself as possible since if someone has taken you out in a remote area with no fonder desire than to see you dead, "being yourself" has nothing to commend it.

Still, it may have been that my own devices did not save me after all. We often take the rational steps only to have the result determined by some happenstance apart from our reach. If we assume some intelligent direction to everything, I suppose that the purpose of such would be one of two things: to keep us humble or to drive us insane. God almighty has apparently never heard of "mixed messages" and what havoc that can wreak on tender psyches. What I mean to say is that if there is a God the father, he could benefit from a rudimentary parenting class. Anyway, what saved me that day was probably not related to what I did but to the fact that it was at that moment that Ronald died.

I had never been present at anyone's death before, not any death of any sort. I've attended several since that time—two beloved dogs, a colleague, and a three-year-old child, and I don't recommend being there for any reason. There is something less of you, too, when it is over. Ronald's death was like the others in its principal features. There was the crisis point, that time when the breathing shifts and the eyes set and you know there is not going to be any recovery. Just then he was holding the Colt .45 he had found in the classifieds, the barrel pointed to the ground near my feet, and he was rolling the cylinder click by click and peering into the filled chambers—he never kept an empty as a safety—as if he hoped to find some answer there. He sighed, and when he exhaled it was different, with his exhalation making a long, low trumpet sound that is sometimes called a death rattle. He looked off toward the far line of trees before he turned his eyes to me, and I could see that they were becoming fixed.

"I'm better than you are. You're nothing. You're just a loser, that's all." I had nothing to say to him in return. I should have consoled him, I suppose, but I did not see that he might be talking of himself, instead taking what he said to heart as if he had struck me, feeling a sort of self-pitying anguish, the sort that is the easiest of feelings and, so, even nearly dead people are capable of its accomplishment. And then he died. That was all. He looked at the gun, puzzled, as if he had forgotten what it was, and he turned back to get into the truck and we drove home. I knew he was dead because he released his grip and I could gather my strength and run. Not to safety. There is no safe place.

That was December 27 and the following week I returned to Vanderbilt alone. Ronald stayed with his parents and never returned to law school or to do anything but farm and keep books for his father. In Nashville I sent applications to more than 150 philosophy departments, and by May I had passed the oral examination necessary to receive the doctorate at August graduation. I did not return to Kansas for the summer but left after exams for Oxford, Mississippi, where I would teach philosophy at the university beginning September 1. I last saw Ronald during spring break, when I brought him his belongings from Nashville. He said that he wished me well and—in a gesture of generosity I never expected—gave me the Colt .45 to take with me for protection.

# THE REMAINS, continued

# 8.

I HAVE BEEN THINKING
about how to tell you the rest so that you can believe me,
although I concede it would be easier for both of us if you
did not. Coming to know what you have not requires an
alteration to your pretty painting of what *is*, as it were. If
it is a little extra shading in a corner, the bother is not
much. But what I tell you here is more akin to Vermeer's
moving the map on the wall, and, so, some destroying will
be required before returning to paint.

I am back at Laurel early this morning on that very
account—new knowing, I mean. Or, rather, new seeing.
The coffin, the empty coffin I saw yesterday, requires explanation. I am hoping that it and the coyote, too, are

sprung forth from the same source as the visions I mentioned before, the ones following the account I wrote ten years ago. Those I have always put off to imagination or, at most, peculiar mechanisms that are triggered when, and to the degree that, I tell the truth. If it is something more, then what I know to be real must be altered and that is a danger. The moment of change is always one of vulnerability, one that might permit the invasion of notions that are otherwise too weak or the escape of truths, too delicate.

Whatever it is, I cannot deny that I *saw* the coffin— its interior, as well—the details of both present as my hand as it writes. The clay and cement over the box did not disappear, but rather the coffin appeared with them, the silver side rods rusting and its domed metallic cover flattened slightly against the concrete liner and, I tell you, it is *empty*. (Well, there is a Bible lying to one side of the center, and it would not surprise me if *that* presence is what compelled Mr. Stark's departure rather than the odious Lucille McEwen, who, you recall, unforgivably tagged his car with the number of the beast. Perhaps that is what all the thumping was about and he never intended I write any account whatsoever.)

All things considered, it would probably be best if I could take Annie and go home sooner rather than later. I might say something to Lawrence again, if they ever arrive. They are a half hour late already. Yesterday I asked him before he left, "Do you really think it's worth the trouble?" and he looked at me somewhat disoriented as though I had wakened him from deep sleep.

"You mean the bucket? I know the one that's on there won't work. I'll try it if you want me to, but . . ."

"No, I . . ."

"Oh, you mean the cost? The county's paying for our time and the rig. You know. They done lost somebody; they gotta find 'em. It ain't no expense to the family."

"Why bother?" I finally got out. "That's what I was going to say. I mean, he's *dead,* and if his body went somewhere else, it must have been a long time ago, right?"

Lawrence stood politely silent, his eyes narrowed as if he were translating my words from one language to another. Then he cocked an eyebrow. "I don't get your drift. The coffin's there. We know that."

"Well, right. I guess, I'm just asking more in general whether any of this is necessary. Do we really need to dig up a whole cemetery to see where a dead man went?"

He nodded understanding of the question but did not answer at once. Instead, he took off his cap and looked at the ground, a gesture clearly meant to underscore his thoughtful consideration of my query. "Well, now . . . ," he started, then stopped, forcing the brim into a sharper peak before he put the hat on again and looked back at me. "Well, I do see what you're sayin', and I'm not sayin' it's not a good point, 'cause it is. But here's the thing. You get bodies disappearing, now, that's not good. Get somethin' like that started, you can't tell where it might lead."

"Yes, I suppose so," I said, and he had me there. He did. I would be the last to dispute that one thing often leads to an unexpected other as that has been my usual experience. No one becomes so wise as to have all the consequences of a particular act laid out nicely to choose. So, I don't know.

But, as I said, the difficulty is with your believing at all, and what you believe determines some good part of whether I can tell you what is true. Believing was once my own obstacle even when, as now, it was there before me, presented by the unambiguous evidence of my mind and senses.

The first of it came without warning and within days of my arrival in Oxford, one of the many times I have been mocked by whatever it is that attends to such matters, inasmuch as Oxford was meant to be my *refuge* from the dead, as well as those living who would as soon see me one of them. I had come south, driving from Kansas to northeastern Oklahoma, then east through the hills and inevitable rain of Arkansas, turning south again at Brinkley then across the Helena bridge and into Mississippi. I got lost attempting a direct route to Oxford that avoided going all the way down to Clarksdale and drove an extra hour more—Chloe sprawled in the cargo—down turn rows and through dreary plantation towns filled with dark staring faces—"Darling" one of the signs said—before giving up and backtracking and entering just the right portal to have Oxford suddenly revealed, a southern Shangri-la that, above all, *feels* like safe ground, hidden and dense with forked oaks, native pines, sweet gums, and delicate dogwoods, with a certain shimmering something in the air. In Oxford the sky seems always blue, the sun shining, even though I know well enough that there are many gloomy gray-brown Mississippi days there as well.

I was more gravely injured than I knew, however, and my judgment impaired accordingly. Anyone who meant me ill, after all, could have found me even while I wandered the Mississippi Delta. That is the tyranny of modern times. We can be reached anywhere. I have known of deaths by telephone, certainly. My elderly cousin Fred, for instance, stuck the barrel of a .38 in his mouth and shot himself while his wife was distracted by a telephone call. He had cancer and shot himself inside a closet—well, inside his mouth while he was inside a closet—an acceptable midwestern suicide, not overly personal. It is just that, if words can reach you, you can be had, escape requiring a certain knowledge of the pursuer, which, in this case, I don't think we have. Have the physicists had anything to say about *that*, I wonder. I mean, are words waves or particles, or one of those virtually real entities whose existence has to be postulated to make all the rest make sense?

Anyway, as I was saying, the first of it came when I had been in Oxford less than a week, on the Friday before classes were to begin the following Wednesday. I was in my newly painted office in Gallagher Hall, an antebellum barracks at campus center that held two lecture classrooms, the offices of philosophy, sociology, and black studies along with two floors of professorial quarters including my own.

I came in through the main door, which led to Gallagher's vaulted rotunda dividing the wings. There, I consulted the glass-case board and turned left to go to the Department of Philosophy, where the secretary (a work-study student gone to her one-thirty class) had left the door open, my office key, and one copy lying in a mail cubby, beneath a typed label: DR. OSCAR.

My assigned space was less an office than a box with green linoleum, a *beige* box, its space fully used by the oak desk and metal filing cabinet supplied from the warehouse, two captain's chairs, and a metal typing table. Built-in bookshelves covered one wall, the wall at the far end comprising a radiator and a single window, its view centered on the thick dark trunk of a native pine. If I leaned over the radiator, however, and looked to the left, I could also see a bosk of small flat-branched flowering dogwoods and a redbud tree.

As I said, the space was freshly painted and the window only opened six inches, but with the door wide open, too, the paint fumes were bearable. I retrieved four banker's boxes of books from my car, as well as the worn Kazakh rug Koehn had donated from his house in Nashville, placing the latter front and center of the desk and stacking the boxes on the floor near the bookshelves. Atop the boxes, I placed the two dozen or more cardboard mailers that were already spread over my desk holding courtesy copies of apparently every philosophy text published in the preceding year.

I began to shelve the books and, relieved that someone had shown the intelligence to barely skim the shelves with paint, was soon locked in that deep concentration necessary to alphabetical sorting. That is why I think that he might have been in the doorway for a while. Anyway, for no reason at all—as if he had spoken to me, although he had not—I abruptly stopped what I was doing and turned directly to see him and, then, I fainted.

When I woke I was on the floor, seated neatly on the Kazakh with my back wedged between desk and bookcase. My right shoulder hurt and my temple was tingling so that I raised my hand to it, expecting a trickle of blood, but it was only scraped and numb where I had struck the edge of the shelves. A man was kneeling in front of me and I stared into his chest. Unaccountably, I was unable to lift my face toward his, although I knew he was a professor from his clothes—loose khaki pants and striped Oxford shirt, the sleeves rolled to his elbows, and brown Hush Puppies shoes. He held my hand in his, patting it and fussing over me, his voice low and pleasant, but he blew out his words in an odd rhythm, in short bursts that reminded me of Chloe's distinctive bark.

"Hey! I am *so* sorry! God *damn*! I am such an idiot! Are you all right, dear?" I shifted my eyes to look past his shoulder to the doorway, but it was empty.

"I didn't mean to sneak up on you like that. Poor thing! Here, let me help you up." He was a sturdy man, easily pulling me to my feet, then gently releasing my hands and stepping away from me. "Now. A proper beginning. I'm Owen Kendall," he said, giving a half bow that brought the top of his head into my downcast view. His hair was wavy and thick and badly cut. "My office is down that way."

I watched his feet back through the door into the hallway and turn in the direction of the rotunda. Clearing my throat to introduce myself, I nevertheless continued to look down toward my own feet, lamely pretending to brush clean my slacks with my hand. Finally, I brought my chin up a few inches. "Hi. I'm . . ."

"Dr. Oscar," he finished for me. "We've all been waiting for you."

His large fleshy hand extended toward me and I leaned forward, too, reaching my hand to his. When they touched, I forced my head up with a jerk, determined to greet him correctly, and our eyes met. It was only then that I remembered what I had seen before. He was dead. Owen Kendall was a corpse.

Yes, of course, I knew already that there were other corpses and I knew who some of them *were* even. What I say to you now, however, is that this was very different. His corpse remains were standing before me plainly visible. And that was not all. I *felt* his deadness, too. I could barely bear the weight of it, as heavy and cold on my chest as if his lifeless body had fallen from the mortician's slab to land on mine. My knees buckled and I let his hand go to catch myself on the desk.

"Are you okay?" he said, and grabbed my arm to help me, but his grip scratched and pinched at my skin, the flesh of his palm vanished, his hand and arm bone now covered by no more than thin skin, stretched taut like a leather hide curing. Farther up, beneath the protection of his rolled shirt sleeve, two flaps of skin loosely crisscrossed his bulging biceps, its dense layers of tissue dried and fragile, the substance having departed first to leave only form, in the way pages burn in a fireplace.

He offered to fetch me a cold drink and left me sitting on the desk while I waited. I was in a state, of course. It is exactly as I said, *seeing* corpses is quite the different event from merely knowing that they are there, although that latter knowledge saved me, at least, the expense of an extensive psychiatric examination, which, I suppose, the ordinary person would have been bound to consider.

(I am "amazingly sane," in fact, given my "fascinating past," or so Carol told me last night. Apparently, it had not always been a foregone conclusion. "Evan's grandfather was *very* concerned about you. He kept tabs on everything you did. He never really approved of those people they put you with. Evan told me he was glad when you turned out to be a girl. He was kind of jealous of all the attention Win gave you before because nothing got by Win. He knew everything."

"Everything?"

"All of it."

We sat sipping our drinks for several minutes. I don't know what Carol may have been thinking, but I was wondering whether the odd glances I had, every visit, received from my former neighbors were not, as I had supposed, on account of unlikely falsehoods that they thought about me but, instead, possibly because of simple truths they knew.)

After that, I saw corpses everywhere and they were, indeed, *everywhere*. The greater number strolled the campus among faculty and students, but the townspeople were host to an impressive number as well, new corpses arising with regularity, one or two new ones each month, at the very least.

They moved easily among the living, who were unaware of them—the corpses, as I have told you, dissimilar in no noticeable respect. What differences there were only marked the usual imprints of culture all of us share. That is to say, for example, in Kansas, where people tend to be more reticent and less talkative, their corpses tend to be the same. But, the farther south, the more animation, the more talk and easy hospitality, and a southern corpse does not forget her manners just because she is dead, any more than a midwestern one suddenly learns how to carry on a charming conversation about nothing at all.

As for me, I was determined to effect a return to my previous state, that condition where I only knew about the corpses and was not forced to see them as well. It was not a difficult project, really, because there was no one method but a hundred that would accomplish my desire. I don't think I have discovered them all even to this day. As I recall, the first I employed was to avoid the intimate eye contact that had brought Owen's corpse into view, an insight that has led to my residual and unfortunate habit of looking at the floor or ceiling when I am talking to someone. All the same, it is the most reliable method of avoidance I ever found because it worked always, whereas the success of other means seemed partly dependent on qualities of the particular corpse. Someone, for instance, might appear to me quite ordinary until a blurred move-ment directed my attention to her feet, where I then saw a transformation creeping steadily up her body, its edge defined like the gray line of a spring rain making its way across a field of wheat. In such cases, I was usually afforded time to leave or, occasionally, the change could be ar-rested and reversed if I only backed away a foot or two.

Teaching, of course, bound me to face a roomful of people and to stay for an hour or more regardless of whether my audience were living beings. While there were fewer corpses among my classes—college students, as I explained about my sister, are still children, so they are working on coming to life, not losing it—those few who *were* dead were more recently so and thus not yet thoroughly decomposed. For that reason, they were also the most repugnant to see. Fortunately, assigned seating enabled me to avoid looking at the worst of them, and in lecture classes I outlined on the chalkboard while I talked and, thus, kept my back to the class most of the time.

There was one dead girl—Alissa Dubman—I actually enjoyed seeing. She was a student in my first Introductory Philosophy class and one of an unusual number of corpses I taught that semester. Alissa was the only daughter of a Meridian family descended on her mother's side from Confederate General Claudius Wistar Sears and the great beauty Susan Alice Gray. So many cousins were subsequently named either Claude or Alice that by the time *she* arrived, the tradition was broken to name her "Alissa." Still, for some reason she had died very young and sufficiently long enough before my class to have become a thoroughly white, polished skeleton. There was a certain elegance in that guise that was pleasing to the eye and useful, as well. Because, you see, Alissa had died before the age of mental independence, she was quite vexed by significant challenges to her accepted guides, and that was how I had noticed her the first day of class. I was reading Bertrand Russell's "ten commandments" aloud. "Have no respect for authority of others . . . ," I read, and heard the clicking, once then again. On the second instance, I looked to see and caught the movement of Alissa's arm trembling . . . and clattering. After that, I used her as a measure of my lectures, considering them below standard if I could not make her click at least once.

Still, the years I spent with the corpses in Oxford were disturbing and bothersome to me, although they were not the worst time in my life as that was yet to come. And I acknowledge that I became fond of Owen, who offered me valuable advice in running the university's maze of pomposity and pettiness and was something of a handyman, able to fix faucets or replace a windowpane. That is to say, he was willing and able to be useful, which is, of course, always an endearing quality in *any* man, living or dead. Too, I discovered that by actually seeing the specific form someone's corpse took, I was often able to guess the source of his death as well.

Owen, for instance, died of *root rot*, a fatal malady quite common among southerners. Like its botanical counterpart, it can leave signs of life aboveground long after death's course has been set below, and there is no curing it. Its sickeningly sweet odor and the gooey residue on its victim's joints are characteristic, and sometimes the ears are yellow or have already fallen off. And quite a few of my colleagues had succumbed to Donovan's death, the very same disorder that claimed Napoleon, in every case their brains and skulls enlarged and in some instances still as well preserved as formaldehyde specimens atop slender dry bodies long ago withered from starvation. These were easily distinguishable from yet another fairly large group, the members of which had unusually *small* skulls, having died of the reverse mechanism from Donovan's and which I dubbed *Jivaro* after that Ecuadorian tribe of headhunters who so masterfully shrunk what they caught, so that once fair-sized heads of adult men and women became the size of an orange, their eyes, nose, and mouth reduced in scale, under the downy cover and long sweeping lashes of hair that remained as it was. That is the way the Jivaro corpse appears as well, his head reflecting the reduced state of the brain, which, instead of receiving all of the nourishment as is the case in Donovan's death, has been allowed virtually *nothing,* apparently as a means to keep the brain from thinking things it shouldn't.

Those who regularly and rotely enforce rules without regard to their underlying principles—bureaucrats and doctors' receptionists, e.g.—are more susceptible to Jivaro, although Jivaro also regularly descends on Bible Baptists whose determination to check any untoward activity of their brains may be the reason the bodies of their preachers—theoretically the *most* determined Baptists—so often careen out of control to disgrace them.

I don't know, really. I could have learned a lot more then about the various mechanisms of corpsedom if I had been willing to look more, but as I said, that was precisely the opposite of my intent, and I have counted it among the successes of my lifetime that I have been able to keep my wits about me despite the uncommon phenomena with which I have been confronted. I did not give in to the weaker course, I mean, and make it a parlor trick or, worse, unfairly profit from the extra sight. I cannot imagine much use that could have been made of visions of corpses, anyway, or even the other odds and ends that came, all those things that I had to see for the while it took me to discover the particular means necessary to re- duce, if not end, them, the simplest of which was this: I did not look.

Nevertheless, after Owen and during the time I could see the corpses, I saw more than enough to know this: there are many, many ways to die—hundreds, perhaps thousands—and that is just in Oxford, Mississippi.

# 9.

LAWRENCE AND DONNIE
have finally arrived, nine thirty, an hour and a half late.
I am waiting to approach Lawrence again while they park
his truck, backing it up to the cedar nearest the grave and
close enough to sit in the tree's narrow penumbra. That
proximity, however, requires the tailgate at center and the
front wheel of the truck to ride over the corner of Baby
Zink's marker, though that is not of apparent concern to
either of them. Oh, I don't think they are unfeeling men.
It is difficult for anyone to juggle it all. I mean, getting to
work, parking the truck, getting the truck in the shade,
digging the grave, *and* properly respecting the dead. I don't
think we really appreciate that complicatedness in what

is done every day, and yet it is part of what pushes us toward the grave before we need to go. The worst of it is that it is even more complicated than most know. So a wheel resting on a polished rock over what is, by now, no more than a pile of bones seems a little less disrespectful than before. Mr. Stark would have thought it nothing at all or, at least, he professed to care nothing for the rituals of the living to honor the dead.

"I will be dead. I will be the least concerned by my death of anyone. They can throw me into the river, as long as I don't pollute the livestock's drinking water." I was only twelve when he told me this and awestruck by his calm indifference to death's terrors. I notice, however, that he is not in his box and, so, he is perhaps not as unconcerned as he thought he was going to be.

Don't misunderstand me. If I am eager to leave Laurel, it is not out of a desire to leave Kansas. I have not often returned here, but that is not for want of loving it, you know. There would be no choice in the matter, anyway. I am constructed from its pieces, and to talk of going away or returning to it makes no more sense than to speak of leaving or coming back to one's own self.

Likewise, I think well of Donnie and Lawrence, so far as I know them. They are hard workers and are driven to do their work well. In Kansas those are assumed attitudes, and it was only when I had grown and moved away, living in this place and that, that I came to know that it is not a piece of everyone. So there is that attitude, at least, that is shared between us, the approval of which is set in me by virtue of where I was born. And it should not surprise you, therefore, that when I was trying to sort through the corpses in Oxford, one of my theories rested on work and that I have never quite admitted that it was as flawed as the unsuccessful others I tried before and after.

I latched on to it when I was first at Ole Miss and needing something that would direct me away from the corpses. My thinking was that my mother had died, in part, because her work was thwarted; my father, after the most important part of his was gone. I chose not to consider Napoleon's death in the most glorious moment of her own work, that being, I decided, an aberration—something like adult leukemia, which strikes suddenly and quickly downs its prey. Well, I was very wrong, but the tricky part is that there is something in working, *something,* that does sustain one in some way for a short time, some element that can align itself with you as an extra rod alongside your spine so that there need be nothing more than that, which is only to say that my theory resembled most others that nevertheless fail—there was some truth in it, enough to mislead.

As it happens, you see, not only does working not serve to preserve or give us life; it may actually present certain dangers, although perhaps not in the way you think. I know you have, at some time, been advised, "Don't work yourself to death," and, like the rest of us, taken that to warn against strain beyond one's physical limits, too little sleep, too much effort. No. That is not it. There is a woman in Oxford—forty, fifty, I don't know really—who doesn't work at all and she is dead as a door-nail. And I don't mean she is a housewife, who is someone who works hard, after all, our modern Sisyphus, endlessly redoing what has already been done. I mean she doesn't work *at all*. On the other hand, there is a driver in New York City who hires out to visitors for low-cost runs to and from the airport or the theater or wherever you might need to go and she does nothing but work. She schedules fares for any time, day or night. "I sleep when I can," she told me. "Five minutes here and there. It adds up." The woman is not a corpse. So there you go.

"A little hard work never killed anyone," my mother always said, and even if she *was* dead, it is still true. No, it is not the strain of the work, but rather the distraction, which, in my case, let harm come nearer to me than it might have otherwise.

By the way, my earlier conversation with Lawrence seeded somewhere inside him and bore fruit. He wants to leave off digging now and has called Evan to come out and take a look. "He needs to see what we're dealin' with here," he said, probing the dirt once more and tapping the casket's concrete liner not far below.

"We know the coffin's there," Donnie added. "Ain't no juice in puttin' more dirt on the grass."

"It *has* been one thing after another," I agreed, and the both of them shook their heads and snorted in accord.

Lawrence got down on his hands and knees and pressed at the sides of the open grave as if to measure.

"Another thing. We're seeing roots. Big ones, both sides. The way they put this down so close . . . I can't say we could get it back. Might be best just let sleeping dogs lie, you know?"

I nodded, looking thoughtful, as if I were just short of being convinced, hoping thereby to encourage him, the both of them, to more and better arguments to raise with Evan. No, I do not consider that pose to be a violation of my stated commitment to what is true. I said I would tell the truth about my life with corpses, not that I am a damn fool who tells everything she knows. Mr. Stark's empty box can speak for itself if it comes to that. Yes, it is still empty and I noticed this visit that the lining I saw before is creamy satin and there are restraining ribbons neatly bowed over the empty spaces where Mr. Stark's arms and legs had once been.

WORK, I WAS SAYING, distracted me into near disaster. It did not happen in a few days or weeks, of course, that sort of dramatic intensity more found in contrivance than nature, and, in fact, I was into my fifth year at the university before I noticed anything untoward. Work, you see. I was busy working and, what is more, I was, as they say, on a roll.

Oddly, I do not remember much of the substance of what it was I was doing or what it was, specifically, that I accomplished. I taught, of course, and I must have written papers and given public talks, served on committees and such, but I only remember the part that was actually me— the way I was filled with it, I mean, the warm-hot feeling of my colleagues' praise and respectful regard, the tight embrace of the students' clamor for my classes and how they hung about my door with excruciating crushes. (The erotic power of even the most trivial authority, you know, can be amazing.)

The corpses were still around, yes, but I knew how not to see them and, therefore, rarely thought of them anymore except as harmless creatures who, as those in my family had been, were occupied with nothing much. I considered them, at most, a feature of *my* life alone, literal skeletons in my closet that would never be discovered.

But, as I said, in the fall of my fifth year, I began to see otherwise, the corpses placing themselves squarely back in my view where I could not avoid them in the same way as before. One Friday performance of *J.B.*, they occupied an entire row of seats, and I remember a Wednesday night's screening of *Last Year at Marienbad* where I was the only living person in the room. And nearly every day at lunchtime, they lined the steps of the Student Union, forcing me to walk between them. There seemed more of them being together more. It was too difficult to turn from them all, and it was this marked increase in sightings that eventually brought my notice to a quality I had missed before: the corpses were quite *purposeful*, resembling nothing so much, in fact, as workers in a nest of ants. What was more, like the ants—who clump together out of peculiar affinities, such as electromagnetic fields—the corpses clustered in *their* own way, always accompanied by the same something and always doing the same thing with it. *Boxes*, the corpses were endlessly occupied with the gathering of boxes.

I suppose that I could have noticed the boxes sooner, but any scientist will sympathize with my failure to see the connection. Consider that gravity was not surmised until the seventeenth century, even though people and objects had undoubtedly been demonstrating its effects since time immemorial.

Once noticed, however, this odd activity of corpses concerned me so much that I called Mr. Stark to get his opinion. He did not agree with my assessment. "Where are you?" he asked, and I told him I was calling him from home. "Do you have a yard? Yes? Well, step out into it."

I carried the phone with me to the backyard. "Okay. I'm here."

"You see the problem, don't you?"

Well, no, I did not.

"Have you escaped boxes?" he asked, and I could feel his eyebrows raising while he waited for my answer.

Finally, I had to laugh. "No."

Well, his point *was* well taken, that being that boxes are everywhere in the most profound and, therefore, most trivial sense as well. That is to say, they were not only numerous; they were imbedded, there being any number of boxes within any house, any room, any yard, anywhere at all because we are also contained within the earth's environment, something as much a box as anything else, although not comprehensible apart from ourselves, and even were we to launch ourselves into deep space, we would require a box of sorts to survive, and supposing that, contrary to all that is true, we did not, we would still be within the bounds of our own body. So his question to me was, if they are everywhere, then what is the problem? Mere ubiquity, he argued, is insufficient to conclude danger. I saw his point, but he was not the one watching corpses carry boxes hither and yon. The corpses were gathering boxes and are still gathering them as far as I know. For what purpose, if not ill?

Anyway, despite Mr. Stark's rational dismissal of any peril, I responded in my customary way, which is to say I ran and tried to hide. Specifically, I told the chair of my department that my office was too small and found one available in the building across the mall, in the music department, where the constant noise and lack of a regimented studentry seemed to repel the corpses. I had been there for several watchful months when I came to a sudden understanding that moved the boxes to second position on my list of concerns and replaced them by the reason I had noticed them at all. It was not that there were more corpses, you see, but only more next to *me*.

This epiphany transpired as I was grading papers in Nathan's, a bakery and coffee shop a block off campus.

I was seated alone and at my usual place, a counter stool, at the far end. From that position, I could see anyone else who might be seated along the length of the wide counter, its original black linoleum banded with aluminum waving unevenly a distance of almost thirty feet, the mirrored wall behind the counter allowing a view of the rest of the room as well. While I worked, I drank coffee and nibbled at a scone to make the abominable spelling and unmentionable thinking of my students more bearable. I was breathing more heavily and starting to get a slight headache, although I think that what I noticed first was the lack of intrusion. While grading papers is an honored task in a university community, reducing unwanted interruptions, the contrary impulse toward women who dine or drink alone is usually strong enough to overcome the other, but no one had spoken to me in more than thirty minutes, even though the bakery was full. So I looked up to see why.

A middle-aged man in a poplin suit had replaced the young woman who had been seated next to me. He was a lawyer. I didn't know his name but I had seen him at parties and near the federal building where he worked and knew him to be a longtime dead. On his other side was yet another corpse. Even the waiter assigned to our end of the counter was dead. I stood up and the mirror reflected corpses filling the three tables arced immediately behind me as well, and the single booth on the wall behind those. All together, there were eleven of them and they were not persons who ordinarily would meet but, instead, of different sorts and stations. The table nearest me, for instance, held parents from out of town, here to visit their college-age daughter, while the booth contained three droopy-eyed and unshaven boys. They were members of the jazz trio I had seen perform at the bakery on Sunday mornings. Two matrons in workout clothes sat at another of the tables, finished with their daily walk and refueling with coffee and a pastry. All of these shared only that they were corpses, every one of them.

"The cream, please," the corpse next to me said, and my attention shifted from the mirror to his supplicant hand then back again when the others all looked our way as if one, their unity magnifying the gesture. I pushed the steel pitcher down the counter toward him and surveyed the other tables beyond, but not a one of those contained a corpse. I rose and walked behind the counter's occupants, using the mirror to scan the faces of those other than the corpse next to me and the one next to him. None was dead. I retrieved a campus newspaper from the rack by the door, then returned looking more closely at the customers seated at the remaining tables and those serving them. It was true. Of the forty-odd persons present in the bakery, those eleven surrounding me were the only corpses.

I don't know why this was the occasion that I saw it. Partly, I suppose, I had suspected the truth all along and, partly, when I found myself surrounded by them, I was struck by the way that I didn't feel; I thought. My mind raced to analyze the situation. Was it a peculiarity of Nathan's Bakery? A certain time of day? I reviewed my actions, too, for unwitting provocations, even considering whether I should replace my customary black pants and brown shirts with some that were brighter in color. But I already knew that none of these alterations would affect the corpses. What accounted for their increase was not that there were more, but that there were more where I was. They were in all the places I was and at any time whatsoever.

I gathered my papers but did not return to campus as I had intended. I drove home instead and went into the bathroom to look in the mirror. I stared directly at the eyes reflected there, first wide-eyed and, then, squinting my eyes to blur the familiar lines of my face. I spread a bath towel over the rim of the sink and lifted myself up to get closer but saw nothing. I was relieved by the difficulty but not convinced and continued to stare into my own face for two hours more. It may have been longer because I missed my afternoon seminar and returned to my office late, sometime after six, to pick up Chloe, who I had forgotten and left sleeping under my desk. Whatever the amount of time, I needed all of it because, as I said, I could not see anything right away.

Finally, a flicker of something besides my usual face began to appear, but I jerked away and spoiled the image and spent another hour simply trying to get to the point where I would remain still and see. By then my joints were stiff from my awkward perch and I was getting cold, and I was shifting in increasingly short intervals to tolerate the discomfort. That was how I happened to back away a few inches, tipping my head back to ease my neck, and there she was. I could see her at exactly the angle that allowed the ridges of my cheeks to be seen in my near view while they simultaneously reflected back at me from the mirror, and when the entire face appeared, I knew at last why I was drawing the corpses. She was a sly one—the one in the mirror—having kept from my view so long but, of course, it was not as if she were some different engaging personality: a German-speaking boy of ten years or some vampish charmer longing to take me over and have some fun for a change. That would be Sybil or Eve, and that would certainly have attracted my attention long before and possibly served as a source of income. No, it was nothing like that. She was *me*, that is all, except she was dead—my budding corpse, silent witness and traitor to every scheme I had for life and avoiding death.

# 10.

I SCREAMED. I'M ALMOST
certain I did scream because I could see it in the mirror—
my mouth opening, eyebrows knitting, and the look in
my eyes. There was no sound, though, except for my own
breathing, which gave me some comfort until I became
lost in trying to determine whether that meant anything
at all, whether I ever actually heard my parents or sister
*not* breathing. Of course, there was no emergency number
to call for information, no professional for care. Indeed, I
would have had to first identify the appropriate profession
and I could not. So I continued to stare in the mirror.

She was not a ghoul—my corpse, I mean—not yet, but
more a waxen figure taking shape, the head formed and

the features grossly defined, still lacking fine details. Her face was the texture of sculptor's clay, an odd color, not white, not gray, but somewhere near either. The eyes were green like my own but without shine and there were brow ridges, a nose and mouth, no more. It was that blank new-ness, in fact, and not any particular movement that gave the impression of work in progress, that she was growing. Well, of course, she did not move at all, having none of those ways in which our live visage betrays our intentions. She only looked back at me with eyes fixed and without expression of any purpose whatsoever. Still, my horror and fear were rising, fighting to be let loose, not because of her look but her presence, although not that alone but the place of her, that she was, I mean, *inside*.

At the same time, I did not want her to go somewhere where she was out of my sight, either, and I stayed looking at her for a while longer. Not continuously, because I had to tilt my head just so and quiet myself in a way that was even more difficult to do now that I had seen what was there. Finally, when I had exhausted my ability to balance on a hard sink top, I went into my bedroom to lie down. I needed to rest and I wanted to be unconscious, although I did not allow myself to sleep, fearful that I would not wake. She was *inside*. I had lived in a world of corpses by staying away, but how could I stay away from myself? Worse, I knew that she was aiming to take me and knew as well that I had no way to stop her. I don't know. I lay on the bed, then wary of that symbolic stance, paced my apartment from room to room, breathing deeply, moving my arms in windmills for circulation. I went back to the bathroom one time, peeking in around the corner until I could see myself. She was not there and, believing for a moment I must have imagined everything, I spun around throwing my hands up in relief and amusement at my own credulity. That was too fast for my corpse, however, and her dead weight struck me contrécoup, making me stumble for balance. Eventually, I wore myself out with it and sat cross-legged on my bed, staring at nothing and thinking not much more. Then, as I said, I remembered I had left poor Chloe in my office and got myself up and drove to get her.

EVAN MUST BE ON his way. At least, I took that to be Lawrence's meaning when he honked the truck horn at me a few minutes ago and waved, holding his cell phone to his ear with one hand, pointing to it with the other. I see, too, that a few of the fence people have finally decided to come inside, three of them peering into the open grave, while Lawrence and Donnie wait, sitting in their truck under the cedar. Before my hand moves to open my car door, Annie is already raised up to look at me.

"No. You have to stay here. I'm sorry." I give her great head a consoling pat, but she peers up at me through my fingers. "I know. You would be a good girl but . . ." The problem is not her, of course, but *them*. The ones around the grave, I mean. I would be spending all my time on them, making certain that they were not disturbed by Annie's overly large presence rather than supporting Lawrence in his argument to Evan to dig no farther. But Annie is a friend and, because of that, my decision to leave her behind is one made with some care. Friends are entitled to one's respectful consideration, and I am always finding some new reason why.

I know that friends can keep you alive during a stretch when there is nothing else. That is a principle I happened on to indirectly—and made use of—following the unpleasant discovery of my own corpse within.

The jolt of seeing her was sufficient to hold me in place for several weeks, understand, for the reasons I said, but when I found myself still alive after that time, I began to consider my situation and what to do. I possessed only one sure way of dealing with corpses—that being mere avoidance—and *that* technique was of little use. However, I was also a logician and knew the value in assuming the contrary in a difficult proof, and after some time I remembered what I knew and decided to treat my own corpse in exactly the opposite way than I had treated the others. I attended her constantly, I mean. I checked her in the bathroom mirror, in the reflection of sidewalk windows, or by simply looking down, able, before long, to summon her at will. I talked to her and let her know what I was thinking. I closed my eyes and cleared my thoughts to let hers come through. True, she never thought anything, but I found out that she *was* hungry.

That was why I began to spend more and more of my time in Nathan's—in order to feed her, I mean, drinking coffee and downing scones, bear's claws, and peanut butter cookies. It was a fortuitous, if not healthy, move because at the counter I could keep an eye on my own corpse in the same mirror where I had so recently watched those of others surrounding me, and I discovered there that my corpse was not a constant entity but could change for better or worse. More than that, I saw in the bakery mirror that not only did it have the simple capacity to change; my corpse waxed and waned without surcease. In the beginning, in fact, it was *that*, not any expectation, that led directly to my spending an inordinate amount of time with friends. I mean, I had to be at Nathan's to eat, and I saw that as long as I kept living others near me, the corpses seemed to gather less in my proximity. So I invited my friends to meet me at Nathan's.

I SHOULD TELL YOU that I have more hope than ever that I can leave here soon. A few minutes ago, Evan came to look at the digger's work and decide whether to proceed, giving me the opportunity to bolster Lawrence's concerns.

"You've done what you set out to do," I said. "You found the casket. Maybe we should just leave it be. Undisturbed."

Evan said nothing, staring down at the excavation, fiddling with coins in his pocket. "I've been thinking about it some more. The thing that I don't get is I know they put him on the *writing* side. We would've noticed otherwise. Grandma was already buried on that side. They wouldn't have made two mistakes."

I took another tack. "Okay. Let me ask you this: Was the liner there?"

"Where?"

"Over there, where you dug before."

"I guess I don't know what you mean."

"The concrete liner. They always make you get a liner now. That's been true for maybe twenty years," I told him.

He shook his head. "No, there was nothing like that. Just dirt. Well, the book, but . . ."

I threw up my hands. "Well? It's one thing for his coffin to disappear, but the liner, too? He just wasn't *buried* in that spot, Evan. The most likely alternative, it seems to me, is that they put him on this side."

Evan mulled this over, pursing his lips, biting them, pursing them again. "I don't know. I guess maybe."

"The proof of it is that we know there *is* a coffin here and there is *not* one over there" —and I may have won the argument right then, because he made no further objections. Still, reason is not all of it and he wants Carol to agree. He couldn't reach her by telephone so he has left to find her.


MY FRIENDS AT NATHAN'S. One was Bennett, an acting student who had once taken my Intro course. He was a fairly new friend back then and thought, therefore, quite favorably of me. He is still a friend, actually, and was the person who introduced me to Judah Connell, but I will get to that later. More important to tell you now is that Bennett was the very first friend whose effect on my corpse I noticed at Nathan's, that occurring during one of our weekly coffee dates. He came eagerly to these to bask, I suppose, in the inappropriate presence of an older woman of semirenown, and I, conversely, to bask in being a part of something that someone else thought inappropriate and, perhaps, a little dangerous.

"Hey, Oz," he exhaled as he bent long legs to the chair then up again in a single, impossibly unbroken motion. In two strides he retrieved a menu from the counter and was back, sitting at our table. "I'm doing my bit from *Zoo Story* tomorrow. I'm freaking!"

"What scene?" I asked.

"The shepherd scene," he answered, not looking at me but glancing around the bakery with his eyes only. That is the way to do it if you don't want to be noticed—without moving your head, I mean. In fact, as long as you don't move your head, it is acceptable to shift your body around any which way to get a better view.

"See that guy at the counter, one, two, three stools down?"

"*Mmhh.*" At that moment I was looking in the mirror and watching my corpse and, so, merely shifted my perspective to another part of the same mirror, to see the one indicated.

"That's Simon. He was out with Rudy last night after practice—the one who played Helen in *Trojan Women* last spring—and now he's given that guy next to him all the dirt. He's a rapist, you know. Two girls already have said that he slipped them something when they were at parties at his . . ." That was when I noticed. Bennett's shift from his art to the other's sleazy crime had taken me rapidly from one world to another, from something pleasing to something abhorrent, and when I returned to my corpse in the mirror, the shift was apparent there as well. She was more vivid, more clearly there even than before Bennett had arrived, and I stared at her for a long moment, hesitant to release my gaze in case she grew again when I looked away.

When I said nothing, Bennett turned his head around to see my face. "I'm not making it up. He's over there now describing Rudy's pussy to that guy."

"Bennett . . . ," I chided. I had moved my hands up over my ears and hunched my shoulders down toward the table.

"What? I can't believe you! It's just a word."

I shook my head, my eyes on the mirror where my corpse looked back at me, pulsating more then less, waiting to see which direction to go next. Bennett's eyes widened and he put his hand on my shoulder. "Oh god. Were you ever . . . ?" His sheepish concern touched me. He was a mess but a good kid, and in the moment I thought that, my corpse receded a little, hovering in her usual guise, staring back at me staring at her.

"No," I told him. "I just wish . . . It would be good if there were a way to undo things like that"—and then watched as the idea of the erased injustice almost erased my ever-present corpse as well.

After that day I continued to invite friends to Nathan's, but less for protection than to learn. I spent even more hours there than before—fortunate, I know, to be in one of those professions where a lack of actual working takes some time to reveal itself—although my appetite lessened with my attention to the project. I talked to my friends and watched our conversations in the mirror, visiting hours a day with them at Nathan's, all of them coming and going, to and from my little laboratory without ever knowing for what purpose. The pattern emerged at once, although I took my time in refining it, coming to decide that my corpse took this or that action depending on what I was doing, whom I was around, and, it seemed to me then, the subject of our conversation.

Once I had observed the phenomenon at Nathan's, I was able to take my studies elsewhere. My college roommate Mogie still lived in Illinois and we talked occasionally by telephone, the distance between us unexpectedly proving to be an asset inasmuch as I could freely observe myself without distraction or detection. What I saw with Mogie confirmed my theory, but only in part. Unlike my friends at Nathan's, for instance, conversation on the same subject that had made my corpse lessen one time with Mogie could actually increase it in a subsequent call and go on to lessen it still later. And although most of our contact served to decrease my corpse, the effect was far more variable than with any other friend I knew. In the course of a single sentence, I mean, my corpse would suddenly blip up, as if it had been stuck with a straight pin, then as quickly draw back again.

I should mention that one day my corpse abruptly stopped showing any effect whatsoever when I talked with Mogie. I mean, it neither grew nor shrank, rather its face fixed in the same expression, the open-eyed stare of a coma. That marked the end of Mogie's capacity to affect me and, I believe, her death. We have not spoken much in the years since, in part because I would rather not know her fate with certainty. If she is dead, however, the culprit is most certainly *histronia*. I have seen that excess of feeling too often since, its presence coming at the expense of thinking or acting either one—distinguishing it thereby from both Donovan's death and Jivaro—and Mogie always took extra consolation from the juice and aroma of her emotions, letting them go to their limits unjustifiably and simply for the thrill of it. The danger is that these feelings are only the starting point of a lasting series of demands. One who is overly susceptible—who complies without check—will find herself doing feeling's beck and call for worse more than better. It is very much like an addiction and as difficult to cure, all the more so because in the case of histronia the forbidden substance is already inside.

Well, the point is that after a time I thought I had come to an understanding of matters that, even though faulty, permitted me to control the corpse within me to a degree and that reassured me some, despite its requirement that I pay even more attention to corpses than ever before. But I also thought that the primary force that directed such change was within me as well, and that view put me in considerable danger.

I should say that seeing the pertinent force as my own marks me, for all my differences, quite clearly as a product of our time and culture. For some years—the task is virtually complete—something has set itself to convince us of what the solipsists could not, that every one of our life's events most profoundly originates in us alone and, for that reason, can be addressed within that same small space. The notion has spread so far and deep that it would require the demise of an entire industry of self-help, which would, no doubt, protect itself with the same ferocity as have oil, sugar, insurance, and all the other predatory and ill-considered businesses. It is true, of course, that we are alone in a very important sense, but we are far more akin to one standing unseeing and unknowing in a pitch-black room that is, nevertheless, filled with other people. Most certainly, that was my case. Far from having been left behind me, that is, my life with corpses was more my life than ever.

# 11.

THERE IS NO SAYING WHAT
would have been different after that time had Judah Connell not crossed my path in Nathan's Bakery because he
did, and so what is the point of wondering otherwise? We
make this choice or that, then end up at the same desti-
nation either way.

Judah, of course, would have objected to being considered anything but an event of enormous impact. He
was an actor. Well, he was director of theater and creative
performance at the university but, first and foremost—he
would have told you this—he was an *actor*. Bennett introduced us one day at the bakery, although I, and every
other professor, already knew Judah Connell's name

through the gossip that had come with his hiring the year before. Most notably, he had been artistic director of Jackson's Pearl River Players until he was caught naked in a bathtub with Georgann Winter, a sporting Woodland Hills socialite married to one of the theater's grand patrons. In many versions, there were bubbles and in some, an additional woman. Whatever way it had been in the tub, the most pertinent fact was certain—Pearl River had booted him out. Georgann had not been Judah's only indiscretion, of course, or even the most indiscreet of them, but she *was* the first with economic implications, and that meant there had to be consequences.

"Uh-oh" was all the warning Bennett gave me, only seconds before Judah loomed over our stools at the counter and positioned himself between us.

"Ben, my *man*! What's goin' on? Who is this pretty lady you have with you?"

Bennett said nothing, audience to Judah's play, watching him turn to address his lines to me.

"Hey. I'm Judah Connell," he said, smiling down at me enough to show a single dimple. He tipped his head to one side. It was overly large, out of scale with the rest of him, and made him seem closer than he was. "Has Bennett here told you he's our Olivier?"

Bennett groaned and Judah grabbed his arm. "Don't, now! You are, *too*. You're somethin' else, man!" Then he released his student with a slap to the back and, responding to a voice off left, raised up and looked over his shoulder. "Okay, I'm comin'. Nice to meet you, Miss . . ." He smiled the dimple-smile again, hesitating.

"Dr. Oscar," I answered.

"O-oh! *Doctor*. Movin' up, Ben." He was already half away. I watched him in the mirror while he moved through the tight twists of the café toward his friends. His progress was not the wooden, rocking gait of most men, but fluid and attentive to what surrounded him in the same way as a dancer to his partner.

"God, he is such an asshole!" Bennett grumbled, but I thought he seemed diminished by Judah's proximity, by the way that Judah Connell had taken up the entire space around Bennett and me, too. I didn't know what I was seeing, really, thinking then that the effect might come from his theatrical training and later putting it off to Judah's being an only child who had occupied center stage from the beginning and was, therefore, especially familiar with its requirements. Well, actually, he was the second of twins but the first was born dead, the umbilical cord wrapped around its neck, and there was a family joke he despised suggesting that he had murdered his brother in the womb because "we all know how Judah hates to be upstaged."

For all this, I might have guessed the terrible truth of Judah, even on such short acquaintance, had I not been distracted by what happened in those brief minutes he allocated to us. For the duration Judah had commanded our table, that is, I had been more alive or, at least, less dead.

My corpse had receded markedly with the first moment of his arrival, and by the time Judah left, she was nearly invisible. So, asshole or no, when Judah Connell called the next day to invite me to dinner, I accepted at once, and six months later we married.

This choice to be with Judah has always seemed to me to be an act of critical importance in what I have come to know. My increase in knowing wasn't achieved at once, of course. In taking up with Judah, I was proceeding, as ever, under a theory—that some part of me thrived in his presence and that my corpse could be kept down that way by far simpler and more predictable means than those I had been using. For a while, a year, maybe two, I found confirmation for this hypothesis at every turn.

Judah was, after all, a very appealing, if not outright handsome, man. He was a natural entertainer, able to dance and tell stories well, his voice capable of projecting to the back of any auditorium and yet, up close, low with a slight catch that kept it from being cloying. When we met, he was approaching the very peak of his talents and his profession, mentoring a half-dozen well-known actors from Mississippi including, belatedly, Mary Ann Mobley, and when the Coen brothers came to Oxford looking for movie sites, they stayed with us. Even in the presence of such notables, however, it was Judah who seemed to take up the whole room when he was in it, making it, as ever, difficult for people to gain a footing in his presence, easier somehow to let him do what he would.

He was not one to seize the spotlight but, nevertheless, managed to put it on others in a manner that served his own lighting best. When that shining attention was on me, my corpse shrank and I did not need to check the mirror to know. I felt stronger, willing and able to give my regard, even love, to Judah. And I felt safe. I shake my head to think of it now, that I—a professor of philosophy, no less— should have made these simple, fateful errors. Not only did I commit the fallacy of generalizing from particulars, but forgot the dictum that everything follows from a false premise. On top of that, my attachment to my theory made me victim to the sort of experimental bias that plagues scientists testing their own hypotheses. My suppositions, that is, affected what I saw, consistencies becoming more visible at the same time anomalies faded from view. Otherwise, I would have been hard-pressed to deny that, from the very beginning, there were events requiring explanation.

It wasn't true, for instance, that my corpse always lessened in Judah's presence. Many times, most especially when there were other people around us, it didn't, and although we ate our first dinner alone, Judah and I spent *all* of our public time thereafter with other people—at dinner, on trips to Memphis, or going to the continual parties common to a southern town and gown. I returned home from these outings with the same aftermath always, feeling markedly tired, desperate to sit by myself away somewhere until I was stronger. Judah, however, seemed electrified, as if he had been infused with some tonic.

I could have, then and there, concluded that my theory was defective, but I did not because I suffered only the short while until I made it home to be alone with Judah, who within an hour or two had rallied me, confirming by that what I already believed true. So I did only what we all do, that is to say, our theories come *first*, directing their own proofs and not the other way around.

(It is interesting to note that those who study such behaviors for a living have been no more insightful than I was. They speak of *introverts* and *extroverts*, one drained by being with other people, the other enlivened. Do you notice how these labels are offered with not the slightest explanation of why such different results should occur, I mean, by what mechanism? The reason none is identified is because there is none, there being no extroverts and no introverts, but only persons engaged in something else altogether.)

It is true that the beginning years of our marriage were a refuge from corpses. Judah seemed able somehow to avoid any association with the many dead at the university, even while he placed us in the midst of people nearly every day. This constant company strained my resources, as I said, but as long as he took the time to later revive me, I clung to the notion that Judah was a balm to my life and never imagined he could be its mortal enemy.

WELL, NOW MY HOPE to leave Laurel before I finish this account is brought to virtually nothing; they have decided to continue the exhumation and, even more, are planning not only to remove the casket to confirm that it belongs to Mr. Stark but to open it as well. It was Carol's victory pure and simple, but then she had more than reason with which to work. For one thing, unlike her husband and the diggers, she is utterly devoid of any unease in disturbing a man's final resting place.

"Why is it now that you want to stop here? They're almost finished," she quizzed Evan, and it was not a challenge but a genuine question.

"We know it's here and that was the reason we dug to begin with. If we keep on . . . I don't know . . . we need to weigh the necessity of what we're doing with all the other."

"The other what?" Carol was baffled by his argument, and I saw then that their difference of opinion rested not on the particulars of this enterprise but more in the usual ethical fissure between the sexes—the morality of men, following abstract principle; that of women, rooted in actual fact. That is why a man who can impale a living entity on a hook to lure yet another living entity to its death is appalled when his wife harmlessly examines the contents of his wallet or, in this case, satisfies her curiosity by unearthing what is, after all, no more than debris. Because the inclinations of women are more practical, they are the ones that most often prevail. Nevertheless, just as my expectation formed for Carol to denigrate Evan's squeamishness, she surprised me and appealed directly to his tendencies rather than her own.

"You know what I think?" We all looked at Carol. "I think we owe it to your grandfather to know for sure. This whole episode has cast a shadow over his name. I don't think he can really rest in peace until it's settled."

"It *has* been something of a spectacle," Evan acknowledged.

"Let's get the coffin up and have Jeff open it. Showing the utmost respect, of course. If it's your grandfather, great. If it's not, we need to know. Keep on looking."

"Where?" Evan was incredulous. "We can't dig up the whole county."

"Evan. Now, listen to me. He's going to be in this coffin. You were certain of that just two minutes ago, right?"

"Yes," Evan said reluctantly.

"Well, then, I don't understand why you are afraid to take a look. To make absolutely sure."

She had him beaten and, now that I think of it, she has had him beaten from the beginning. It is he who must convince her, you see, otherwise he would not have dug here at all, and Carol will only be sure when she sees the body herself.

But what I was starting to tell you was something else, how matters have become more complicated and unpleasantly so, making this contretemps between Evan and Carol of significantly less interest to me than it was. Odd, isn't it, how we can be totally undone in one moment by, say, the inconvenience of a button popping off, then made totally indifferent to it seconds later when another, more substantial concern appears? That is what happened to me, standing on one side of the pit and intent on the argument between Evan and Carol—my buttons—when the three fence people, the ones I mentioned before, transformed my priorities. They had moved closer, you see, until they were clustered in a half circle about Carol, pressing at her back and shoulders, leaning in and forward as if they were ready to protect her. Their intrusion seemed curious to me, partly because Carol was oblivious to their wrapping around her and neither Evan nor the diggers so much as glanced their way. I looked at the visitors more closely than I had before. They were an older woman, whom I did not know, and two men—*boys*, really—that I did. The taller dark-haired one was Tommy Frank and the other, "Horse" Brown, and they had been in high school with my sister. There was something else they shared with each other as well. Both had died in 1961 and been buried here, in Laurel.

So I am back in my car, back with Annie, less bothered now by seeing Mr. Stark's empty coffin and one coyote than I am with why it is that I should once again be seeing corpses while Evan and the others see nothing at all. I did, in an exercise of caution, check the mirror again, but I do not see my own corpse and I can think of nothing more to do than carry on with this.

NEARLY TWO YEARS PASSED before I entertained any idea that all was not as I thought with Judah, and that only because by then I had undeniably declined and was continuing apace. I no longer recovered as completely from social outings, even with what seemed the same attention from Judah. And I had been seeing shadows. You know what I mean, the ones that move in the corner of your field of vision but disappear when you turn to look at them. We all have those from time to time, and I am not suggesting you need be alarmed, but when they are interrupting you every day, sometimes rising up so vividly and suddenly that you are distracted from deepest concentration, or when they come so close you feel them tapping on your shoulder, then perhaps you might give it some thought. I was tired, too, undeniably weaker, and there were chills that woke me nightly and, then, refused to be warmed.

No, I did not throw down my belief in Judah's benefit to me to start fresh with some new theory. Instead, I made adjustments—the smallest possible—and the first of these was that I stopped going to the parties.

"If it's all right, you go on to the Shaws' tonight. I don't feel like it," I told Judah, who surprised me with his angry response.

"What? I can't tell Robbie Shaw that. All our friends. They're goin' to think my wife doesn't care enough about me to get dressed up and come out at night . . ." Then he caught himself and softened his tone, cajoling, threatening at once. "Look. I'm looking after your interests here. People don't forget something like this. Next time you go to the dean wanting something, he'll tell *you* he doesn't feel like it."

So I did go to that party with him, after all, walking in the front door with him and greeting the hosts and two other people. Then, however, I drifted away from Judah, circling around the long table of beef tips and folded refrigerator rolls, through the kitchen, where I apologized to the help for disturbing them before exiting out the back door to the car. I sat there for two hours before returning through that same back door, through the kitchen and help, and again to the party, circling the table in reverse and finding Judah, who was ready to go.

I followed the same procedure for every party thereafter, and when several months of this abstinence did not arrest my decline, I moved to change other parts of my life with Judah as well. I made excuses to miss going out or to leave early when we were engaged for dinner; I devised endless ruses that needed me to leave on lengthy errands by myself when we had houseguests. Nevertheless, the only noticeable effect of any of these evasions was Judah's rising level of irritation with me.

"I married you for three reasons," he told me. "First, you look good. Second, you like sex. Third, I thought you wouldn't be a problem, but I have to tell you, I don't know about that last one anymore."

I persisted nonetheless—the desire to live tends to supercede the one to please—although I might have capitulated in time had I not received unexpected help. That is

to say, in the gentlest of terms, I began to put on weight—
my corpse had to be fed, you know—which led, eventually, to the elimination of reasons one and two for Judah's
marrying me as well. As my size increased, our scheduled
dinners decreased and Judah's weekend plans less often
included me until, at last, I saw only people during my
work on campus and, of course, Judah.

Incremental alterations and incremental decline, visible only after accumulation, allowed years to pass by as
nothing stopped my downward course. The shadows and
weariness and chills continued at the same time new diffi-
culties presented themselves. For one, I began to see my
corpse more clearly—she increased, little by little—until
I could spot her at any time whatsoever even without ad-
justing my gaze. I *felt* her as well, a great cold stone lodged
inside and so clearly present that at times it seemed more
likely that she was the one looking at me rather than the
other way around.

Judah and I had been married almost seven years by
then. That was also when I left my job teaching to take a
sabbatical, although the usual purposes of such scholarly
leave—a book or major article—were no longer within
my capacity to fulfill. Instead, I followed the original intent of a time for renewal and I rested. Or, rather, I *occupied* myself. Every weekday, mid-morning, I took a long
walk for a specified amount of time or a specified distance,
although never an outside walk such as the university
campus, which is filled with oak and cherry and dogwood

trees and really quite beautiful, but entirely too non-specific. Rather, I walked the painted concrete apron circling the basketball coliseum, for thirty-six circuits or for exactly one hour, whatever appealed to me most that day. It was a penance I paid for my fat, no more than that, but I continued to increase in mass each week despite it.

(I did try not to eat at all, but that can only be sustained so long. Until lunch, to be precise, although the hearty meal I made myself then was of no particular effect. I was always very hungry, even after I had eaten. The true source of my hunger—my corpse—was incapable of satisfaction.)

On Sundays I drove. Most times I took Maggie with me, stopping on Sunday mornings alone at the airport mart, where the owner fried doughnuts to glaze. I always bought four of them—two for me, two for Maggie. Then I filled a large paper cup with coffee, stirred in an envelope of hot cocoa mix, and drove us to where the road dead-ended into the reservoir, staying there for at least an hour while Maggie sniffed and explored and I read the Sunday paper.

Otherwise, I played games at my computer—clicking at bouncing balls, falling blocks of color, a deck of cards—to supply the comforting weight of hours of repetitive mindless motion, which is good practice for the long sleep as well. I was still up to reading but I could only abide books about impossibility, particularly books that detailed life as it should be. I read *Utopia* by Thomas More, *Walden Pond*, and, of course, Plato's *Republic*. I don't remember them all—the Holy Bible, I read that again, too—but my favorite was *Lost Horizon*. With this last, I was regressing, I suppose, to a childhood obsession left over from my Sunday school days where I learned that when we all got to Heaven, what a wonderful day it would be. "What will we be doing all day?" I had asked, and was cheerfully assured that we would be sitting in circles singing songs of praise to the Lord, which sounded less to me like Heaven than it did Sunday school. The other children, however, seemed well satisfied. I think now that they were probably of the mind that it would be enough to come face-to-face with God Almighty, in the way that one can spend a lifetime living off the experience of seeing Mick Jagger in a restaurant.

In the end, however, I was not rested and I was certainly not renewed. I was dying. To be more precise—in a college town there will always be some insufferable ass who responds, "We're *all* dying"—I had come to that last point, to one unexpected event away from being a corpse just like my family, like Napoleon and so many others.

I thought that no one else knew of my dying, but, looking back, I realize that almost everyone must have known, most certainly little Genevieve Vanessa Dupree—Jenny Van—whose family had moved in down the street that year.

She pestered me endlessly. She was just six then and a very cute little girl with long streaky hair that was never combed but always tangled, and she had a sprinkle of freckles over her nose, just one narrow strip in a line so straight that it looked as if someone tried to spray a board in front of her face and part of it sprayed over on her. You could not mention the freckles, though, because she lacked any decent sense of humor about herself, although she thought it acceptable to treat me as if I were the funniest person she had ever known.

"Oz," she said to me one day, "why do you always go like this?" —and then she threw herself into a chair, gasping and wheezing for a few seconds before terminating the ruckus with a large sigh.

"Is that supposed to be me?"

"Yeah. You always do that. It sounds funny."

"I'm glad you're entertained."

"No I'm *not*," she said, indignant, then, "What's 'entertained'?"

I arched my eyebrow and rested my face in my hand, index finger curled over the bridge of my nose. I sighed and shifted positions. I gave every nonverbal cue of dismissal I had accumulated in almost forty years, but she was only six then and didn't know the language yet.

"Oz? Oz-z-z-z-z! That sounds funny!"

I didn't laugh and it was then that she asked me.

"Are you going to die?"

That is what I mean. Just why would she think of that? How could she know what she was asking? I suspected that her mother or father, both of them doctors, had put the idea in her head, doctors' families being known for their continual discussions of bodies and their innards, not abstract bodies either but always the body of particular individuals, any one of whom they or their children are likely to see at the grocery store, school, or church.

"We are *all* going to die," I responded. I know.

She looked puzzled for only a moment, then recovered. She was very bright for her age. "No, I know *that*. I mean like right now. Or, you know, maybe Wednesday?"

"Why do you want to know?" I asked her, and she confirmed my worst suspicions because she was suddenly evasive, shrugging her shoulders, brazenly opening one of my desk drawers to snoop right in front of me.

"Well." She pulled my special MontBlanc pen from the drawer, the one with a gold and malachite body. "Can I have *this* when you die?"

I sat back in my chair, exasperated, covering my eyes with my hands.

"Are you crying?"

"No. Go on home," I urged her, and finally she left.

Now that I think of it, I don't know how or why Jenny Van latched on to me, but it must have been her cat nature because I do not have children and I have always found them *all* something of a nuisance, not really anyone themselves, especially at Jenny Van's premature age; all I could think of when I saw her was that it was entirely likely that, absent some fortuitous intervention from someone who actually knew what he or she was doing, Jenny Van would continue not being anyone for the rest of her natural life.

Anyway, I will tell you that I found that state of tenuous existence, the one just before death, to be the most painful of all. At last, I had a sense of what was being lost. It was as if I had slipped toward this place for years, walking into an increasingly barren and rocky landscape as the animals, trees, and bushes became rarer and rarer. Finally, I had topped the crest and looked to see nothing but the same nothing as far as could be seen, and only then did I understand. I tried to think of something to do, but I had no thought of how to trace the course that had brought me there. And there was no one to ask, no one who had come to that final point and then returned to tell of it.

My thinking was this: if I simply turn around and walk back, and if I do that every time I come to the brink, won't that save me? But, even then, I knew too much to answer "yes" and believe it. When walking blind, you might, for instance, come to a brink already occupied by another, and that other might be waiting there with no better purpose than to throw you off.

# 12.

I HAVE A PHOTOGRAPH
that I keep to remind me. I took it to capture my appearance at my lowest ebb, barely past the first point of my own
recognition of where I was. I wanted the truth, not what I
had previously believed for the sole purpose of continuing;
I stacked a few books at the corner of my desk, a long table
really, and set the Polaroid camera on top. The first picture
got only my neck, so I lowered my face to the table, resting
it atop my hands. I watched it develop—faint charcoal
gray across white, then the color—unable to believe that
what emerged was a true likeness of me despite a certain
resemblance in the eyes. Let me describe it as best I can.
In the picture, my hair is chin length, bleached to a red-

dish bronze that, in this picture, looks like wet straw, nothing better than that. My skin is pallid, the surfaces of my cheeks flat and fat beneath my eyes, which have been made smaller because of the flesh surrounding them. They are blue eyes, shading toward green and with a dark gray rim, emphasized by my dark brows, my natural dark brown.

I had grown to an immense size and now everyone thought differently of me, no longer lean, but in a different package altogether. It is a habit we have and I don't fault them. I have decided, in thinking it through, that a certain aesthetic sensibility must have some evolutionary survival value and that we are repulsed by obesity because it is, everyone seems to agree, generally unhealthy. See? I rationalized it away. But I must admit to a certain feeling during that time, inconsistent with my conclusion, one of injustice. If there is time, I will tell you about the man who had literally drooled on my bare tanned shoulder one summer's night, all the while telling me how he longed for communication with a stellar mind and that he had "never met a PhD with eyes like" mine. Seven years later he had nothing to say to me at all. Perhaps the excess of flesh was an opaque curtain that kept me and my starry thoughts from showing. Anyway, there were some compensations. I became mostly free of the sometimes oppressive attention of men, and I was not given the opportunity of joining Oxford's new wife-swapping club.

My friends called me the same as always, perhaps even more. They wanted my advice on how to live their lives.

(Yes, *my* advice. I am convinced that irony, on some days, was the only thing that held me from the grave.)

Little Jenny Van could be excused the error, perhaps, on account of her tender years. I remember once during that time when she showed up at my house after school with one brow swollen and her eyelid puffed red. A play-ground accident, plain and simple, and I laughed at the sight of her. It made her angry.

"Don't laugh. I don't like it when you laugh at me, and now everybody's going to laugh because I have to have my eye like this and I can't see very well." She was about to cry and I really could not abide her crying because her nose always ran and her voice became high and whiny and she couldn't hear anything reasonable.

"Oh, it'll be okay. Tomorrow, or the next day, it won't be so swollen. You'll get a little dark line over your eyelid, and after a week or so, that will go away, too. Isn't that right, Maggie?" Maggie wagged her tail and sneezed. "See? Maggie said that she had a black eye once and it went away just like I said."

Jenny Van forgot her trouble almost at once. "How do you know what she's saying?"

"Well, when Maggie sneezes that's a signal that she's going to think something that she wants to tell me, so I listen really hard and I can hear it inside my head." Jenny Van touched her swollen eye and then stared at Maggie a long while.

"Oz, how do you know *everything?*" she asked me finally, and I had to tell her that I didn't and to go home and not come back until she didn't look so funny.

She and the others, too, imposed an extra burden by this false consideration at the same time nothing of value was offered in return, when my only feeling of substance was a deep and abiding shame. I wanted to think that they did this without intention, but I became more uncertain as my death approached ever nearer.

Oh, I know. Those were high-class worries for someone who had more pressing concerns, who was engaged in little more than dying. I was not indifferent to the cause of my affliction. I had considered the sorts of death I knew and ruled them out, one by one. I was not dying Donovan's death nor was I in death throes on account of my old injuries from Ronald. Midwesterners have a tendency to live far from home—either physically or psychologically—and, so, are virtually immune to root rot. I ran down the sorts of death I knew, ticking them off and, still, given all this considering, I was slow to see the evidence that ever increased to point at Judah.

I did notice the puzzling effects of him—persons who were tired after being too long with him or who unexpectedly developed a headache or the woman who became nauseated. Once, I remember, Judah was at our front door giving last thank-you's and good-bye's to Jeanette Theiss, the energetic director of the department of piano, and he held her hands in his, stroking them as they talked. Suddenly, she pulled them away, rubbing her palms together and massaging her fingers.

"I need to get out of this air-conditioning. My hands are freezing!" she said.

"Cold hands, warm heart," Judah said, and he was giddy, practically floating, as he held Jeanette's shoulder and walked her to her car.

I saw all of this and, yet, there is not one but a dozen ways to describe the very same event. I mean to say the fact that our point of reference is our own somewhat arbitrary choice is not merely a feature of Einstein's theory of relativity. At the very least, my view of Judah required that whatever he effected in these others was not intended. I imagined that it was instead, perhaps, an accident of sorts and accounted for by some unknown subatomic feature of life. In short, my thinking did not bring me to the truth, but rather truth was brought to me and only when the very thing I had worked to avoid— corpses—found their way back into my life.

Oh, it was not to do with me, I don't think, but an accident of circumstances, which, in this case, was the gift of an unusually large endowment to the School of Fine Arts. That, in turn, led to numerous gatherings—at the university, money and meetings always increase in direct proportion— and those included discussions that Judah was conducting among members of his department in the privacy of our home. As with any group of professors, there were corpses.

I watched them from my table by the kitchen windows. I wasn't accumulating information but watched them for no better purpose than entertainment, and I felt no need to leave. I had determined, if nothing more, that in the space-less universe of the dead, mere distance accomplishes noth-ing, and it was fascinating to watch Judah's manipulation of the others, his artful combination of logical fallacies, flat-tery, and lies. (I was the only one to hear both Judah's dis-paraging comments about his colleagues before the meeting and his compliments to them to their face, otherwise I would have been as fooled as they.) I saw other things, too. With my own decline, my ability to see the dead had per-versely increased so that I could see not only the corpses, but others who, like me, were corpses in the making. And I sometimes even saw odd pieces that I thought might be maladies or conditions within others, although I was never able to sort through all of it. I simply watched, as I said, and in watching, I began to see what Judah was doing.

It was late November and quite cold and Judah had laid a fire in the den, drawing up armchairs on either side of a small sofa in front of the fireplace. Henry Gates and Larry Russmeyer were there with him, Henry alive and in reasonable health, but there was the shadow of a begin-ning corpse in Larry. Their meeting concerned a new per-formance center and which of two proposed building sites the department was going to support. It had lasted longer than most, with Judah and Henry each arguing his side of the matter for Larry's benefit.

"I agree that the University Avenue lot is closer in and that, perhaps, it is more pleasing aesthetically, Judah, but we have to be practical, too," Henry said.

"Why? Why do we have to be practical, Henry?"

Henry laughed. "Well . . . what is it you're proposing as an alternative? Foolishness?"

"No, I'm serious now. If practicality were the only thing, we would stick the toilet out here and put this fancy vase in a closet where it wouldn't be broken. Indeed, if practicality were the only thing, you and I would be out of a job."

Henry laughed him off and rose to pour himself an-other glass of wine. Judah knew he would not sway Henry, however, and his attention remained where it had ever been, on Larry. "Larry, I know *you* can appreciate the sub-tleties of my point. Maybe you can explain it to Henry better than I can."

Larry sat silently for an awkward moment, a quiet man compared to either Judah or Henry, and it may have been then that I first noticed the corpse inside him.

"I agree with you, Judah, that it's not the only thing," he said finally, and Judah sat back, pleased. But then, "It's a balance, isn't it? Even a sculptor has to work within the limits of his material. Henry's annex road site is a little more removed, not as historical as the other, but other-wise it is vastly better suited. And it's not unpleasant. So what I think is that, unless we intend to mostly sit outside and think about where we are, it makes more sense to choose the site that, on balance, has *both* aesthetics and practicality."

Well, that is not all Larry said or any of them, for that matter, but I have given you a fair summary of the discussion, and the important point is not *that*, in any event, but what Judah did next, which was to rise from his chair and move to the sofa next to Larry. Then, stretching his right arm along the back of the sofa, he rested his fingers lightly on Larry's shoulder. Larry's body jerked sharply, as if Judah had struck him. I looked to see Henry's reaction but he had none.

"I can't believe you really think that. Is that what you really think, Larry?" Judah asked him, and curled his fingers farther around Larry's shoulder. I saw it quite clearly then, his corpse, not the same shadow as before, but risen to the surface and plainly visible. I watched it increase further still, Judah's hand on Larry's shoulder while the corpse slowly enlarged.

"Maybe not," Larry said. "I really haven't decided yet." But it was not until he slumped back against the sofa, defeated, that Judah withdrew his hand. The meeting ended shortly thereafter, I recall, everyone agreeing to meet again on the matter later in the week.

I turned these events over in my mind for hours—did I mention that feature of deadness, the ease of obsession? Judah had done the deed intentionally, that was clear now, and it had been so horribly direct, as if, I mean, he were pulling or sucking the life out. Taken with the incidents

I had seen before, what I saw demanded only one conclusion: Judah was capable of inflicting mortal injury on others and, if on them, on me as well. Still, that is not what I believed. I couldn't deny the injury to Larry, but I also knew that Judah had delivered me from injury more than once and, for all I knew, he was helping me still, holding other unseen forces at bay, forces that would have killed me long before except for him. Regardless of what he might have done to anyone else, I trusted him to not hurt me. I suppose that is the simplest way to put it.

I DON'T KNOW. It is difficult to describe events that were only experienced in their true form many years later, not then. At the time I saw it all much differently, so it sometimes seems that in telling you, I am also telling myself for the first time. I admit, for instance, that my ability to see corpses turned out to be a valuable ally despite my opinion of it then. But those times are done, and I am not at all pleased that I am once more seeing the dead everywhere around me. I didn't really explain the extent of it before, when I saw Tommy and Horse, that is, standing there behind Carol. When they appeared, I quickly looked away—old habits don't die but merely submit to the yoke, reappearing in any moment of inattention to the rein—but there was no avoiding them. Wherever I turned my eyes, corpses came into view. Many of them lay slumbering beneath their stones, but just as many were sitting bolt upright or lounging in some spot nearby. And even more—this would surprise you—were not in their coffins at all. So here is the situation: Everyone is dithering over Mr. Stark as though his disappearance were an anomaly. Better, I suppose, that they don't know that Cleora Harrington and at least ten others are missing as well and that even more are hanging about, not where they were put. And, yet, that is the other thing I need to tell you—it seems, somehow, that they *do* know.

In the quarter of an hour after, for instance, several more of the supposedly "interred" came over to take a look at the excavation and, each time they did, whomever they passed—whether the diggers or Carol or Evan—took a step away as if to allow the spectator a clear view into the open grave. One of them, in fact, the one that stayed on the longest, forced Lawrence to make a little circle around her both when he went to get his cell phone and when he returned, even though it was equally clear that he did not see anyone standing there.

I suppose I should be grateful it is not exactly the same as before, these corpses not the rotted carcasses of that time as I would have thought. Oddly, they seem refreshed, almost healthy. Still, I am not pleased to see them, and it serves me right for coming here for no better reason than a message that, with a little patience, I might well have received soon enough in the secure environs of my Oxford home.

Well, as I said, I can see nothing to do for now but contain myself within this car and write. It was not that different then. My will to oppose death had declined with the possibilities I could imagine for escaping it, and of what use is will without a way? I wished to be left to myself was all, death certain to arrive at any moment, but I was not to be granted that peace. An approaching death takes care to announce itself, you know, in unexpected thoughts, disturbing dreams, in the quality of air we breathe. Thus, Judah's attention was inevitably drawn to me and, without explanation, he began coming home at exactly five o'clock each afternoon. "I thought I'd come home a little early," he said, and smiled at me the first of these days. "Sit here in front of the fire, enjoy a little libation and time to talk." He fixed a scotch for himself and poured me a glass of merlot. He sat on the sofa, the same he had shared with Larry, and patted the cushion next to him. I sat with him there for an hour or more, the fire warm and Maggie sleeping on the floor at my feet. We talked of ordinary matters, or at least those that ordinarily mattered to Judah—his success with a new production, compliments given him or good reviews received, and, most often, his friends and colleagues about whom he gave detailed evaluations focused on the weaknesses that made them "second rate," the academic equivalent to Ronald's "losers." Then, he left again, off to see to his nightly plans.

Every day after, Judah continued this same routine. I had not sought these daily visits but found myself heartened by them nonetheless, even supposing, contrary to reason, that they were undertaken for my benefit. It was not long before I saw that they were not, although the transformation to something less benign occurred beneath my notice. Judah was accomplished at transitions and he artfully changed the subject of our conversations bit by bit until, at last, they were no more than scheduled assaults comprising his loathing and discontent.

One evening he shared with me his pride in how well he had conducted himself under the difficult conditions I had created. "You know? . . . I have been faithful to you when most men would have said 'Fuck it.' But I have to tell you that if I find someone who rings my bell, I'm gonna jump right on her."

Some years later, when others thought it didn't matter anymore, I was told that by then in our marriage, Judah had already enjoyed having his bell rung any number of times. Of course, it was easy to be "faithful" when your definition excluded one-night stands and anything done out of town. But I did not know these things then and so did not think them. Rather, I accepted Judah's self-flattery at its word. Why would I do otherwise? I had no reason to doubt him and I think even he believed himself at times.

And I eventually learned from Bennett that Judah's disloyalty extended to mocking my appearance among his students and colleagues. It was enough hurt already, when he sat facing me on the little sofa and declared, "I don't love you. I can't love a pig," cutting quite deeply even without knowing that was what he told others as well. Still, I faulted myself for his distress as well as my own, so

I sat there, taking in whatever he cast at me and saying nothing at all. I made no effort to stop him, no attempt to explain. I only breathed myself in, the way a man sucks in his gut before a picture is taken, and tried to take what was left of me, all that was alive and feeling, down to a solid mass deep inside where the pain was far away and made bearable.

No, I never told Judah about the corpses, or that my own corpse was so great as to be nearly all of me, or any of my life with corpses at all. That would have been only to share the truth, and truth, without more, was of no particular interest to Judah. He was not a philosopher. He valued what was true only insofar as it was also of use, and, as to that, he already knew what he needed to know.

"God must be punishing me," he said, shaking with self-righteous fury, and I could not deny that it was a possibility.

For my part, I was ready, waiting to die. I was quite certain, if nothing else, that I was hopelessly wounded and defective, incapable of living in any worthwhile manner. Dying was what I deserved and would, I concluded, be better for everyone. I did not die, however. Instead, we continued this daily routine for weeks, first breaking it only in late January when Judah surprised me one day, coming home after lunch instead of later in the afternoon. I was doing nothing much, sitting by myself on the sofa, trying to warm my constant chill. Maggie was sleeping lapped over my feet.

"Are you having a meeting here?" I asked him, but he said, "No," and I did not press him further for an explanation. He went to the bar and fixed himself a scotch and came in to sit next to me. He said nothing for a long while, looking into the fireplace, sipping his drink. I watched him, waiting. Finally, he turned toward me, smiling, almost tender, as if he were about to extend his hand to grasp mine or to caress my cheek, and I smiled back at him, grateful for this rare affection however slight.

His face suddenly hardened and he leaned toward me, placing his arm on the sofa back between us. He tipped his large head down toward me and fixed his eyes on mine.

"Don't do that. Smile that satisfied smile as if you had any reason to be smiling. Haven't you understood anything I tell you? You disgust me. You are worthless to me." His hand dropped from the sofa back to my chest in one short sweep, too quick for me to avoid him. His fingers spread over my breastbone, the tip of his index finger resting in the hollow of my neck, and I felt my body jerk once, then again, harder. My skin grew cold and tight, its boundaries expanding to contain my corpse that pressed steadily outward and in minutes, or seconds, I don't know, I was little more than a hide stretched taut across cold, weathered stone.

He held me there, tightly in place. My breath came in short, painful gasps, and so shallowly that the reflexive panic of suffocation was beginning to rise. Maggie whined, then stood, placing one front paw on the sofa between us.

Judah pressed harder against me, and it was then that I felt something moving beneath my skin, as though his hand were inside me and wiggling the fingers. Maggie moved forward farther, trying to widen the small space between Judah's leg and mine and, for a second, Judah lost his grip. Inside me, however, the same movement persisted, fluttering about, untethered and desperate, and I recognized it finally as my own, the last living part of me. But then Judah reasserted his hold, his hand coming after the bit of life and taking hold of it. I could feel him tugging at it, trying to pull it out of me right through my skin and into his own. He strained to hold on while Maggie's thick body pressed harder between us.

"Get off!" he shouted at her, and pushed at her wide head with his free hand. She lowered her chest onto her paws and her chin tight into the cushion, squeezing her eyes shut against his force, but she did not move away. He turned his face full into mine. "Make her get down!"

I stared back at him, unable to say anything, letting go what I no longer believed and putting in its place what I could no longer deny. I was not safe from him. Judah meant to steal my life in the same way he had the others. He had not come to me as the benefactor I thought or even as a mere spectator there for morbid curiosity but stirred by the possibility of picking at my carcass, a vulture hungrily descending in the penumbra of death, but before life is gone.

"Tell her 'no'," he ordered again. I was still in his grasp, but there was something new that pulled me back, an opposing will resting in a solid line, starting near my throat and winding down through my chest and legs to Maggie's soft ear draped across my knee and her body pressed against my shins. For a moment there was stasis, Judah and I holding the prize unmoving between us, as though each of us were aiding the other in keeping it aloft. Then I felt a lessening to his hold, if barely perceptible. I put my hand on Maggie's head and looked at him. "No," I said.

My voice was stronger than either of us expected and Judah's eyes widened a little. The color drained from his face. His breathing grew less regular. I don't remember the order exactly, but at the moment he lifted his hand from my chest, I pushed myself up from the sofa and Maggie backed off to sit in front of us. I took her by the collar, out the front door and to the car, then drove to the reservoir.

I was finally rid of the trust that had nearly undone me, never allowing Judah again within arm's reach or speaking to him beyond the most basic necessity. I slept alone and I kept Maggie with me at all times.

Judah never mentioned what had happened at any time thereafter, nor did he give any sign that he even remembered. He was, as I said, an actor. But he moved to the guest room without being asked, and he no longer bothered to throw me the bits and pieces of life that he had given before, that he had so skillfully used to trick me during all those years. He may have meant it as a punish-ment or even a way to accomplish my death through omission, having failed to do it directly. If so, he miscal-culated. I no longer needed what he had once been will-ing to give me. I had unexpected new nourishment for the fragment of life that had survived. It was not of the na-ture, or sufficient, to sustain an ordinary life but more like a chocolate bar in a snowstorm, something that might get you through one night, and, in one sense, it had been pro-vided to me by Judah himself. It was this: I began to imag-ine Judah dead; I began planning how to kill him.

# 13.

FOR ALMOST THREE MONTHS
I thought of little else. I stopped playing games. I barely
ate. I talked to no one because no one knew of my plans
for Judah or could *ever* know. I engaged in thought experi-
ments quite often. If one morning I woke up and Judah
were already dead, lying there beside me with his thin lips
stretched, shiny, around an open mouth, eyes fixed on the
ceiling fan—I thought of that. What would I feel? What
would I do?

I wouldn't touch him but ease softly out of the bed.
Then I would call Joe Bishop, the doctor Judah called
when he wanted something to get him up or bring him
down. Then the funeral. I was certain I could act the part

for that small time, and if the funeral were the end of it, well and good. But it never is. One cannot be the grieving widow for a day only and, so, the expectations come, surging against you like breakers and, sooner or later, braced or not, one of them will topple you. And if they don't really push just that way, then they are a limit and you are the calf escaping the pen only to discover he is still in the pasture. Also, I was no longer sleeping with Judah. The experiment failed.

I thought of the other, too. I mean, that one morning Judah woke to find *me* dead. He would come to the master bedroom where I slept, dressing from his closet there as he did every morning, and just as he turned to thread his belt through the pants loops, he would see me lying too still and he would know. It was almost too perfect—no loose ends, no aftermath for me, and I knew that Judah would be an excellent widower, knowing how to mourn—how to return, for instance, briefly to my casket beneath the mortuary awning without fanfare—knowing that all eyes are on him anyway. Reaching out with a soft touch good-bye, then his lip trembling, walking away to his own car. The mourning period would have had to be brief, of course, because he would need to make dinner plans, unable to spend that, or any other, evening alone. But there was a problem with this side of the experiment that kept me from its conduct. I was not inclined to suicide—one either is that sort or not—and waiting for a fortuitous accident or cancer risked taking too long. My decreased appetite had already substantially reduced my fat and could, in a few months more, leave me emaciated, the thought of that inevitably invoking the certainty—and annoyance—of Judah's increasing sexual appetite as he saw my form approach fatlessness and approximate more closely that of a twelve-year-old boy.

My considerations were not altogether theoretical. There is a lot of intraspousal killing, you know, and no time in my own life when I did not know of at least one case of it. I was only eight years old when Carolyn Krehbiel, my sister's classmate and very beautiful in that way that high school girls with lavender angora sweaters could be in the fifties, killed Denny Yeager, her male counterpart, the Apollo to her Venus, after only two weeks of marriage. She didn't like the way he looked in the morning and she had hurled a Pyrex pot of hot coffee at Denny, then cracked him over the head with a counter meat grinder as he clutched at the buried glass splinters and scalded skin already blistering on his face. At least he died quickly and the mercy of that is why Carolyn only had to go to Oklahoma for a year or so, visiting aunts there being the usual solution for Kansas girls who needed to get out of town, although the more common cause was conception not murder.

A few years later, however, Nona Welch did hard time for killing *her* husband, even though it was done with a lot more good reason. She had endured Warren's wanderings, the demands for nightly copulation the entire fifteen years of their marriage, as well as his habit of screwing farm animals, larger shoats who could still be picked up and held steady and in full view of anyone who might be around. But she killed him the day she took their eleven-year-old daughter, Sharon, to town to let the doctor stitch up the outer rips and tears her father had inflicted, leaving the rest to nature. When she came home, she loaded his shotgun, and when he walked in the door, she was sitting in his recliner across from the television set and she shot without rising. The buckshot hit Warren gut level and tore tiny holes in the walls of his intestines before it lodged in the flesh of his back. It took him two and a half weeks to slowly die while the poison of his guts leaked into him. Nona dutifully sat with him to the end, of course, and then the sheriff took her in.

I had the requisite equipment. Although our automatic coffeemaker might prove unwieldy, Judah owned a serviceable shotgun. It sat in the corner of the hall closet and, thanks to my farm upbringing, I knew how to use it. And, of course, I still had Ronald's .45. But I also knew that murder could be accomplished on a shoestring. I remembered the Lederer murder, or *about* it since that occurred at least thirty years before I was born, and in that case, the only weapon needed was a skeleton key.

Carol reminded me of that—well, of the Lederer house, I mean—because that is where I got the scar. "Grandpa Stark went ballistic when he found out about . . ." Carol ran her finger from her forehead to chin, tracing the path of the narrow ridge down my own face. "You can hardly see it. Did you have some work done?"

I shook my head. "I didn't know that he knew."

"Not just him, everyone. Evan told me. My cousin married Mike Stoner, you know."

She meant Mike who caused my injury, there in the same house where Mr. Lederer had killed Alma because, it was said, she was skinny and didn't fix up, so that he could marry Betty Sue Dykes, who was plump and powdered and every day wore a grosgrain bow in her hair to match her outfit. He locked Alma in the basement, where she had either succumbed to brown recluse toxin or died from starvation, and twenty years later he himself had died in the house undiscovered until weeks after, when his decomposed remains were found in the dining room.

"I don't know how you had the nerve to go in there," Carol said. "Evan carried me up there kicking and fighting once when we were seniors. I gave him back his class ring and his jacket and everything. I was so mad."

I went there not once, but maybe half a dozen times— I can't remember for certain—returning across the county to my old home to lead the way for the Branscom girls and their boyfriends, Gordon and Kenny. We staged elaborate tricks to frighten their friends, thinking that the entire history and setting of the place seemed constructed for no other purpose and would be shamefully wasted if we did not take advantage of it.

The first time, we only wanted to see the son's crate, the shipping box for his coffin sent home from Pearl Harbor to Mr. Lederer, who was by then a widower twice over. We were expecting the crate to be in the barn and unexpectedly found it sitting on the porch beneath the parlor window instead. We all ran away so fast that Linda tripped over a fallen barbed-wire fence, hidden beneath the leaves, sprained her ankle, and skinned both elbows. It was months and many more visits after that when we brought Mike Stoner, a hateful boy who was annoying Lois with lewd remarks every time she entered American government class. We had been trying to lure him to the Lederer place all year.

The boys dared Mike to walk through the house alone, "through the middle all the way to the back door, by yourself." He entered the front hall and, as we had planned, the rotten floor forced him right and into the parlor. I was waiting for him there, hidden behind the heavy drapes, which were themselves hanging on a wooden rod precariously supported by iron hooks. I gave him time to get to the center where the boards were weakest and, then, rustled the drapes. I heard him spin and his breath suck in, but he did not run away—I'll give him that—lunging instead at the curtain where he wrapped his arms around them—and me—and pulled down. The whole of it—curtain, rod, and several hooks—descended together, their combined weight dropping straight down less than an inch in front of me except for one of the hooks that protruded to gouge a straight line from the top of my forehead, along the length of my nose and, skipping my mouth, caught its last chunk from the tip of my chin. As it did, my blood spurted onto Mike, who fainted, collapsing onto the floor and convincing us that, despite everything, we had achieved a stunning success.

After that, Kenny and Lois began calling me "Oz," for the Wizard of Oz, who had pretended great power only to be exposed as a mere mortal when Toto pulled back the curtain. Because my last name was "Oscar," I suppose, the nickname stuck. "It was just an old house," I told Carol, and was thankful she understood that I meant to end the discussion.

Anyway, it was not my injury but the earlier murder I thought of when I was making plans for Judah, plans that were inconveniently interrupted when Mr. Stark died in April. There had not been nearly enough time to have concluded matters. So it was for that reason that I put Judah's fate aside for a while and, instead, wrote the account about my life with corpses.


CAROL IS BEING BRAVER than she thinks, walking up and down the rows of graves while we wait for the diggers to finish. My opinion of her thinking, by the way, has risen and for no other reason than that she will believe anything at all, try on anything, any idea, and not dismiss it at the front, which, given how things are, seems to me far more rational than Evan's engineer outlook on things and far more likely to arrive at truth, which is, after all, the only good use we have for rationality. And when in the course of all these beliefs, she happens across a true one, there is something that tells her and stops her.

This very moment she walks the cemetery in the company of a half-dozen corpses without knowing it, without seeing. Still, they are having a fine time amusing themselves at her expense, because almost everything any one of them does gets a rise from her. She knows there is *something*, but her ideas of what is and what isn't don't provide the container to let her see it. Tommy and Horse are two of them. As I said, both were killed before I left here. Horse died playing chicken on Highway 50 in his red '58 Chevy Coupe, and Tommy's family was struck by a train near Partridge where the crossing is up a sharp grade from the highway, discouraging precautionary stopping, and, back then, there were no signals. You would think that a train coming on the prairie would be apparent for miles, but that is what I am telling you: We can look right at something and never see it. They are taking turns now, blowing on the back of Carol's neck, making her brush at it, and, once, Horse lay himself down directly in her path and she lost her footing going over him and had to catch herself—in a wonderful coincidence—against his headstone. She doesn't know much beyond that, but at least some of the truth is actually getting through. In fact, I am certain that had she been the one confronted with *my* experiences, she would have seen earlier than I did what was what. My early years as a boy got my own intuition off to a late start.

The two men, Lawrence and Donnie, show the differ-ence sex can make. They notice so little that they aren't attracting nearly the attention Carol is. Indeed, after walking around the dead observers so carefully at first, Lawrence has started charging right through them. Oh, once, one of them positioned himself directly in front of Lawrence and waved his arms and jumped up and down, and Lawrence *did* stop and turn back to his truck for some-thing, but I can't say for certain that one had anything to do with the other.

As for me, I continue to check the mirror every ten minutes for assurance, but it is really better if I ignore the situation for now. As it is, these few lines have taken nearly an hour to get down and recalling those troubling days with Judah unaccountably caused me to sob out loud, upsetting Annie and making every one of Carol's dead companions stop in their tracks to turn and look at me.

I need to correct what I said earlier. I was rationaliz-ing, slipping back into old methods of thinking. I said that Mr. Stark's death and what came after interrupted me, but I had more than sufficient time to have finished off Judah before then. The truth of it is that I had delayed the deed, partly because I suspected that killing Judah would injure rather than enliven me. I have since learned that my sus-picion was correct, that when we harm another on pur-pose, the execution of our intent can form a vector from us to the other, forcing a part of our life down its line to be destroyed as well. Mere consideration of causing harm, however, is something else, falling into that group of acts that expand our world of possibilities rather than constrict them, although I don't recommend this course for everyone. For the ordinary person, there are more sensible and pleasing ways to increase potential. I was nearly dead, however, and that state had left me with only vestiges of feeling and, then, only the most primordial. That is to say, I felt fear and I felt anger, no more than that.

I also admit that I was not in a hurry to be alone, that I shared a little of Judah's distaste for solitude after all. We all do to one degree or another, I suppose, because we are lonely in living our difficult lives and want some company. Jenny Van understood this perfectly. The day after I returned from Mr. Stark's funeral—and his demand I write of the corpses—Jenny Van came to visit me.

"What are you doing?" She often just walked on into the house so that I had to throw the bolt even in the daytime, but I forgot that sometimes, having other things to think about, other things to decide.

"I'm writing a book. Well, an account, really."

"About what?"

"I don't know."

"What do you mean?"

"What do you mean, what do I mean? What is it that you don't understand?"

"What is the—you know, the thing—what is it about?"

"*I don't know.*"

She sighed and looked unhappy, and it perturbed me more than a little that I was made to feel a failure at a task I did not undertake to do, that I had no interest in doing, which was communicating anything of substance to a thoughtless child. But, at least, I was up to facing her down and I sat stone-faced, staring at her until she spoke.

"Could *I* write a book?"

"Certainly. I think you should begin right away. Why don't you go home and ask your mother or father for some paper and a pencil and start writing."

"I can't. They're at the hospital." She rubbed her index finger hard along the edge of my desk. "Do you have some paper?" I did and that is how she came to spend the afternoon in my office, writing her book about that day, part of the preceding day, and her birthday party one month before, using my services for spelling and punctuation, but I understood completely. She did not want to be alone and she most certainly did not want to be alone when thinking about what she knew and had seen and what she might write in a book.

As for my own project, I thought all I had to say would be complete within a week, even allowing for my little neighbor's frequent interruptions. Instead, I wrote and rewrote and strained to remember what I did not want to remember at all. It was October before I stopped with what I had and took the manuscript to Owen Kendall's friend at the university press. He agreed to publish it that spring as part of a series of novellas, "assuming it's fiction," he joked. I didn't tell him it was, but I also did not bother to correct him.

The morning after I delivered the manuscript, I opened my eyes to the difference. I was awake and not in my usual lethargic haze that required two cups of strong coffee to remedy. Still, I stayed beneath the quilt's soft cotton, not anxious, but more like a gravely wounded soldier who has just regained consciousness and, while glad to be alive, is afraid to know all of his circumstances—perhaps a leg is missing. There was more noise than I remembered. At my ear, the table clock pulsed on the bedside table, the book-case shelf across the room suddenly snapped from the dry air, and a shirt slipped softly from its hanger in the closet, *plop* to the floor. The heat pump hummed, and then the flow of air pushed through the floor vent. Maggie pushed herself up at the side of the bed to be patted, then dropped with a sigh and clunk to the floor to sleep some more. Out-side the window a blue jay was perched in a low sweet gum branch, screeching its cat alarm while the intended prey— a house finch and wren—twittered and flitted at the bird feeder, quarreling over a few sunflower seeds. I lay, listen-ing, for almost an hour more until, finally, I could no longer bear the suspense. Throwing off the covers, I swung my legs over the side of the bed and I stood. Nothing was missing.

In the days that followed that first morning's vigor, my health slowly, steadily returned, and nearly all of the unpleasant disturbances I had endured resolved and went away. Within months I had returned to my normal weight as well and my corpse, still visible for some time after, eventually receded from view until I could not see her at all. At the same time, my ability to see other corpses also declined, and by mid-January, when I was finally able to return to campus, I did not recognize many of my dead colleagues, most notably Owen, who had to speak before I knew who he was. His corpse visage had disappeared, leaving behind what must have been his appearance as he had been alive, middle-aged, sturdy with a slight paunch, and sporting a bad haircut.

Mr. Stark had been right about that much. Telling the truth, even a part of it, had saved me, and the salutary benefits I had already received would have been reward enough. But consequences are not flowing water from a tap to be turned on or off as one pleases, and these first pleasantries followed the same unpredictable and uncontrolled course as my first feelings had done many years before. That is to say, they were little more than a dribble and, then, the faucet suddenly opened full force.

# 14.

THE FEATURE OF OUR EXIS-
tence I am set to reveal to you is not so different from the
fact of death that, once known, informs almost our every
act. Oh, we don't occupy ourselves endlessly with our approaching death—most of us, anyway—but neither do we
behave as if we were immortal. Well, in exactly the same
way, there is another natural feature of our being here, a
transaction by which the living live and become dead or not,
a simple occurrence that once known changes everything.

My own knowledge of it was one of the many unin-
tended consequences Mr. Stark has imposed in my life, in
this case, partly a result of writing the account he demanded of me and partly a result of my haste in doing so.

All that truth telling was too much for my unconditioned system and provoked an overreaction so that I began seeing things that I ought not, things that are there but not ordinarily seen.

This capacity did not descend on me without any warning whatsoever, through high drama—a burning bush, a statue come to life. I see that now. There were gentle proddings of light and shadow to alert me beforehand, thoughts and dreams, too, or the odd juxtaposition, but I ascribed them to the vagaries of random thinking or my ever-active imagination or, more often, failed to see them at all. I was a professor of logic, after all, and a midwesterner to boot. Seeing corpses was an eccentricity that had been slipped in on me, but by this point I knew something of the territory and I had no plans to enlarge it. That decision, however, was not mine to make.

Jenny Van was almost eight then and still appearing in my office like clockwork every day at four.

"Oz?"

"Um."

"Why don't you have a baby?"

"Why don't I have one at some unspecified time in the future or why don't I already have one?"

"What?"

"You have to say things clearly, Jenny Van, or you cannot ever hope to be understood."

She laughed, brushing her hair from her face, and giggled as if she knew something that I did not. I wished she would not come anymore. Every time that she did, I found it agitating since I did not consider it my responsibility to give her space for living outside the confines of the child-hood her parents had constructed for her and, indeed, I was not certain I had the strength. She didn't even have a pet, you know, because her father was allergic to cats and her mother, afraid of dogs. Being busy doctors, of course, they did not have time for therapy for themselves.

After a half hour or so, I persuaded her to go home and I was left alone working at my desk. Five minutes later I looked up. I thought she had come back for something. Later I realized I had heard nothing at all but had simply known that someone was there and inferred the return of Jenny Van on some excuse that she was bound to give and that I would, as usual, find to be insufficient. And I later recalled, too, that it was in exactly the same manner that I had been subjected to Owen Kendall's corpse my first days in Oxford.

Anyway, I looked up and to my right, across the room to the only doorway, and someone *was* there, a child, but it was not Jenny. He was younger, maybe five or six, very pretty, with dark eyes and brown hair having a slight curl to it. His skin was smooth and gold, his chin dropped nearly to his chest, and he was looking up at me through long, dark lashes.

"Hello?" I tried to say, but the word broke in half in my throat in the way words do when we are about to cry. The boy did not answer me or seem to hear, although he continued to look straight at me, his brow furrowed and lips pressed together tightly. He was so serious, I thought, for such a little one, seeming regretful at having interrupted me, or perhaps he was only puzzled about what it was he *had* interrupted.

We stared at one another for a long while, then he turned his head to his right as if someone had called him. He hesitated, looking back at me a last time, and then turned toward the summons and left. I didn't call out to him. I did not move at all and I couldn't tell you, even now, what I was thinking in the first minutes or even the first hour that he was gone. I may have tried, for brief seconds, to hold on to the thought that he was some new interloper from the neighborhood and no one I knew at all, but that was not possible. I had recognized the look of his face, my own familiar expression in his, and, in any event, what mother does not know her own child? It did not matter that he was taken without knowledge or consent, because he was and there was nothing to be done now. A great truth had simply rolled into place, one already known and immutable, and I was left to bear it. Yes, that took some while to do and, with that, I would like to leave the subject because I only relate this incident at all to explain what began the whole business of the extra seeing.

This unexpected vision proved to be the vanguard of a multitude of unbidden sights. Few, if any, were as dramatic as the first, but less was required to get my attention now, and I became better able to recognize their hallmarks, the

most persistent of these being one thing overlaying another, so that I saw what I ordinarily saw but with something other added to it, as in a photograph from film
exposed twice over. I recall that, the following afternoon,
I walked into the screened porch at the back of our house
and discovered it filled with furniture of several different
sorts. Our bentwood rockers and glass-topped table were
still there but so were a large wicker sofa and two matching side chairs, all with bright floral cushions, as well as
two white metal lawn chairs, partly rusted through. They
were mixed together, over and under—I had to close my
eyes to it. It was dizzying. The conglomeration extended
out the door, too, where the solitary weeping birch I had
planted five years before was pressed against a six-foot
camellia in full bloom that I had never seen.

There was some hazard in this because it was not, you
see, as if I had been given more peripheral vision, for instance, which could be useful and easily managed. In fact,
I injured myself merely getting out of bed one morning,
when I felt my feet touch long coarse fur over downy
fuzz—causing me to move myself away from the bed in
one great leap and badly twisting my knee. Maggie sat up
and we looked hard at each other—I, bent over huffing
and holding my hurt, while she peered out from under
thick gray and black strands lying over a pearl gray under-
coat, a wolf's body hanging over hers like a mantle.

It is difficult to explain exactly how it was or all that it
was. Nearly everything was different in some way if I

turned my attention to it, and it was not any one thing or person or place. Too, it could be seeing or hearing or feeling or all of those. And unlike the boy, almost none of it meant anything to me or conveyed any information from which I could make some sense. In the grocery store once, I saw a man coming toward me in the cereal aisle and he was wearing a hat, an English bowler, that was out of place with his T-shirt and jeans. I knew the hat was not there in the usual sense and, yet, in my first sight of it, I still felt a profound sorrow spreading down and through me as if it were something poured into a hole in the top of my head. Why? I don't know and the futility of these disturbances was one of the reasons I had to stop them.

Well, I am getting ahead of myself, because what I wanted to tell you is about what I came to know on account of this extra seeing, the common feature of our existence that I mentioned earlier. I saw it many times before I knew what it was, the first time while teaching an undergraduate epistemology class that spring. Looking out over the fifteen or twenty students who sat facing me, I had noticed that each person in the group appeared larger than he or she was ordinarily and, also, less dense, as if an image of that person had been projected onto a screen before me but not yet brought tightly into focus. Too, they were, each of them, sufficiently large to be overlapping one another, and I thought that I might only be seeing the same double exposure that I had seen other times. The movement, however, was different. The students' larger versions grew smaller, then larger, swerved one way, then another, and over them all hung a haze of mixed color—blue, purple, yellow, and pink. I thought the color might be no more than illusion or an artifact of the constant movement but it was not.

Some time later, but the same week as I recall, I was in the union cafeteria line at lunch and I saw it again or what was very similar. The woman serving from behind the counter passed a sandwich on a plate to the student in front of me, and as the plate was delivered from her hand to his, both persons were suddenly in motion. Their bodies were no longer fixed and solid but moving and fluid, as if they were oscillating, in and out, bright then dim.

Yes, I was curious as to what was transpiring between these people, or *among* them in the case of my class, but I was also less willing than ever to come close enough to find out for myself. Whatever was happening, I figured, had been unknown to me before and might as well stay that way. I devoted my efforts instead to my steadily recovering health and to settling myself so that these strange sights would go away altogether.

To that end, I took walks several times a week in the country, far removed from other people and their constructions and, for that reason, less likely to present the sorts of unexpected sights and feelings that came otherwise. Nevertheless, it was on one of these walks that I was first made a participant in exactly the phenomenon I had witnessed and I began to understand what it was.

It was May then, more than a year following Mr. Stark's death and more than six months since I had finished writing of the corpses. I had driven to a road several miles out in the county where I had not been before, deliberately setting out to walk an undetermined distance and to end up no place definite. I parked in the drive of a small UBE church, set back a city block from the gravel road in front and surrounded on three sides by its cemetery, and walked west from there. On the right was an unfenced low expanse of saw grass and thistle that rolled, finally, down to a creek. To the left, a sharp bank rose up to a high pasture and ran alongside it for more than a quarter of a mile. Cedars and white oaks grew along the fence line, shading the road as well as the bank where dozens of oak leaf hydrangeas drooped creamy blossoms over the debris rained down from the trees overhead. I was near the one-lane bridge crossing the creek when I heard the hoofbeats above and looked up, expecting to see a horse or cow. Instead, I was thrilled to see something unexpected, more exotic, a lone llama rushing to the fence to see who was on the road below.

He was a big fellow, sorrel with a white blaze, and amply sturdy for packing rugs and baskets up and down the steep slopes of the Andes. He held his long neck rigidly upright and looked down his nose at me, his curving cream lashes shading gray-speckled eyes that were blinking slowly.

"Hello, pretty boy," I greeted him. He lowered his head over the fence and nibbled at the Japanese kudzu starting up the post. I climbed the bank toward him, stepping through the hydrangeas and the sprawling branches of a recently fallen limb. He waited, picking at the kudzu, his gaze fixed upon me.

I was less than ten feet from him, I suppose, when I remembered that llamas spit when they are annoyed and I stopped where I was, uncertain if I wanted to come close enough to risk being sprayed. I immediately regretted the thought because, as if he had read my insult, the animal abruptly turned away from the fence and walked a short distance away, turning his rump to the road and his head away from me.

"Come back, boy. I'm sorry," I called, but he stood his ground. I continued to pick my way through the grass and the sharp branches of the limb to come all the way to the fence, reaching for the post as leverage to pull myself up to the barbed wire. I took fresh leaves from the vine and held them out to him, but he did not come. So I stood there without moving, kudzu in hand, for ten minutes, maybe more, until, finally, my karmic debt was apparently paid and the llama turned to walk back toward me.

He ignored my outstretched hand and stepped right up to the fence, pressing his broad chest to bend the wire. We were very close and I braced for the putrid spit, then forgot my concern altogether when, instead, he lowered his head and reached his soft nose to touch and wriggle across my chest, gave a short snuff, then dropped away. I felt a gentle pulse outward as my body took in what the llama had given, dispersing it evenly like a dried sponge soaking up water. The unexpected infusion made me smile, then laugh to let go of what was extra. I think I had received more, you see, than I was able to accept.

Well. I did not know immediately what had transpired. Still, I had seen the same transaction before and, now, I had felt it as well, and before too much time had passed, I was able to guess what it was—*life exchange*, which is to say the principal means by which we live, giving and taking life, one from the other in a continual unconscious transfer. It is a necessary supplement to life we may otherwise generate or lose and the sort of natural process that, like breathing, must be done to live—there is no refusing—and just as you can only hold your breath for a short while, life cannot be taken in and kept to yourself. It must move, flowing out of one to another, then back again from the same one or someone different. If we have been unaware of the particulars, it is only because the process seems to be instinctive for those raised in the ordinary way.

That is not to suggest that this exchange is as automatic as breathing is. Rather, it appears to be learned, at least in part—you remember the finch's song—and some of us have more talent for it than others. There are those, for instance, who habitually gain in their exchanges with others and whom some call "extroverts," and ones who habitually lose, "introverts," accounting for the way the former are invigorated by social contact and the latter, depleted. Some of us have more to give, perhaps having

the sort of life metabolism requiring very little and allowing us to share our bounty with others. Those are the
*sources*, such as my friend Lucy Cupp. Likewise, there are
those who never get enough no matter how much they
use up and, so, grab and take life without reciprocation—
the *stealers*, such as Judah. And, of course, more than anything else, there are those who lack judgment or
consideration and take too much or give too little or take
without asking, assuming you will take back.

Well, you see at once, don't you, that this makes all
our relations with other humans risky business? That is
why, I gather, we are moved to call the dog our best friend,
because given a choice between the two—dog and
human—we would never choose the friend who could
steal our life over one that might only pee on the carpet
from time to time. Animals, in fact, are less variable in
these matters than we are and, therefore, place themselves
at a disadvantage only when they exchange with us. In
that transaction, it is always we who are more likely than
they to take too much. The llama passed life to me, for instance, without taking *any* in return, and this altruism is
especially true in the case of dogs, accounting for their exceptionally short lives, although cats, who more com-
monly refuse to engage in any sort of exchange, not only
live longer lives, but have nine of them.

Anyway, you see the difficulty. Whereas, ideally, this
exchange might proceed under a sort of communist principle—to each according to his need and from each

according to his ability to give—instead life is flowing in larger part to those who have more ability to take, and from those less able to refuse. Our efforts to shield ourselves from such dangers are crude and mostly to no avail. Physical distance is an ancient device, but less effective than you would suppose. The same is true of emotional distance or any sort of disguise such as clothing, makeup, or even fat. Perhaps, if you really wanted to understand, you should consult the physicists directly, but it seems that regardless of where we go, we are, as far as cause and effect are concerned, all in exactly the same spot.

Also, now that you know about this process of life exchange, you can understand the complicity I had in my near death, another reason I may have hesitated to kill Judah. I do not mean that I caused my own decline toward death in the direct manner that Judah had, but I had acted in a way that made me ripe for the taking. I call it *death mask* or sometimes *curtains*. Either way, it is all the same because what I did was exactly that, I spent my years behind an impenetrable curtain where I hid away the living part of me, lacking the will to let it see the light of day. That was an error of some magnitude since my withdrawal from the ongoing life exchange held not only death at bay, but life as well. Well, it's no use regretting it since I did it and for reasons compelling to me then: I did not want anyone to see me and I did not want anyone to know how I really felt about anything and, most especially, I did not want anyone to know the truth about how I didn't feel at all.

MR. STARK'S CASKET is almost in view, and Lawrence and Donnie are inside the grave now. They have lifted the coffin from its liner and are removing the last shovels of soil from atop it as delicately as if they were spooning sugar into afternoon tea at the Connaught. Evan went to get Jeff Preston from the mortuary; Kenneth Miller, the Methodist minister, arrived a few minutes ago. As to this latter event, were I not involved with a high degree of my own concerns right now, I think I would be up to making a formal protest on Mr. Stark's behalf. It was not enough, apparently, that they insulted him at his burial, but now must repeat the injury at his unearthing, as well.

Yes, the fence people remain in force and, yes, it has occurred to me to walk over for a little better look at them. However, I have not. I have enough information to consider for the moment. Whether they are alive or dead, come here from their homes or a nearby grave, is of no import to what I have to tell you. Although we have been together nearly three days now, none has shared my view along with the space and would not likely believe me if I were to plainly tell them otherwise. That judgment is not the failing of either of us necessarily inasmuch as we are proceeding from different facts altogether—as much as if we were watching different movies in different rooms, the reasonable and justifiable observations in one place nonsensical in the other.

Once you have had a view of the different room, however, there is no ignoring its existence. With my knowing of life exchange, any pretense that it was not there put me in more danger than I already was. It was not a difficult inference to the truth, you see, that I was put at a disadvantage by my strange beginnings. I knew I could receive life, yes, and that others could take it away from me. But I had never learned how to give or take life intentionally or those ways by which life is generated or anything else that might offer protection to me in a world filled with this constant moving exchange. What was worse, I was a professor of philosophy and subject to the special hazards of that profession. More than their academic colleagues, philosophers increase that natural disadvantage in life exchange by rigorously directing the work of their bodies to the service of their minds. The skull not only protects the brain, you know, but makes the head the part of our body that is least receptive to life.

Well, in a way, my problem is not that different from yours, is it? We need other people to live and, yet, they might well be killing us, all at the very same time. Imbalance is inherent and it is pervasive. And what is more, this asymmetric process is likely governed by pure physics, quantum particles flowing one way or another, so that, as time passes, we may expect the disparity will only get worse not better. With sufficient time, I mean—and our life expectancy continues to increase—there must eventually be human black holes amongst us, those whose mass has become so laden with life that it is irresistibly pulling the life from others into themselves until the others are completely emptied and expire. In fact, without some correction in the way physical death has served so far—it is difficult to know what to hope for—we will be a world peopled by black holes and corpses, no more than that. Then, of course, the black holes would have to turn on each other and the strongest, upon pulling the last of everything in, would be so dense as to collapse into itself and finally explode, shooting all of that trapped life back out into all parts of the universe to begin once more. I think that states as well as I can the principle structure of my cosmology and my cosmogony, too, that our continual exchange of life is an ongoing repeating process, an infinite oscillation that moves between extremes, on one end billions of living beings and, on the other, one black hole before the point of disintegration to begin the swing back to a world that resembles nothing so much as a single, immeasurable sonoluminescing bubble dancing about in the fluid universe.

# 15.

THEIR WORK COMPLETE,
Lawrence and Donnie stretched a banker's green tarp over
their excavation, concealing what was there until we were
all gathered at Mr. Stark's grave once more. There are only
the seven of us now, including the diggers. The fence people
are still outside, of course, and Annie is watching from the
car, her head resting out the open window. The Reverend
Miller, Carol, and I stood on the near side, Evan and Jeff
Preston at the far end while the diggers knelt and took
either side of the tarp, then laid it back on itself in two-foot
sections. I thought they handled it exactly right, too, having the appropriate solemn faces, the same lightness of touch
and exactness of movement as soldiers folding the flag.

None of us spoke while they worked, but when the light first caught the corner of the casket below, I thought someone ought. Here, where we were standing so close to what had been solemnly interred ten years before, with the proper attention to sacred detail and the intent it never be disturbed, well . . . ends necessarily reflect the means used to reach them and that verity always advises some attention to ritual. I silently gave greeting to my old friend, hoping he was there to hear it, and was trying to think of some words to say when Carol spoke first.

"I don't remember the top being that dark." She looked unhappy that her expectation had been disappointed. "I thought we got the desert taupe and not the heritage bronze one."

"I'm pretty sure that's it, honey. At that time it was the next to the most expensive one old Floyd had. Jeff?"

Jeff squatted beside the grave and patted the packed soil wall, testing it. "Everything looks okay. It won't be anything to open it up. I brought along a casket wrench."

He trotted off toward his car, leaving Evan and Carol to wait awhile more before their disagreement could be settled, before they would see whether Winfield Evan Stark waited below. I did not share their suspense, of course, and, for my part, prayed to whatever powers direct such that before the coffin was opened to its empty interior, Mr. Stark would come back and take his proper place in it. Amen.

When Jeff returned with the wrench and a pair of pliers, he dropped into the grave and straddled the concrete liner, bending down over a circular bolt at one end of the casket. "This little cap needs to be unscrewed first," he said, trying the pliers. He tapped it lightly and once again but, failing to move it, he came out. "It's kind of rusty. I might need a little spray," he said, frowning. "I've never seen one rust like that. They're guaranteed not to."

"Why don't you try something bigger . . . a hammer, maybe?" Carol suggested, but Jeff said he didn't know if he'd feel right about that and that it would only take a few minutes to go back to town and get the spray because "I know right where it is."

That was twenty minutes ago and Lawrence has since volunteered that he has WD-40 on his truck but he didn't say anything because he didn't know that was what we wanted. A moment ago Jeff called Evan to say that it would be a little longer before he could come back to the cemetery; a lady had come in to the funeral home unexpectedly and wanted to select a different casket for her mother.

Still, the matter will be settled very soon now and at the same time I have delivered on my promise to tell you of the corpses since all that remains to say is that, since writing the first account, I have managed to survive. No, as I explained, I do not have the usual capacities, the usual defenses. But I have done what I could and, at first, that was only keeping a distance from others and keeping Maggie near. Within the same year, however, I moved to the country a few miles from Oxford and gathered animals about me. They can be trusted to supply me with the life

I need and not take more than I am able to give. In return, I tend them, keeping them fed and healthy, preparing the wild ones to return to their natural habitat.

I *attend* the animals, too, with sight and touch and sound, hoping I am giving them some small portion of life by that, but I don't know. I do not see any of it anymore, the life exchange or the other, either one. I pursued my efforts to mute the visions until I succeeded in doing so, avoiding idle looking or close attention to anything unless it was absolutely necessary. If extra sights came anyway, I looked away or analyzed their composition and, with either approach, they usually disappeared. In other words, I developed a habit of perceiving the world in the accepted way, and within a few months what I was seeing was the same as anyone else. Well, it was, at least, until my visit here, in Laurel.

I am glad to be going back home, to be with them again, all of my charges. It is wearing to be around so many people this much time and without any animals other than Annie. I called Jenny Van to let her know we will be back late tomorrow and she assured me everything and everyone was "great."

"I had two exams this week so I took the raccoon and the squirrels to Dr. Shilling to board," she told me, but said, "I'll pick them up after school, so they'll be here when you come."

I trust her but, also, in the proverbial way, tie my camel. She is almost seventeen now and will be a senior

MY LIFE WITH CORPSES

in high school next fall. Still, she spends entirely too much time looking in the mirror at herself and flirting with boys who are completely unworthy of her, and it nearly always takes her a month to read the extra books I assign her—*The Golden Bough,* presently—rather than the week it should. She is still capable of being a pest. However, I admit that she has made some progress. I have been collecting some materials on suitable colleges for her, in anticipation that she will ask my advice. I planned to tell Jenny Van about life exchange before she went away to school—perhaps the corpses, too—and maybe I should have told her from the beginning. But she has seemed to be in no danger and I didn't want her, so young, to bear my same cares. I liked to watch how, knowing nothing at all, she has managed to learn quite a lot. She always jumps straight into things, supremely confident of the most ridiculous notions, then abandons them without regret or embarrassment when she knows better. She is not afraid of much and seems happy to be here and, watching her, I can sometimes imagine what my own course might have been in a life that was normal. Well, I suppose it doesn't matter anymore because, now, of course, *everyone* will know.

Judah? Surely you agree that he deserved killing, so it is not a blow when I tell you he is dead, although not by my hand. He died within the year I wrote my original account, quite suddenly and of natural causes. I found him myself one morning when his department called looking for him. He had failed to show at auditions for his new play. I went upstairs to the guest room where he slept and there he was, in bed and dead as earth. I had nothing to do with it. Really. Well, I did follow Disraeli's practice of putting the names of his enemies on a piece of paper and locking them in a drawer by writing Judah's full name on a little Post-it note and putting it in our safety-deposit box at the bank. What Disraeli intended I don't know, but it was only a few months following that day that Judah was gone.

I must admit that I think more kindly of him now. For one thing, he left me, if not a wealthy widow, then well-enough fixed for a good deal of freedom. For another, being dead is far more lovable than being alive. It is only then that all of our irritating, changeable, unpredictable aliveness stops obscuring our good qualities so that we can be appreciated. We can be fixed in bronze for easy observation and approval and all can stand over us exclaiming their conclusions about what we were like, what we did, all of the certainties of us. There is no longer the danger that we will suddenly get picked up on a DUI or exposed for embezzling and make them look like fools for ever saying one good word about us. No, it is much safer to admire the dead, and I can appreciate now that Judah was a very fine actor.

The life I did take was that of my dog Maggie, who in her tenth year contracted a peculiar form of nerve cancer that tore away at her until, at the last, no pain medicine was sufficient to soothe her. As she was entirely too big to carry anywhere, I called the veterinarian to come to the house and administer the poison. Oh, I know it was the "merciful" thing to do, but that does not mean there was no price because there was. I could feel the paying of it while I sat on the ground with the weight of Maggie's heavy velvet head against my thigh, stroking her flank while the anesthetic paralyzed her insides until she gave a last shuddering groan.

"It's just the death rattle," the vet said to me, thinking, I suppose, to reassure me. "She's already dead."

But what I am saying is that in the course of her dying, I gave up a little more of my space to death, too. That is all.

The coffin is open at last. It is five o'clock now, and while some of the fence people have gone, there are nearly as many as before. Inside, we are next to the grave, clustered tightly at one end, fortunate that it is not a boat on water.

Evan, who is in front, points to the coffin. "What *is* that?" he asks, leaning closer and squinting his eyes to see.

Jeff is not looking but has knelt gathering his tools. "I'm sorry. I should have prepared you. We never put clothes on the bottom. Nobody does. I guess *some* do, but . . ."

"No. Come here," Evan insists.

Donnie gives Jeff a hand up and we step back to let him get to the end of the grave, where he positions himself between Evan and the Reverend Miller.

Evan points to the half shadow that divides the open lid from the closed. *"That."*

Our eyes all follow the trajectory of his arm downward. Jeff drops to his knees and leans halfway into the ground to look. "That stuff with the hairs? That's probably adipocere or . . . but, you know, I'm surprised. He's dried up pretty neatly. He must have been, you know, on the skinny side . . ."

"Jeff. Leave that, okay? Look there. No. Further up. Do you see the jacket sleeve? Okay, look across where the tips of the finger bones touch, above the knees there."

Jeff puts his arms on the sides to brace himself and leans over farther. "Oh, yeah. You have to adjust to the dark a little. Get just the right angle. I don't think . . . *Hey!*"

Jeff jerks both arms out of the grave and pushes his body away from the pit, his weight thrown full force against Kenneth Miller, then Carol, then me and the diggers behind. We are toppled like so many dominoes.

A gasp goes up over by the fence, then the low buzz of conversation. Evan, the only one of us on his feet, does not seem to hear them, instead looking down at our disorderly pile in annoyance, his lips pressed in a slight smile, an "embarrassed for you" expression on his face.

Jeff is still on the ground with the rest of us. "Criminy!" he laughs. "I didn't know what had me." He holds his arms aloft for us to see, and they are covered over with dark brown pods the size of popped corn. He shakes them to the ground and they begin to crawl.

"They're alive!" the minister shouts, and he and Carol shift suddenly backward on their heels, bumping each other and me, and we all fall in a heap once more.

"Everybody take it easy, okay?" Evan frowns at us, glancing toward the fence. "What are those, Jeff? Beetles?"

"Nah. Locusts, aren't they? There're a bunch of them. Must have been a nest. I don't think they're hurting anything."

Annie jumped from the car when Kenneth Miller hollered and is huffing beside me, straining at her collar to reach the little creatures on the ground below. I hold her head up while the procession of bulbous shells on legs makes its way from the open grave. It will not be ending any time soon, the numbers are too many, and every member seems intent on the same objective, the old cedar nearest to us.

Evan waves us up to gather at the graveside. "Reverend Miller?" he says, and the minister steps forward, folds his hands in front of his groin, and begins to pray. It is the Lord's Prayer, *again,* apparently the pledge of allegiance of graveside services, but it is not, perhaps, the same affront to Mr. Stark after all. That is what I am trying to see, and, with my head lowered, I can take another good look at the open coffin below. No, I still do not see it.

They see Mr. Stark or, rather, his remains. I do not. That is it, plain and simple. I see the patch of blue serge that Evan mentioned and, below that, the rusting droop of cream satin liner with two leg ties neatly knotted and bowed. But, it is the other—fingertips and undressed hairy leg bones and whatever Jeff said may be clinging to them—well, no. Our views intersect only in what is *not* Mr. Stark—the coffin, his clothes, and there in the half-light, the restless, wriggling mass emerging from the dark pit below, hundreds of crawling casements, their long wait over. Not beetles, or locusts either, of course, but *cicadas*— Plato's cave bugs—determinedly climbing out of the dark earth and up the tree to split their dull nymph shells and come forth, growing their deep red eyes and glossy brown wings in a few hours time so that they can fly away for their short lives in the light.

# THE RETURN

WHEN THE RAIN IS COMING down solid silver, straight down from a same-colored sky, it isn't safe to keep moving. If it had held off a few hours more, Annie and I would be all the way home or in Memphis, at least, and in either event past the Arkansas rain. Instead, we are here, beneath the six-lane overpass east of Little Rock, sealed in our own concrete vault by the watery curtain at either end. Truth be told, I am not in any hurry to leave. Annie is on the backseat, deep asleep on her pillow bed, with her eyes scrunched tight and her square nose burrowed into the soft flannel, and I am taking the time to look around.

For now, I am looking no farther than within the confines of this car. So far, I am only brave enough for that.

Still, depending on the direction of my attention, there is more to see here than you might think. Wait. Let me put that better. There is more *here* than you might think.

It is important to be precise, you know, even though something of a burden. Yesterday I was the only one who departed Laurel Cemetery discontented, because I was also the only one who required more of events than easy explanation. For everyone else, matters were concluded when they saw Mr. Stark lying in his coffin, and after the minister's prayer, no one was inclined to linger.

"Well. That's that." Evan clapped his hands and raised his eyebrows at Carol, who acknowledged his triumph by saying nothing. "Thank god, we're out here in the middle of nowhere. People would be talking about this for the next six months," he said, as if all those standing at the fence were not there.

Carol invited me for dinner and when I declined, insisted that I at least join them for drinks before, and then they left. I watched them go, the minister with them, but there was nothing to tell me with certainty how many they saw at the fence or if they saw any at all. As I said before, they seem to see both when they do and sometimes when they do not, and what they did yesterday was consistent with either conclusion.

Jeff Preston stayed on fifteen minutes more, conscientiously picking out wayward nymphs before rebolting the casket. Meanwhile, Lawrence and Donnie, with me standing over them to supervise, scooped out the rest of the cicadas, several hundred altogether, and deposited them on a pile of moist dirt near the old cedar whose root had fed them for seventeen years.

I admit that I was the one facing *several* anomalies whereas they were only lacking an account for the book. I mentioned it later, when I was sitting in the kitchen, drinking wine with Carol while she prepared dinner for herself and Evan.

"Oh, that." Carol shook her head, laughing. "I should have known."

"What's that?"

"Well, don't you see? Evan cannot resist making a fool out of me whenever he has the chance. He got Lawrence and Donnie to say they found it, make me believe it when he just made the whole thing up."

"He told you?"

"He doesn't have to tell me. We've been married a long time. I know. When he gets here, *you* ask him, okay?"

Evan did not understand the question, at first.

"Why don't you keep it?" he answered, then catching his error, wrinkled his nose at the subject. "Oh, I see. You mean the other. Who knows? Somebody's joke probably. Right? We won't know for years, then someone will own up. Like crop circles. But I mean it, Oz. You keep the book."

I glanced at Carol, who gave me a wink. "I told you," she whispered.

Well, when you encounter people believing what they need to believe, it is not a good idea to point out the fact that those beliefs are resting on weak timbers. It is also of no use. So I left them with their view of "how things are" still intact and lay awake until two o'clock this morning trying to figure out my own problems.

At daybreak I returned to Laurel Cemetery. I walked there. It is only a couple of miles out, although too far for Annie so I left her behind in the room, sound asleep and upside down, her feet propped against the side of the bed. I wanted to go on foot rather than in my car—to be a pilgrim rather than a pilot, I suppose—and in less than half an hour, I was there, standing before the main gate, south and under the iron letters that spelled "Laurel."

A few people were already standing outside the fence and there were others moving around inside, although I couldn't see anything clearly, the sun still too low to overcome the cedars' dark curtain. The cicadas had been audible even from the mile corner, but most of them had apparently not left Laurel because, now, the noise was deafening. Their rhythmic buzz easily masked the morning sounds I had heard walking—field mice skittering through stalks of corn, the purr of red-winged blackbirds in the ditches, flying cattail to cattail, and even the shrill *skrawk!* of pheasants rising from pasture. It would not be better any time soon, so I raised the latch and went inside. I walked down the south drive, a small group gathering behind me, and when I turned off toward Mr. Stark's grave, they followed.

Lawrence and Donnie had filled it in, packed the soil firmly in a low mound, and then sprinkled grass seed on top with clippings spread over that. They had done the same for the earlier dig, as well. I placed the book atop the first mound, leaning it against the headstone—having taken it as Evan suggested and bringing it with me to the cemetery to give back. I have thought a lot about the corrected error that I told you and have decided the only reasonable explanation is that, whatever its source, this little volume is not *my* account, at least not one of the volumes published back then.

Then I stepped back a few feet and stood straight, taking a deep breath before trying but, almost with my intent to see it, the coffin below came into view. It was empty. Mr. Stark was still not there.

The south drive and eight rows of graves lay between Mr. Stark's grave and the Shanline plot, which was a little to the left, the last one before the row of lilacs. I started across, ignoring those who continued to follow me but careful to avoid stepping on the graves and the caskets below. Some were empty but even more held perfectly preserved bodies, all fully dressed and lying, not immobile but *unmoving*, as if they were sleeping.

When I reached the Shanlines, I went to the near end of the bushes Carol had pointed out to me and walked around to the other side. The fence behind was not close, as it had appeared, but at least twenty feet away and the big cedar, nearly half that distance. The space was open grass and mostly unused, but between the tree and lilacs, there was one large family plot bounded by a low fence of ornate wrought iron and containing two white sepulchres, aboveground New Orleans style.

I walked toward the plot. The nearer crypt displayed a relief of Mary holding the infant Jesus. "French," I thought, well before I was able to read the carved letters on the bottom that said "Emile Chartiers," giving me back the momentary satisfaction of the lucky guess. The other crypt belonged to his wife, Marie. There was a statue placed between the sepulchres, urns at the four corners, and three small headstones, all children, two of whom had died stillborn, the third fighting for the Union in the Civil War. Marie and the soldier lay peacefully in their graves. The others, however, were not there.

The Chartiers were the long-departed family that Sheriff Thompson had told me about, that had given up space to my family, and the graves for my parents and sister were immediately outside the iron fence in a tight space no more than eight feet square. A flat rectangle of composite concrete marked each grave, each carved with a name and the years of birth and death, the latter being in every case, of course, 1963.

I expected the three coffins to appear as easily as that of Mr. Stark. Minutes passed, however, and I could see nothing but the grass and concrete on the ground before me. I was set to give up when I felt a movement that had not occurred before. It was both inside and not, as if my entire field of vision—my sight of it and what I saw, too— had altered to the left by a half step; instead of looking, I was simply taking in what came. The color changed first, from the spring green grass to a ruddy shade and then to dark brown and black. Then the ground or, rather, what I saw of it began quivering and rolling until it was a tiny sea and, at its center, a coffin floated into view. My breath caught and there was only grass and the stone as before. I gathered myself once more and waited. This time, as though the seeing of it had been a lesson learned, the coffin appeared in less than a minute and, shortly after, the others as well.

I could see them clearly, despite the early light, and they sat only inches apart, the one on the left slightly out of line with the others, a little higher and not straight. There were no concrete liners and the caskets were not even that, after all, but rather packing crates of the sort used for transporting coffins, like the one for Mr. Lederer's son that I had seen on the porch years before. All of them were empty.

It was what I had expected, what I had guessed in the early hours of the morning and returned to Laurel to see. My corpse family was dead even before the grave, so their remains in the crates below were likewise dead. If I did not see them, therefore, it was only for the same reason I do not see the corpses anymore. Of course, that meant that those I *was* seeing—Tommy, Horse, and the others—

were not corpses at all. They were alive. Well, they were the life left of them, I think, and the same must be said of those figures lying still in their coffins. I am seeing extra again, although only life but more of it than is ordinary. Yes, I have questions still but satisfaction, nonetheless, in one step taken. It is almost never like closing a door, you know, but rather making the choice as to which one to open and walk through.

I went out the same gate I had entered and turned to wave at my entourage and those still leaning on the fence. They looked after me but did not wave back. None followed me to the road; I waited a moment to see if one might. I had wondered why the others lay in their caskets, eyes closed, when they could be up walking about with these, and now I wondered why those walking about stayed. Why had they never taken what was alive in them and left the bounds of Laurel Cemetery? Most of the world, after all, lay outside that fence.

So I left Laurel and now am exploring what there is here, in this small space. I have been more than an hour at it and have determined that there is probably more than I could know. It is not only the additions from other times and places, you see, but also the infinite manifestations of what is right now. When the steering wheel, for instance, is viewed just so, its grained finish magnifies, dispersing into the mostly space it is. Seen another way, it cannot be distinguished from the dash behind it and the feel of it is likewise variable.

Double exposures seem to be my special talent. The door face and console sport images of the hands that assembled them, and once I heard a faint cough near the glove box. The leather seats are interesting, at least they were for the time I saw open field and blue sky and plush-faced calves and before the other that . . . Well, let's say I have taken the last step over to being vegetarian and leave it at that.

I have also been enjoying the happy sight of Annie's puppy ways and her wolf ancestor, but more than thirty minutes ago, I suddenly felt her shoulder's arthritic ache in mine and it has yet to go away. Special care is apparently required when dealing with a life intact.

No, I have seen nothing of my old friend Winfield Evan Stark, not at Laurel or here. Yet I know that a part of him must endure, one that is at least capable of sending me a message—more a demand, really—and otherwise causing a sizable disturbance in his old hometown. He must be very pleased with himself, even laughing, I suppose. I hope so.


THAT IS ALL I CAN TELL YOU. Well, I believe it is all that I have to, and it is certainly all that I *want* to tell. Of course, there are any number of other details of my life that remain untold. Telling the truth is, by its nature, selective, and I have been telling you about my life with *corpses*, not my life.

You understand, don't you, that you may do what you please with this information? Or, perhaps, you will do what you can. In either case, there is no need of proof or formal justification to me or to anyone; those standards are still beyond all of our reaches anyway. I am not giving you data from a physics experiment but telling you the Truth, and surely you see by now that these two enterprises are wholly, irrevocably different.

The rain is starting to let up. A few more hours, now, and I will be home to . . . well, to whatever may be there, although I don't expect to see any corpses. My inability to see what is dead persists, although I suspect it will return if I seem willing and that I will someday catch sight of them again, my own corpse included. Like bones in the coffin, she is within me somewhere, as much a part as the rest. That is true of everyone, you know. We are all carrying our corpses with us, ready for the memorial service.

You want to know of death? Well, I shall save my breath.
When you know life, why then we'll talk of death again.
—CONFUCIUS

# ACKNOWLEDGMENTS

It is humbling to try to identify those who have signifi-cantly contributed to the completion of a work thought to be as solitary as a novel. There are so very many. I acknowledge and thank them all, including those whose help I have for-gotten or who have helped me in ways I never knew. I am especially grateful to the following:

Helen Sheehy, an old friend, who first suggested to me that my short story, "My Life with Corpses," should be con-tinued into a novel.

Philip Spitzer, my agent, who provided thoughtful ap-preciation of my work, along with experienced and profes-sional guidance.

Walter Bode, the talented editor for both my novels and to whom thanks is due at least thrice over—for his valued friendship, for his intelligent insight and skill in editing, and, finally, for his unfailing good humor while he patiently waited for me to live all that I needed to write this novel.

Dr. Jerome Burt, Sibyl Child, Suzie Daggett, Mary Anne Duchin, Marty Dunbar, Mary Greer, David Haight, Rita Harrington, Dorothy Howorth, Barbi Jackson, Dr. Ted Kendall, Vail Kobbé, Gerald May, Jack Meier, Dr. Peter Nelson, Dr. Gerald Paske, Frederik Schultz, Georgia Stevens, Gail Turner, and Virginia Westbury, my good friends, each of whom unselfishly gave time to read or be read to or discuss or listen or criticize or praise.

Maggie and Harry, my departed canine companions, for their comfort and inspiration, and little Gershwin who has succeeded them.

And, finally, Dr. Felipe Gaitan and Adriana, for their constant love and faith in me, not to mention their special ability to live with the sort of person who could write this book.

WYLENE DUNBAR
*October, 2003*